I0615435

Hank Dooley:
The Life and Love of a Big-City Cop

Written by

Stephen P. DeLuca

Hank Dooley: The Life and Love of a Big-City Cop

Published by Stephen DeLuca
180 W Main St Westminster, MD 21157 USA

ISBN: 978-0-9960905-1-3

Printed in the United States of America by Lulu Press

The following story does not take place in your city. It takes place in *my* city. Any similarity to anything that ever happened in your city is purely coincidental.

Hank Dooley: The Life and Love of a Big-City Cop

Part I
<u>A Tale of Two Eddies</u>

Chapter 1

The City was in its typical mid-morning mode of hectic commercial activity. Cars, buses and trucks. Delivery boys, merchants and customers. Grocers, shoe repairmen and druggists. Squatters, renters and owners. Insiders, outsiders and the invisible. Under the hazily ascending sun, everybody was going about their business or poking their nose into someone else's business.

Nobody likes having someone else poking a nose into their business, despite paying taxes to cover the handsome salary of thousands of professionals to do just that thing. One of those professionals was emerging from the greasy door of the Riviera Luncheonette with a take-out paper cup of coffee in his left hand. Squinting in the bright daylight, he crossed the sidewalk, ducking between the parked cars.

"Hey Dooley! Your shoelace is untied!"

The man paused in mid-sip, rolled his eyes and turned over his shoulder. "You still tryin' to play that trick, Smacky? It didn't work the last fifty times and it ain't gonna work now."

"Yeah, I know, I know. But, it's the truth this time, Dooley. I swear it."

"Uh huh. Well, I'm not looking down, so you're wasting your breath. And a smoker like you should be counting the breaths he has left in him."

"You should look at your shoes, Dooley. How do you know if it's tied or not unless you look? You don't want people to think you can't tie your shoes properly, do you? I mean, if a shoe is untied, what does that say about the man?"

"Smacky, shove it up your ass. That's what it says about the man."

"I'm just tryin' to save you some grief, that's all! You might trip and fall."

There was a gap in the traffic and Dooley was able to cross Lingstrome Avenue. "Stay outta trouble, will ya, Smacky? I don't wanna have to send for the boys to draw a line around you. Know what I mean?"

"I sure do. But, what about your shoelace?" Smacky called out over the noise of the passing vehicles. "Seriously, you're going to trip over them one of these days."

He waved his coffee cup above his shoulder without looking back. "See ya round, Smacky." He wanted desperately to look down at his shoelace, but he was afraid Smacky might see him do it. He upended his cup and gulped down the rest of his coffee instead, finishing with a robust 'aaahh'.

"Hi officer. Got a match?" It was the voice of a bedraggled and nervous woman. She looked like she had once been attractive.

"No, but I can rub two sticks together."

"I wouldn't go around bragging about that if I were you. Your name's Dooley, isn't it?"

"That depends."

"On what?"

"On why you're asking."

"I'll take that for a 'yes'. Sergio said I should talk to you about—about this problem."

"What's 'this problem'? And who the hell is Sergio?"

"Don't worry about who Sergio is. He's just a friend. The point is, he said you can be trusted. Is he right? He said you were a square cop. He said you wouldn't double-cross anybody. He said that a close friend of his said, 'Hank Dooley did right by me when no one else would.' He said 'I'll never forget Dooley, as long as I live.' And now he's dead."

"That's nice. I don't remember him either." Dooley couldn't fit his coffee cup in the overflowing wire trash basket, so he let it drop to the sidewalk with the rest of the garbage there.

"Look, cop, was Sergio right? Can you be trusted?"

"That kinda depends, too. For example, lady, I wouldn't want to leave me alone in a room full of money, you know what I mean?"

"I do. Look, Dooley, I don't have time to beat around the bush. Let me come straight to the point. There's this man, see?"

7

"Yeah?"

"Yeah. He's important. I mean he's real important. *Real* important. Understand?"

"Wait a second. Let me guess—he's real important."

"Are you poking fun at me? 'Cause I can..."

"No, no. I'm not poking fun. I was just—You're right, I am poking fun at you. Forget it. Look, just go on, will you?"

The woman paused for a second and stared at Dooley to make sure he wasn't laughing at her. "All right. So anyway, this guy, he's got this thing. It's kind of like...a preference, you could say."

Dooley waited for the punchline, but there was none. "A preference? A preference for what? Rare steak? A stick-shift? What?"

"No, no. Nothing like that." She stopped and thought for a second. "Well, actually, yeah, you could say a stick-shift, if you catch my drift."

"Your drift?" Dooley looked around at the traffic on Lingstrome Avenue and wondered for a second if life was passing him by. "I'll be honest with you, lady. I don't know what you're talking about. Stick-shifts and Sergio! Why don't you just come out with it?"

"Okay, Dooley, if that's how you want it. Here it is in a nutshell. This real important guy is certain of something, you know?"

"No, I *don't* know. Of what? That the Rangers are going to win the Stanley Cup? What, for chrissakes?"

"I thought you were a smart cop, but I guess it's true like they say, that there are no smart cops."

"Look, lady, you came to me. I didn't ask to play this stupid guessing game. Well, what then? What's he certain of?"

The woman looked around suspiciously. "Sometimes his zipper doesn't work properly."

"His zipper?! What the...?" Dooley glanced at his wristwatch without really noting the time on it, then started pushing past the woman. "I gotta go. This

8

obviously doesn't concern the police. Tell this guy who's so damn important to contact a licensed sex therapist. That's what he really needs."

"Look, Dooley, can we go somewhere? I don't feel safe talking here."

"Can you please let go of my arm? I paid good money for this jacket."

"This piece of crap? Sorry, Dooley. I can't let you go. You gotta hear this. It's not safe here, though."

"What are you worried about? You're with me. You're perfectly safe."

"Uuugghh!" The woman suddenly slumped against Dooley.

"Now what is it? Are you all right? Stand up and stop leaning on me. Here, get up." Dooley struggled to get the woman back upright, but she continued to slide down his body, coming to rest in a heap at his feet.

A voice from the side of the alley, next to the delivery entrance to the local drug store got Dooley's attention. "Hey, Dooley, are things that bad these days that you gotta get 'em pie-eyed before they'll tumble for you?" The man laughed at Dooley's predicament. "Be a gentleman. Take her home and let her sleep it off first."

"It's not like that, Twitchell. Put down that hand truck and help me. She was tryin' to tell me something, and then, she just tensed-up and fainted." Dooley gave up trying to lift the woman and let her unfold slowly on the pavement.

Twitchell set aside his hand truck at the back door of his pharmacy and made his way over to them. "You telling me your pick-up line is so good, she just fainted dead away? Hey, wait a second. She's bleeding, Dooley. Her jacket's soaked through."

"You're right, Twitchell. She's been shot! Look, here's the bullet hole." Dooley poked around the neat little hole, then he dropped the woman and rose to his feet.

"Not a bad looker. Who shot her, Dooley?"

"Beats me." They both stood over the woman's body, staring down at her. "I don't even know who she is or what she was tryin' tell me. I didn't even hear the gunshot." Dooley looked around and scanned the windows and rooftops across Lingstrome Avenue. He could see nothing unusual. No one seemed out of place, and nobody was visible on the rooftops. The shot could have come from anywhere—even a passing vehicle.

"Hmph. You don't know a helluva lot, do you? Even *I* heard the gunshot. I thought it was a car backfiring. Look, Dooley, I've got to get back to unloading my truck. I got a kid manning the cash register. You don't still need me, do you?"

"No, I guess not. Go back to your drug store, Twitchell. I know where to find you if I need you."

Twitchell walked back to his hand truck. "Good luck, Dooley. I have a feeling you're going to need it." He chuckled again.

As a small group of curious onlookers gathered, Dooley walked to the police call box and phoned in the incident, requesting the coroner's wagon.

Chapter 2

For emphasis, Captain Homily dropped a large folder stuffed with reports on his desk and he gestured in a sweeping motion, with both hands, at piles containing many such folders. "Look, Hank, you come in here with this crap and meanwhile our citizens are being raped and murdered by the carload." He reclined and folded his hands across his beltline. "You're one of my best detectives when you put your mind to it. Things are bad, in case you haven't noticed and the new Mayor is about to release the latest statistics." He held up a slim volume, bound in plastic with a clear front. "Guess how much crime is up from last year."

"I don't know, Captain. Nine percent, ten percent?"

Homily stared at Dooley, deflated by the reply. "Only four percent, actually. But we can't be complacent about this. This City runs on trust. We can't afford any increase at all—even four percent. This is serious!" He dropped the report on his desk.

Dooley was taken aback for a moment. Four percent didn't seem that serious. "This woman was murdered, Captain. That's serious!"

"She was a drug addicted hooker. Who cares if she was murdered? I sure don't. Good riddance. Probably did her a favor."

"Well, *I* care."

"You would. You're a hopeless romantic, Dooley. Some not-too-unattractive woman dies in your arms– of course you care. If I was a sap like you, I'd care, too." Homily sighed and picked up one of the numerous files. "Look, Hank, here's a file—a little boy, six years old. His arms and legs were pulled off and he was choked to death on a giant hairball made from his own hair." He put the file back on the desk. "Doesn't that break your heart?"

Dooley was unsure what to say, so he settled on something fairly neutral. "That's picturesque."

"Picturesque, eh? The whole city is aghast and the newspapers are running this on page three everyday. And things are so bad that this case is actually *low* on my priority list. I need you to forget this trollop and get back to work on some of these other cases that haven't been solved yet. Here's a file—a

11

woman's fallopian tubes wash up on Bulton Beach. Some little kids thought it was a sea creature. This can't go on."

"But, this woman…"

"Dooley! The previous Mayor was hanged from a lamppost on the Horace Street pier in broad daylight last October and this department hasn't a clue who did it yet. You can't work on this dead broad thing. That's final. Do you understand me?"

Dooley searched Homily's eyes for some trace of equivocation, but found none. "I suppose I don't have much choice, do I, Captain?"

"No, Hank. Not this time. Look, I'll make you a deal. When we get the ex-Mayor's killers, I'll let you pursue this trollop's murderer. Okay?"

"What case do you want me to work on in the meantime? The ex-Mayor?"

"You see that box of files there on that chair?" Captain Homily pointed toward the wall. "Those one hundred and fourteen cases are now yours."

Dooley looked through the box, noting some of the names on the folders. "These? These are Pfeiffer's cases, aren't they? I recognize a couple of them."

"They *were* Pfeiffer's cases—that is, until he was murdered."

"Pfeiffer? They got *Pfeiffer?*" Dooley was shocked.

"Last night. Every one of the investigations he was working on is in that box there. They're all yours now."

"You don't seem too broken up about it, Captain."

"I am. I'm very upset—brokenhearted, even."

"You don't look it."

"Well, I am. I'm distraught." Homily was back in his reclined, arms-across-the-beltline posture.

"Then, why are you smiling?"

"Am I? Well, I don't mean to be. I'm not really smiling. I've got a cramp in my cheek." He reached up and pressed on his cheekbone. "Don't give me any trouble, Dooley. I've got enough as it is."

"I'm not tryin' to give anybody any trouble, Captain. I'm just tryin' to figure out what's what. Pfeiffer was the straightest arrow on the entire force. You knew him as well as anyone. I mean, you worked with Pfeiffer—what, twenty years? You're even godfather to his daughter. And..." Dooley stopped abruptly.

"What?"

"Do you realize that you're smiling again?" Dooley scratched his ass.

"Am I? Sorry, must be another one of those cramps."

"Must be," Dooley said absently. "I'll get cracking on these cases, Captain."

"Good. Now, get outta here. I've gotta call the Mayor. His office left two messages while I was out."

"What's the Mayor up to?"

"Something about his wife. I don't know. She probably wants police presence for some function. Hello? This is Captain Homily. I'll hold." Homily cupped his hand over the receiver. "Keep me up to date on your progress, Hank, will you?"

"If I make any."

Dooley picked up the box and schlepped it out of the Captain's office and down the hall to room 237. His asshole itched for some reason, but with both hands occupied with the heavy box, he couldn't scratch it. He set the box on the desk and began unloading the folders from it, reading the summary pages as he set them down.

The first one was an explosion at a dress shop on Front Street that killed four women. The investigators determined that it was blown up using several sticks of dynamite sewn into a petticoat.

The second file was the murder of a clown who was performing tricks in front of a group of kids at a church carnival when he was exploded by a grenade rigged to his trick oversized mallet that he used to hit himself on the head.

"The old disappearing clown trick." Dooley muttered his pithy comment under his breath.

He continued pulling the files and scanning their summaries. There was the case of a priest who was stoned to death by a gang of girls from the sixth grade of St. Peter Parochial School. There were several related cases of gar-roted bums, each of whom was murdered in the old Lancaster Hotel flop-house during the Fourth of July weekend. It went on and on like a roll call of horror and death, nothing particularly unusual in the bunch. He decided to put the files in piles on his desk, categorized by the offense, then by neighborhood, trying to make sense of it all.

"Hey, Hank!"

"Hi, Perk. Come in."

"Dooley, Dooley, Dooley. I haven't seen you in the office for a while. Where have you been?"

"The usual. Wearing down the sidewalk."

Perkins pulled up a chair and sat down wearily. "Any luck on that—what was it?—you know, the Junior High School thing?"

"No, it was the Emily Warren Elementary School."

"Some kid went postal or something, wasn't it?"

"Poison cookies at recess."

"Oh yeah, that's right! Any breaks?"

"Not a one."

"What brings you back here?"

"Homily wants me to work Pfeiffer's cases."

"That's interesting."

"How's that?"

"Can I move this box over, Hank? I gotta put my coffee down."

"Sure, put it on the floor. Why'd you say that was interesting?"

14

Perkins crossed his legs and put his hands behind his head. "Oh, well, only because Homily didn't even want Pfeiffer working on them. At least he didn't want Pfeiffer making any progress on them. And Pfeiffer was working on some pretty big stuff, I gather. Maybe with links to the mob."

Dooley cocked his head. "I don't understand."

"Well, I just think it's interesting that he wouldn't want Pfeiffer working on them, but when Pfeiffer gets iced, he wants you to work on them."

Dooley rose to his feet, peeked down the hallway, then, closed the door. They continued talking in hushed tones. "Did Homily tell Pfeiffer he didn't want him working on these cases?"

"Not in so many words, but he kept throwing up roadblocks and interfering; distracting him whenever he could."

"What do you mean 'distracting him'?"

Perkins shifted in his seat. "It's hard to put your finger on it. Whenever Pfeiffer started getting somewhere with a case, the Captain would suddenly give him some urgent assignment that would take him away for a few days or a week." Perkins paused to strike a match to light a cigarette. "When Pfeiffer got back to the original case, suddenly the trail had gone cold." He shook out the match.

Dooley shook his head. "Yeah, but we get stuff thrown at us from every angle all the time. There's nothing too strange about that."

Perkins sat and stared at Dooley with a slight smirk. "You think what you want. You know how good Pfeiffer was. Would you believe he hadn't cracked a case in five whole months? I'm telling you not one single case. Not a murder, assault, shoplifting, soliciting or jaywalking."

Dooley got a chill. "Five months? That *is* odd. You know what else? Homily was smiling when he was telling me about Pfeiffer."

"You're kidding! No shit? Smiling?"

"Yep, like the woman in that painting by Mona Lisa. Sort of complacent."

Perkins leaned forward. "I thought he and Pfeiffer were…" He placed his index and middle fingers together.

"That's what I thought, too. If anything caused a rift, I sure didn't know about it."

Perkins whistled and leaned back again. They both got a start when the door opened and Sanchez poked his head in.

"Hi guys." Sanchez took a second, sizing up the situation he walked into. "What's up, my man? You two look like you got caught with your hands in the cookie jar."

"Maybe we did, Sanchez." Dooley glanced at Perkins.

"Look, Perk, my man, I gotta talk to that insurance guy again. You wanna come along? Maybe we can do the ol' double-team, eh?"

Dooley started putting the files back into the box they came out of. "You buying life insurance, Sanchez?"

"No, this insurance guy. I think he killed the landlord of his office building. We talked with him twice already, Dooley, and everything he says makes perfect sense and matches with the evidence, but I just don't believe him."

"Bullshit, Sanchez. You just don't like him. Maybe I'd better go along or you'll end up breaking his arm for a confession." Perkins put out his cigarette. "Good luck, Hank."

"Whatcha wishing him good luck for?"

"Homily gave him Pfeiffer's caseload."

"Ay, caramba!" Sanchez grimaced in sympathy and sucked air between his teeth.

"Well, good luck with your insurance guy. I've gotta hit the streets and solve all these cases before lunch. So, you'll have to excuse me."

Chapter 3

As usual, Dooley didn't know where to start. He was handed an impossibly large number of unsolved cases, which he was supposed to work on in addition to his own large caseload. Or was he really supposed to work on these cases? After all, didn't Perkins say that Homily threw up roadblocks to keep Pfeiffer from making progress on them? If that were the case, why would Homily expect him to solve any of them? Dooley took the box with him to his car and headed for the one place he knew he could do some clear thinking: The Riviera Luncheonette.

Dooley ate many—no, most of his meals there and found the conversation with Marty, the proprietor, enjoyable and even useful. But, more importantly, Dooley was accustomed to drinking endless cups of the Riviera's famously terrible coffee. It was an awful, bitter brew, percolated in a machine that, like most of the diner's equipment, may never have been cleaned in all its years of operation. Rumor had it that the Riviera was protected by the mob, so a Health Department citation was not a problem for him. The coffee itself was of crude quality to begin with, but its brutal method of preparation only served to marginalize it to the point of toxicity. Dooley loved it, but only with several teaspoons of sugar added, which acted as a kind of passport to get it past his body's natural defenses.

Dooley had come to believe that he did some of his most creative and intuitive thinking under the influence of this concoction. Besides, it was his only real vice— at least the only one he could talk about— so he indulged it whenever he could. He had become superstitious about its use after he cracked a particularly inscrutable case by drinking so much of it one night that he passed out behind the wheel of his car as he drove home, fortuitously crashing head-on into the guilty party and killing him. It was hard for anyone to believe that this was just a wild coincidence. The man Dooley crashed into had not even been a suspect during the investigation, yet here he was—guilty as sin and dead as a doornail.

Lugging the box of files, Dooley headed out of the office and down the stairs to the garage level of the police headquarters building. He wondered about Perkins's account of Captain Homily's treatment of Pfeiffer. How did Perkins know about this stuff anyway? He wasn't particularly close to either Pfeiffer or the Captain. Maybe it was just Pfeiffer complaining because he'd had a run of bad luck? Dooley had never known Homily to be an especially crooked Captain. He couldn't imagine him covering up any crime nor having any motive for doing so. As for causing the death of a fellow cop—that was inconceivable. Nevertheless, Dooley felt very uneasy about the whole

17

situation—especially since he had felt that telltale itch as he walked out of Homily's office.

Dooley drove over to Lingstrome Avenue with the box of files on the passenger seat and left them there when he went into the luncheonette.

"Hi, Hank."

"Whaddya got, Marty?"

"It's up on the blackboard." He pointed over his shoulder with his thumb as he placed a cup of coffee in front of Dooley. "If you're getting lunch, stick with the tried and true." He dropped the sugar dispenser next to the coffee cup. "You can't go wrong."

"I can't remember, did I eat breakfast here this morning?"

"Yep."

"Then, gimme the meatloaf."

"Right-o."

"Not much sugar in this dispenser."

"Don't worry, Hank, I got fifteen dispensers."

Dooley loaded his coffee with an ample infusion of sugar, stirring all the while to make certain it was mostly dissolved. His experience with coffee told him that large quantities of sugar had a harder time dissolving than did small quantities.

"What's the matter, Hank? You look distracted. Need a refill yet?"

"Yeah, I'm on this case that I think is worth pursuing. No sooner had I left here this morning than some woman gets shot right in front of me. Hell, she was talking to me when she caught the bullet!"

"I thought I heard a commotion. Nothing unusual, though. What's the problem?"

Dooley prepared his second cup of coffee. "No problem except the Captain doesn't want me to bother investigating it. Thinks it's too trivial or something. He's got me working on other stuff in the meantime. I had this huge box of files next to me in the car on the way over here and I looked over at

it while I was waiting at a red light and thought, 'what a load of crap!'
There's no way I'm going to be able to make any headway on *any* of these
cases. Then I thought of the woman who died in my arms. Who's going to
solve that one if I don't? Nobody, that's who. And the Captain's fine with
that."

Marty served up the order of meatloaf. "I still don't get it. This woman who
died in your arms—is she important?"

"Who knows? Probably not. She said she had something important to tell
me, though. The Captain gave me a whole box full of another detective's
cases instead. And they're all as cold as shit."

"Ready for more coffee?"

"Sure."

"What was so important that she had to tell you?"

"I have no idea. You better give me another sugar dispenser. I couldn't get
her to come out with it. She looked sincere enough."

"She was an addict, wasn't she? Couldn't have been too important." He
poured another cup of coffee for Dooley. "What about those cold cases you
just got? Maybe there's something worthwhile there?"

"Maybe." Dooley dug into the meatloaf, washing down each greasy bite
with a healthy swig of hot coffee. He was already thinking of spending as
little time as possible on Pfeiffer's old cases and going after the killer of the
ragged woman who died at his feet that morning. He lifted his head from his
meatloaf and coffee and gazed through the grease-coated windows of the
Riviera and across the busy avenue to the alley where it occurred. "Marty,
you ever hear of a guy named Sergio?"

"Can't say that I have. Who's he supposed to be?"

"I don't know. That woman this morning said that Sergio told her to contact
me. I don't know what to do about that woman. Nobody knows who she is.
Nobody's contacted Missing Persons, looking for anyone matching her description."

"How'd you guys figure out she was a drug-addicted hooker?"

"She had needle marks and a pocketful of condoms. But mainly, she just
looked like one."

19

"Ah, of course. Well, Hank, what are you going to do next?"

"I'll find a Sergio."

He perused Pfeiffer's case files that night, looking at the crimes, the circumstances and the players. Nothing moved or inspired him.

The only case that held any sense of intrigue was the massive extortion ring operating at the ballpark. Fans were being systematically robbed and beaten, bank accounts were drained, family heirlooms bequeathed and inheritances were signed away to known racketeers. Needless to say, attendance at the games was dropping. Pfeiffer had found that perhaps as many as twenty eight thousand people had been victimized so far. Why hadn't anyone stepped up to the plate? Why wouldn't anyone talk to the police?

It seemed a hopeless blind alley until he came across a little tidbit buried in the routine reports Pfeiffer gave to the Captain. According to Pfeiffer's notes, a man named Sergio Cuchenoso was undecided about cooperating with the investigation. Given a little more time and a slight nudge or a threat, he might have caved in and helped bust up this ring. Dooley was exhilarated. This was too good to be a coincidence. How many Sergios could there be in the City, anyway? Dooley had no clue what connection, if any, the drug-addicted hooker had to this Sergio or the extortion ring, but he was determined to find out. Cuchenoso's address was scrawled into the report and crossed out and written over, but he thought he could make out 21 Piano Street.

Chapter 4

Dooley drove out to the address in Pfeiffer's file, hoping that this Sergio might be *the* Sergio the woman was referring to with her dying words. The houses and apartment buildings here were definitely solid middle-class. He pulled up in front of number 21, which turned out to be a semi-private apartment complex that took up most of the city block it was on. There was a pair of ornate columns marking the entrance to the courtyard.

Dooley walked through the courtyard and entered the apartment building, which seemed to him swankier than he would have expected for a character such as Sergio Cuchenoso. Cuchenoso was supposed to be a low-life who wouldn't have been able to pass muster enough to rent the incinerator room of a place like this. The courtyard had tailored lawns and shrubs. A concrete mermaid fountain sent water arcing a couple of feet in the air, making a pleasant dribbling sound. An old lady tottered slowly along the path, walking her Pekingese.

The actual apartment building had a marble lobby with plush furniture and Rococo-style murals. Dooley checked the directory, then took the elevator up to the third floor.

"Yes? Who is it?" It was a woman's voice—perhaps an old woman—that answered Dooley's knock.

"Detective Dooley, police, ma'am. Can you open the door, please?"

"What do you want?"

"I need to speak to Sergio Cuchenoso. Can you open the door, ma'am?" He waited a few seconds. Nothing. "Ma'am, it's not going to do you any good to cover up for him."

"He isn't here. Go away."

Dooley was impressed. This was clearly going to be difficult. The old woman was a tough old bird. "Look, lady, we're going to catch up with him sooner or later. It'll be a lot easier for everybody if you just let me in now." Dooley waited. Still nothing. Dooley pounded very hard on the door. He could hear the neighbors shuffling around behind closed doors, peeking through their peepholes. One person opened their door a crack, leaving the chain attached, of course, in order to watch what was going on.

21

"Open the door or I'll have to bust it down, lady. This is your last warning!"

"Go away or I'll call the police!" She sounded genuinely scared.

Dooley was suddenly worried that he'd give the old woman a heart attack. "Ma'am, I *am* the police. Just open the door. I need to speak to Sergio Cuchenoso. If you let me do that, I'll leave you alone."

"I don't believe you. I don't know what you're talking about. Go away!"

Clearly he would have to calm the old woman down and relieve her fears before he could get anywhere with her. He would have relied on his extensive training if he could have recalled any of it. "Look, ma'am, let's start over again from the beginning." Dooley was fighting his growing frustration. "Sergio Cuchenoso lives here, right?

"No, you're wrong."

"I appreciate you wanting to protect him, but you're just making everything harder and you could get into trouble, too."

"But, I've done nothing! Please, please leave me alone!"

Dooley felt bad for the poor old woman, but forged ahead with his grim task. "I'm going to ask you once more. Are you going to let me in?"

"Oh, heavens!"

"Is Sergio Cuchenoso in there?"

"No!" She was audibly crying.

Dooley was exasperated. "He's listed at this address: 21 Piano Street, apartment 3B. That's this apartment. Can you open the door now, ma'am?"

"No, it isn't."

"It isn't what?"

"It isn't what you said."

"What isn't what I said?"

"21 Piano Street. This isn't 21 Piano Street."

"What do you mean?"

"This is 21 Plano Street. Please, please go away. I'm not well. Oh dear. Please, please."

Dooley paused, then turned and walked away. He didn't start muttering to himself until he was out of the building and back in the courtyard. Dooley spotted a boy standing in the entrance to one of the buildings and amusing himself by playing with his yo-yo. "Hey, kid, which way is Piano Street?"

"How should I know, Mister?" The boy ran into the building.

"Hey, come back here! Stupid punk kid." Thinking that the service station on the corner would have a map, Dooley walked out onto the street and down the block. There was a Sunoco sign visible down the street and Dooley headed for it, wondering all the time how he could have confused the two street names. If he had gotten Cuchenoso's address wrong it might have made more sense to him.

There were no customers at the pumps when he got there, so he walked into the grubby, little office. A young attendant was sitting on the small putty-colored metal desk and buffing the contacts of a spark plug with an emery cloth.

"Hi officer."

"Hi, pal. You guys have a street map here?"

"A street map? Whaddya need a street map for?"

"Long story short, I got confused between Piano Street and Plano Street. So I'm trying to figure out the quickest way to Piano Street from here. I don't have much time. You have a map here?"

The attendant continued buffing his plug. "I tell'ya, we're all out of maps, officer. If you're short of time, I suggest just going the usual way. Forget about the quickest way. Short-cuts never pan out anyway."

"Yeah, well, I would normally take that advice, but I'm kinda up against it this time. Hey, maybe I don't need a map after all. If you just tell me which way *you* would go, I'll compare that to my way and see if yours is shorter. See what I mean?"

"Sure, I see what you mean. That's a great idea. Except, I wouldn't go to Piano Street. I've got no business there." He kept on buffing.

"What if someone told you to go to Piano Street?"

"I'd tell them to fuck off." He finally looked up and smiled.

"Well, forget about Piano Street, then. What if you had business somewhere *near* Piano Street? How would you get there?"

"I wouldn't go. I'd send Faustino instead. This job is bad enough without having to run errands everywhere in creation." He blew on his spark plug.

"You don't like this job much, do you?"

"Why do you say that?"

"'Cause you don't seem too interested in helping customers. That's why."

"You haven't bought anything. You're not a customer."

"Who's Faustino?"

"He's a guy that pumps gas here. Why?"

"Where is he now?"

"He's at his sister's house, I think. She was having problems with her driver's license or something. Why do you want to know? He in some kind of trouble?"

"Is he coming back soon?"

"I don't know. I doubt it. He just left about twenty minutes ago. His sister lives right off of Piano Street, as a matter of fact. Why are you scratching your ass?"

"What do you care? On what street?"

"Uh, I don't know. Somewhere near Piano Street. Say! Is that why you came in here with all that Piano Street jazz? Ha! Pretty clever, cop."

"You seemed pretty sure about the street just a second ago."

The attendant squirmed a bit and dropped the spark plug. "Well, I'm not so sure. I only know about where it is. I mean, how would I know? She's not

24

my sister. You know what I mean?" He gave a small giggle as he bent to pick up the plug.

"What's your name? Is it Eddie?"

Eddie looked distressed. "How'd you know that?"

"It's on your shirt, kid. Okay, you don't know the street. What neighborhood is it in?"

Eddie walked around Dooley and wiped his hands on a dirty rag. "I'm not sure. I don't know. You wouldn't expect Faustino's sister to be living there, that's all."

"Why's that? Too upscale? Too poor? Too many Chinese? What?"

"No, it's not that, so much." Eddie faded out and stared out the picture window, across the street and into the distance. He was unfocused.

Dooley was starting to lose his patience and he got a little louder. "Then, what is it? Too far from her brother? Too much traffic? Too much altitude? Gimme something, Eddie."

"Well, you just have to know Maritsa. Then you'd know what I mean."

"I guess you know Maritsa pretty well, huh?"

Eddie snapped out of his trance. "No, I wouldn't say that. I just hear Faustino talking, that's all." He turned from the window and noticed Dooley scratching his backside. "You should cut down on that scratching stuff. It's gross, man."

"Don't worry about my ass. If I were you, I'd be worrying about *your* ass. Look, the fact of the matter is that I don't know Maritsa. So, since you seem to know her so well, why don't you just fill me in, huh?"

Eddie dropped the rag. "I'd love to keep chatting, officer, but I've got a customer." He darted out the door to a waiting customer in a Chevy Impala.

When another customer pulled up to the pumps, Dooley decided to drop the question-and-answer session for the time being and head back for a cup of coffee and to report in to the Captain. On the way back, he thought of what had happened that morning and afternoon, concluding that none of it made any sense. He still couldn't figure out how he had gone to Plano Street instead of Piano Street. He also concluded that he didn't really have his heart in any of the cases that he inherited from Pfeiffer and was dreading facing the Captain. He stopped at the Riviera Luncheonette to fortify himself beforehand, then, when he could no longer delay the inevitable, dragged himself to headquarters to face the music.

"Dooley! Where the hell have you been all day?"

"Plano Street." He decided not to lie to Homily—at least on this one point.

"What in blazes! Plano Street? That's just about the only street in the city that *hasn't* been part of this crime wave. What were you doing down on Plano Street? You have a girlfriend there, or something?"

Dooley was fidgeting with his cuff. "I was following up on a lead, Captain. Unfortunately, it turned out to be a dead end. I talked to several people there, including an old lady, a gas station attendant and a street-wise punk kid." He continued fixing his cuff. "Nothing panned out."

"Which case was this?"

"Uh, the—um…"

"Not the stadium racket?"

"Yeah, that's the one."

"The guy that Pfeiffer was trying to get to testify? What was his name, Cucinello?"

"Cuchenoso. That's him."

"I thought he lived on Piano Street. Why were down on Plano? You confused Piano and Plano, didn't you?"

"No, no, nothing like that! It just so happens the woman who lives near Piano has a brother that works at the service station near Plano and I went down there to dig a little. That's all. It seemed like a decent lead and we needed a break in the case. I took a chance."

Homily sat down and was now half-hidden by a high stack of folders. "Well, no matter. I don't give a damn anyway, because I'm taking you off all those other cases."

"What? Why's that, Captain?"

"That drug-addicted hooker that died in your arms yesterday morning."

"I thought I was wasting my time with her. Isn't that what you said?"

Homily dropped a thick folder on the desk, in front of Dooley. "That was before I found out who she was."

"Who was she? Some washed-up actress?"

"She was the Mayor's wife."

Dooley was stunned. "So, she wasn't a drug-addicted hooker, after all."

"Oh, she *was* a drug-addicted hooker, all right. She just happened to be the Mayor's wife, too."

"It's no wonder crime is up, when even the Mayor's wife is a drug-addicted hooker." Dooley picked up the folder and started flipping through it. "I wonder how a guy like that could get elected mayor of a large city like ours?"

"Two-thirds of the electorate voted for him, Dooley."

"Yeah, but why?"

"He promised to fight crime."

They both paused, speechless, then they began to chuckle at the awful irony.

"Captain, seriously, you and I have been cops for a long time, now. What the hell is happening to this City? I don't remember things being this bad. I've read the stories of the lawless gangs back at the turn of the century, but I never thought we'd live to see the day…"

"Take it easy, Hank. This whole thing is going to turn around."

"When?"

"It's already started. You can't see it yet, but I'm in a privileged position on the inside. You'll have to take my word for it. A special task force has been set up to handle some of the more out-of-control aspects."

"What sort of task force? Who's in it?"

"I can't talk a lot about it at this time, Hank, and I trust you'll keep it under your hat for the time being. Let's just say it's a merger of two of the major enforcement bodies. The two complement each other nicely."

"It'll be refreshing and encouraging to see things sliding back the other way. When do you think we'll start seeing things turn around?"

"They already have. Some of those cases I dumped on you yesterday had already been cracked and the culprits punished."

"Why'd you dump them on me if they were already solved."

"I had to keep someone on them, because they weren't solved officially, yet."

"I don't get it."

"You will. Hang in there. Keep on the Mayor's wife's murder. That's still unsolved."

Chapter 5

"Back at the scene of the crime, eh, Dooley?" It was Twitchell, the pharmacist, unloading his step van.

Dooley waved at him. He had decided, once he had studied the file on the former First Lady, that the first plan of action should be to revisit the crime scene, diagram the alley and gather information so that he could make a detailed reconstruction of the event. Dooley was surprised that his recollection of that encounter was vague and confused. He had been taken by surprise and succumbed to the common malady from which almost all witnesses suffer.

Dooley moved to where he recalled standing with the Mayor's wife and began making notes as he looked around. He was about fifteen to eighteen feet down an alley that ran between Twitchell's Drugs and Ferdinand Savings & Loan. The alley dead-ended behind the drug store and was surrounded by other buildings whose entrances were on Foster Alley. In all, the entire area of the alley was an irregular space of approximately fifty by eighty feet. Because the back of the alley was a cul-de-sac, obscured from the street, the buildings all had police locks on their doors and iron bars on their filthy windows. Pigeon droppings covered all the perchable surfaces. The drug store kept a dumpster in the back and near it were some odds and ends pieces of refuse. On the ground next to the dumpster, in the most private recess of the alley, were two piles of human shit and some tissue.

"What a place for the wife of the Mayor to croak."

When he finished diagramming the alley and the buildings, he turned back toward Lingstrome Avenue and the businesses across the street. He re-ran the conversation he had with the Mayor's wife in his mind like a short movie. Her back would have been exposed to Lingstrome Avenue and especially to the businesses on the extreme right of the opening, where Dooley's eye was drawn toward Tiny's Tavern.

"Hey, Dooley, I thought you guys were going to let this one go, seeing that she was just a hooker and an addict?"

"Why would you think that, Twitchell?"

"I don't know, it's just that I didn't see anybody for a couple of days, so I thought, maybe…"

"Yeah, it would've been that way, but she turned out to be a VIP."

Twitchell seemed stunned for a moment. "A VIP? That's interesting."

"Yep, a VIP. So, she got bumped up a few notches, from 'forget about her, she's just a prostitute and a drug addict' to 'get on it right away, Dooley'."

Twitchell was standing, frozen to the spot with two stacked cartons in his arms. "So, you think there might have been a motive other than humanitarian?" He chuckled.

Dooley clicked his pen and tucked his memo pad in his jacket pocket. "You seem to be a lot more interested in this murder than any of the other dozens of murders that happened in this alley over the past eighteen months. Why's that, Twitch? Wanna switch careers from druggist to detective?"

Twitchell suddenly snapped to attention. "No! Nah, it's just that—well, I don't know—all this violence. I just was wondering, you know." He nodded at Dooley as if they had an understanding.

"Hey, Twitchell, you were here when she was shot."

"Yeah, that's right, come to think of it. Gee, I guess I was lucky, huh? I coulda been shot, too, if I was in the right place—or the *wrong* place, I mean." He made a move to bring the cartons into the store, but Dooley kept the conversation going.

"Exactly where were you when I was talking to her? Do you remember?"

Twitchell rested the cartons on the railing at the rear door, then made a big show of rubbing the back of his neck and then his chin. "Let's see. Hmm. Yeah, I was unloading the truck just like I'm doing now. I was probably standing right here. Yeah, I bet I was right here, puttin' boxes on the hand truck. Yeah, that's it." He beamed with pride at what he obviously thought was an excellent answer.

"You don't remember noticing anything before or after, do you?"

Twitchell had picked up the cartons again, but stopped short at the new question. "Like what?"

Dooley slowly closed the gap between them. "Oh, like anything odd, somebody acting strange, looking extra alert, maybe carrying a bundle or walking funny. In a hurry or lingering too long. You know."

Twitchell's gaze drifted up into the distance and over somewhere to the left. "Hmm. You mean aside from the sound of the gunshot? Nah, I don't, sorry. Hey! Now that you mention it, I do remember something. There was a guy who I noticed walking up and down the street that morning, all nervous-like, looking around. I didn't give it a second thought 'til you just asked, but maybe he did have some connection to this case, after all." He was beaming with self-satisfaction again.

"You ever see this guy before? Do you know who he is?"

Twitchell knitted his brow. "I don't know. I'm not sure. No, I don't think so."

Dooley was wondering where this was leading. His asshole was nagging at him. "What'd he look like?"

"He was old."

"Old? How old?"

"He was very old. *Very* old."

"How old is 'very old'? What? Like eighty? Ninety?"

"He looked older."

"Older than ninety?"

"I'm tellin' you, this guy looked about as old as they come." Twitchell shook his head. "Man, he was old."

"What did he look like?"

"Old."

"Yeah, I got that part, Twitch. Give me some characteristics, will you?"

"Let me think. He was pale, he had a big red nose, dark bushy eyebrows, thin white hair and a baggy old suit."

"What color?"

"He was white."

Dooley rolled his eyes. "Not him! I mean the suit, for chrissakes!"

31

"I don't know—gray, maybe. Maybe kinda olive-colored. I don't know. Do I look like a fashion designer? Listen, Dooley, I gotta finish loading these boxes." He picked up his cartons and started into the store.

"Okay, but if you think of anything else, you know where to find me."

Twitchell disappeared inside and Dooley strolled toward the street. 'Twitchell's recollection of this old man's face seemed remarkably detailed,' he thought to himself. He scanned the businesses across the street. Tiny's Tavern, toward the right, seemed the most likely location for the origin of the fatal shot, so Dooley turned in that direction, intending to pay a visit to the owner, but before he could get across Lingstrome Avenue, a familiar face appeared in the crowd.

"Smacky! Hey, Smacky!"

Smacky looked for a second like he wanted to disappear, but when he realized he was stuck he relaxed, dropped his shoulders and waited for Dooley to catch up to him. "What did I do now, Dooley? Spit on the sidewalk?"

Dooley finished getting across Lingstrome Avenue, avoiding being flattened by the rushing cars and a city bus. "Smacky, you were around the other day when that woman got shot down there in the alley. I recall that we spoke not two minutes before she caught the bullet."

"I didn't do it."

"I know that, Smacky. The thing is, you were around. You might have seen something that could help me. What do you say, Smacky? You think you remember anything from the other day? Something that sticks out in your mind?"

"Nah, I don't remember nothin', Dooley."

Dooley put his arm around him. "C'mon, Smacky. Be a pal. You never know. You could be a hero. Maybe there'll be a reward. Maybe a few thousand smackers for ol' Smacky, eh?" He pounded him on the back for emphasis.

Smacky lit up like a Christmas tree. "A few thousand!"

"I heard they're talkin' about ten or fifteen thousand." Dooley waited for that to sink in. "This is a really big deal."

Smacky snapped out of his trance. "For that tramp? Don't bullshit me, Dooley. I wasn't born yesterday, you know."

"No bullshit, Smacky. This so-called 'tramp' came with credentials. She was a VIP, despite her shabby appearance." Dooley could tell he was losing him. "C'mon, I don't have a lot of extra time on this. Honest. I really don't wanna have to haul you in and beat it out of you. You and I were on bad terms for a month that last time."

"Two months."

"All right, two months. I don't want those kinda bad feelings again, do you? C'mon, man."

Smacky knew he wasn't going to get any ten thousand dollars. He thought, however, that there might be at least a fifty-dollar bill in it for him. So, with his mouth watering, his memory came galloping back. "You know, come to think of it, I do recall a couple of little things from the other day. On their own, mind you, they wouldn't add up to anything, but taken together— that's a different story."

"What are those couple of 'little things'?" Dooley held his breath in anticipation.

"The first thing was that the traffic light was out that morning."

Dooley let his breath out. "Uh, huh."

"The other thing was that Tiny's Tavern opened twenty one minutes early that morning." Smacky paused, expecting a reaction, which he didn't get.

"So?"

"You don't get it. Edgar never *ever* opens the door before ten o'clock."

"You know this for a fact, huh? And you think he might be somehow connected with this incident?"

"Why not? He had to fight the mayor's office tooth and nail last month to keep his liquor license. He had to pay all kinds of fines and kickbacks for…"

"Go on, Smacky. What about those fines?"

"Oh, nothing."

"I thought you were about to say something."

"No, I just realized—what would his liquor license problems have to do with this murder? Nothing, right?" He giggled nervously.

"I don't know, Smacky. You brought it up. Could there be a connection? You tell me."

"You're the cop. Not me." Smacky was looking everywhere but at Dooley.

"I thought you didn't know who the woman was."

Smacky tried to think of a lie, but was fresh out.

"You knew she was the Mayor's wife, didn't you, Smacky?"

"I suppose I did."

"Why the game, Smacky? You might lose out on that reward."

"The word is these guys are playing for keeps, Dooley. I'd kinda like to keep living, you know what I mean?"

"What else do you remember, Smacky? You remember any unusual people that morning? Anybody acting odd? Carrying strange bundles? Loitering? Anything?"

"No, nothing."

"Somebody mentioned a guy wandering the street who was really, really old. You remember anybody like that?"

Smacky replied without missing a beat. "Yeah, old Mr. Kinder."

"You know this guy?" Dooley was surprised at the quick response. "This Kinder guy, is he very old-looking?"

"Yeah, he's really old-looking. But, he couldn't have done it. He's practically blind. He'd have to be right next to you to shoot you." He laughed at the thought.

"Was he acting strange that morning?"

"Strange? Like what?"

34

"Acting suspicious, nervous, anything like that?"

"Yeah, but that's the way he always acts. He's a nervous type. He can't see anything, so he's afraid he's gonna be mugged, so he acts agitated all the time. I think he figures it'll scare off the muggers. Like he's crazy and will go ape shit if they try anything on him."

"Does it work?"

"Well, as far as I know, he's never been mugged. So, yeah, I guess it works. Criminals can be a pretty superstitious bunch."

"You know this guy pretty well, huh?"

"Not *that* well. We both lived in Alberghetti's rooming house before the City tore it down. I'd do some shopping for him, maybe pick up a prescription for him, if he didn't feel up to going out. He'd give me a quarter tip for my trouble."

Dooley smirked. "Just a *quarter*? And you still did him the favor? Come on, Smacky!"

"Well, I might've miscalculated his change or forgot how much the meatball sub cost. After all, Dooley, I had to go out of my way. I gotta charge for wear and tear on these shoes, too."

"I thought as much. You said you got his prescriptions for him?"

"Yeah, sometimes, but very rarely. He didn't like me to do that for him."

"Why's that?"

"I think maybe 'cause I came back from the drug store with the wrong thing one time—capsules or something. Boy, that ticked him off. He was acting like he could barely lift his head when I left, but when I came back with the wrong pills, he jumps up and storms outta there like Jesse Owens's long-lost brother."

"Why didn't he get a family member to pick up his pills for him?"

"No family, that's why."

"Bachelor?"

"No, he'd been married, but he was widowed. He had a daughter, but she died young."

"What drug store did he use?"

"This one, right here." He cocked his thumb across the street. "Twitchell's."

Chapter 6

Dooley walked up the dusty wood stairway to the second floor and to old man Kinder's apartment. The building was probably as old as Kinder himself. It was one of those three-story walk-ups, with an inexpensive limestone façade on the first floor and good quality brick above that. The windows were topped with limestone lintels, decorated with phony keystones. The building probably looked handsome when it was new, but that was aeons ago. Now, it was ugly, with the later addition of the fire escape and the decades of grime. The beaten and deformed steel garbage cans out front did a lot to enhance the overall brutal character of 171 Thistle Street.

Dooley reached the top of the creaky stairs and was at Kinder's door, on which he knocked loudly.

Kinder yelled harshly from within. "Go away! I don't want any!"

"I'm not selling anything. Open up, Kinder, it's the police. I've gotta ask you some questions."

"Who is it?"

"The police. Detective Dooley. Come on, Kinder, open up."

"Dooley, huh? How do I know you're a detective? You have a badge or something?"

Dooley pulled out his badge and looked at the door. There was no peephole. "I'll show it to you, but you'll have to open the door first."

"Okay, I'll open the door, but you must promise me no funny stuff."

"What do you mean, 'funny stuff'?"

"Promise me, first."

"Okay, no funny stuff." Dooley rolled his eyes, but the door opened once he'd promised.

"Okay, show me the badge."

"I am showing you the badge."

"Where is it? You say you're showing me this so-called badge of yours. Where?"

"Here—right here. I'm showing you."

"Of course you are. My eyes aren't quite as good as they used to be." Dooley was sure he still hadn't seen it. "Well, officer, what do you need from me?"

"Can we step inside?"

"Yes, certainly." Kinder gestured with a sweep of his hand. "Come in. Sorry, I only have the one chair there."

"That's okay, I only need one." Dooley sat on the chair as Kinder sat on the edge of his bed. Kinder did look incredibly old. His skin was thin and weathered and his eyes, clouded by blindness, had that watery, gray-yellow quality of decrepitude. His posture was poor and he walked stiffly. He looked like he was living well into extra innings. "I don't want to waste your time; I know you are a busy man." Dooley figured that Kinder had no pressing business for the foreseeable future. "I'll get right to the point. Your name surfaced in our investigation of the murder that took place behind Twitchell's drug store the other day."

"Certainly you don't think *I* had anything to do with it, do you? I'm sure, Officer Dooley, that you can tell by now that my eyesight is not what it once was."

"Yeah, you just told me it wasn't."

"Even if I knew who this person was, I would find it virtually impossible to find this person in the street."

"I'm just here to ask questions, Mr. Kinder. The facts will come out. A blind man can kill, too, you know." Dooley took stock of the man's apartment. It was one medium-sized room with two windows. It contained a tiny kitchenette, a table, the aforementioned chair, a cot, a nightstand, a small dresser and a small bathroom.

"You think you know better than me who is capable of killing, Officer?"

"I find it interesting that you assume that your poor eyesight is more of a handicap than your extreme old age." Dooley saw that the nightstand was covered in pill bottles, surrounding a small picture frame.

"I'm not making any assumptions. I know that my eyes are my biggest handicap. I'm not as old as I look."

"What about your health? Is it good? How about the old ticker? I notice you're living on second floor here. That's a long flight of stairs outside that door."

"What are you saying? You really think I'm a killer, don't you?" Kinder looked at Dooley for a long moment. "Well, you're right. I *am* a killer. Though I haven't killed in a long time. You seem surprised. Do you find that hard to believe, Officer Dooley?" He lit up a cigar. Dooley waited because he was sure that Kinder was winding up for a big pitch. Through a cloud of blue smoke he delivered it "I beat a furniture deliveryman to death with his own hand truck when I was just three years old." He bragged while pointing his cigar at Dooley for emphasis. "When I was in the service, I strangled an old woman with an unwashed sock, just for the contents of her purse." He puffed on that foul-smelling, cheap cigar. "You want to know how much it was worth to me to have done that? Three dollars and eleven cents." Kinder paused to drink something from a paper cup. "I killed a busboy one time. I killed him right there in the restaurant by shoving a meatball sandwich down his throat."

Dooley started thinking that the busboy got off easy. That cigar was giving off such a terrifically noxious stench that he started to wonder if Kinder was going to be able to claim another victim soon. Aside from the urge to vomit, however, he had the urge to scratch his ass.

"I killed myself twice, Professor Dooley..."

"Detective."

"Sorry. ...Detective Dooley, but they brought me back both times." He was waving that murderous smoking cigar around as he spoke. As he continued, he was getting more excited and waved the cigar with increasing dynamism. "I killed a plumber who was installing a toilet for me, just because he farted loudly in my foyer. I killed my Aunt Louisa when she tried to change the station on my kitchen radio." Kinder paused for a moment to catch his breath and slumped a bit as he relaxed. "I killed a dwarf."

"You ever slay a giant?"

Kinder shot back, after the second it took him to realize he was being ridiculed. "You think it's funny? It's *not* funny! Killing is grim work. It's lonely work. And there are no repeat customers."

"You came back for seconds."

"You're a smart aleck as well as a cop."

"Why'd you kill the dwarf?"

"I don't recall. That's not the point, anyway."

"What is?"

"You'd like to know how I'm involved in this awful murder in the alley."

"Yes, I would. Are you going to tell me?"

Kinder got up from the bed and rose to his full stature. "I don't know who it is that told you whatever they told you, but I do know they are lying to you. You believe me, don't you?"

"Mr. Kinder, I'll let you in on a little secret."

"What's that, Professor?" Kinder puffed his horrid cigar.

Dooley crossed his legs. "I have a funny asshole."

"What kind of thing is that to say to a man? What's so funny about your asshole?"

"You could say it talks to me. That's right, Kinder, it talks to me. It tells me when somebody's not telling the truth."

"And how does your asshole perform this extraordinary circus trick? Does it reach up and tap you on the shoulder and whisper quietly in your ear, 'this man's lying, Professor'?"

"Not exactly, old man. It itches me. That's how it tells me."

"My friend, that's not what you think it is. If you'd wash it now and then it might not…"

"Oh, it's clean, all right. I wash it all the time. If you have any doubt, I'll let you inspect it."

Kinder threw up both hands, palms forward. "That's quite all right, sir. I'll take your word for it."

"I thought you might. Anyway, my asshole has been talking to me about you."

"Are you calling me a liar, Dooley?" Kinder visibly tensed up.

"No, Mr. Kinder, I am not."

Kinder relaxed. "Good."

"But, my asshole sure is." Dooley expected him to blow his top, but Kinder smiled wanly instead.

"Your asshole is right, Doctor Dooley. There has been only one man I ever wanted to kill. And I couldn't even kill *him*." He put the smelly butt of his cigar in a cheap tin ashtray on the counter next to the sink, then walked over to his bedside table. "I had a daughter. This is her picture, here. She was the loveliest girl. Look. You can see that, can't you?" He showed Dooley the picture. Dooley got the impression that she was a slut. Kinder turned the frame back and looked sadly into it. "Innocent and good, she was. But, *he* ruined her. He ruined her and then he killed her to keep her from ruining *him*. I won't rest until that devil is ruined. It's what I live for. It's what keeps me focused. I'd do anything to bring about his demise. Anything!"

Dooley's asshole had stopped talking. "Who is this—this devil?"

Kinder sat silently on the edge of the bed, still holding his beloved memory in his hands, but staring off into someplace. Dooley called his name a couple more times, but got no reaction.

"Well, Mr. Kinder, I guess we'll be talking again." Dooley headed to the door. "In the meantime, I'll let you get back to your business. Don't bother getting up. I know the way out." Kinder hadn't budged as he let himself out of the single room apartment and into the comparatively fresh air of the musty hallway.

As he slowly creaked his way down the stairs, he pondered the old man's sanity; quickly deciding that Kinder was at least as sane as anyone he knew. Since he was just a couple of blocks from it, he decided to grab some coffee and maybe a slice of pie at the Riviera.

The Riviera was empty as usual. "Hey, Dooley, willing to wait for a seat? Ha, ha!"

"Has anyone *ever* had to wait to sit down here, Marty? Or, more to the point, would anyone ever *want* to wait for a seat here?"

"You think you know everything, but this place was a real happenin' joint back in its heyday."

"When the hell was that? This place never had a heyday, Marty. Gimme a break." He took the third seat at the counter, but not before spinning the first two as he passed them. Marty slid a cup of coffee in Dooley's place at the same time. "They built this place with the grease already pre-installed."

"When I bought the place it was pretty nice."

"So, you're the reason it's such a crappy luncheonette?"

"I'm not the tidiest guy around. I know that. I've sort of let the place get a bit dingy, but I pass inspection every time."

"Marty, I know you pay for those certificates."

"Yeah, but they wouldn't give 'em to me if the place was *that* bad. It's a little early for dinner. What do you want?"

"I was thinking of a slice of pie, but that pie doesn't look too good."

"Don't have the pie. The crust is moldy underneath. How 'bout a cheese danish? I got 'em fresh yesterday."

"Sounds good. Better give me a refill." Dooley dangled the empty coffee cup from his index finger. As the coffee was being poured, his mind popped back to old man Kinder. "You ever serve a guy named Kinder? He looks unbelievably old; stands about five foot two; grayish complexion from too many cigars; blind as a bat."

"Hmm, doesn't ring a bell. What's his story?"

"I don't know. I think he's guilty of something."

"We're all guilty of something, Hank."

"You better give me another refill."

"How's the danish?"

"No better than I deserve. When did you buy this place?"

"Nineteen fifty-five. I signed the papers on August 9th. My wife didn't approve. I told her to go fuck herself. She fucked someone else instead. She never listened to me."

"Which one was that?"

"Wife number two. Arlene."

"What was wife one? Phyllis?"

"Florence."

"What happened to her?"

"She left me when she found out I was sleeping with Arlene."

"How'd she find out?"

"Arlene called the house. I told her never to do that, but…"

"I know, she never listened to you. Here, I need another refill."

"I keep telling you, Hank, you oughtta get married. There's nothing like it."

"I haven't found the right girl. I don't think I'm the marrying kind. It's hard to be the wife of a cop. They don't understand the whole criminal society and how we fit in. Sometimes I don't either, to be honest with you."

"Yeah, but Hank, you don't even go out on dates. That kind of life can drive a man nuts."

"I do all right, Marty. I'm kinda awkward in the whole dating-social scene. I wouldn't know how to act. All that door-holding and chair-pulling and stuff."

"It's not like that. Most women don't care about that bullshit. They just want a good meal and a few drinks. Let them do all the talking. Then, you take 'em back to the apartment and you're home free."

"Yeah, but then they expect you to call them the next day and you gotta do it all over again. No thanks." He pushed his cup forward. "Better fill 'er up."

"I don't get you. I like being married. It adds an extra zing to having affairs."

"Can't argue with that." He finally bit into the section of danish that contained a blob of cheese. "Mmm."

"You found the cheese?"

"Yeah. I thought I never would."

"It's good, huh?"

Chapter 7

"Back so soon, Dooley? You musta made some progress, huh?"

"I'm not sure, Perkins."

"Captain Homily is going to expect some news if he sees you here."

Dooley plopped in his chair heavily. "I'm not worried about Homily. If he asks, I'll just tell him the truth. These things take time. You can't expect to get blood from a stone—at least not on the first squeeze."

"Well, my fine-feathered friend, you'd better get blood from somewhere, because Homily wants it. He needs it. The newspapers are crawling all over him for the killer. They're planning some kind of giant memorial ceremony for her. There's going to be a big procession from 19th Street, down Robinson all the way to City Hall."

"She was only the first lady for a couple of months, for chrissakes! Nobody knew who she was or what she did. She was a hooker and a drug addict."

"Doesn't matter. She has come to represent something for the people. They identify with her. That's the important thing. They sympathize with her. She was one of them."

"That's a sobering thought."

"What's a sobering thought?" It was a third voice, from the doorway.

"Oh, hi, Captain. We're just talking about, you know, this whole First Lady murder thing."

"Speaking of this whole First Lady murder thing, Detective Dooley, what progress have you made so far?

"Uh, I—uh, let's see—I'm narrowing the field of suspects. I've already interviewed three possible witnesses and got a hot tip on a fourth. You can't get blood from a stone, Captain."

"If you don't dig up a suspect soon, I'm going to get blood from *your* stones, Dooley. What do we know so far?"

Dooley shifted uncomfortably in his seat and picked up a file, flipping through it. "Well, we know the following..." He suddenly glanced at his watch. "Oh, geez! Is that the time? I'm supposed to be meeting a potential witness right about now. I'll have to fill you in later, Captain." He dropped the file back on the desk and dashed out of the office.

In his haste to get out of the office, Dooley had no idea where to turn next, so he gravitated back to Lingstrome Avenue where, if all else failed, he could grab a few cups of coffee and do some deep thinking. However, on the way there, Dooley decided to visit Tiny's Tavern, situated directly across the street from Twitchell's Drug Store and the alley in which the murder occurred.

Tiny's was the saloon equivalent of the Riviera. Instead of decades of grease, it was decades of beer and bourbon that coated every surface. It was a tidy place, however. Because nothing much ever happened there. Down-and-outers drowned their pitiful little sorrows, paid their tab and left.

"What can we do for you?"

"Where's Eddie?"

"Who's Eddie?"

"What's your name, kid?"

"My name's Edgar. What of it?"

"Who's the guy that's here in the afternoons?"

"Me. I'm here until at least six o'clock."

"You open this place up every day?"

"I do"

"What time do you open up each morning?"

"Ten o'clock."

"Every day?"

"Every day."

"Ever open earlier than ten?"

"Never."

"You sure? My asshole's itching me."

"That's a disgusting thought."

"That may be, but you should be very concerned about it, my friend."

"And tell me why I should be concerned about your itchy asshole."

"Because, Edgar, it's telling me something. Right now, it's telling me that you opened early the day before yesterday."

"Your asshole told you that?"

"Why'd you open early that day?"

"Why don't you just ask your asshole?"

Dooley positioned himself face-to-face with him, took out his detective's badge and pressed it into Edgar's face. "I'm asking you. Why *that* day?"

"I had to go to Motor Vehicles that morning and it took less time than I thought it would. I didn't have to wait long for the bus and I got here early. So, I opened early."

Dooley removed the badge from Edgar's face, which was now embossed with a mirror image of it in magenta-colored flesh. "What business did you have at Motor Vehicles?"

"I had to turn in my plates. I sold my Matador."

"And did you turn in your plates?"

"Funny you should ask. Actually, I forgot to take 'em with me. I left 'em home. That's why it took so little time."

"You expect me to believe that shit?"

"Why not?"

"Look, I don't need my asshole to tell me that load of crap didn't have a shred of truth in it." Dooley grabbed the kid firmly by the upper arm, squeezing just a little too hard for comfort. "Now, why don't you play ball, huh? It doesn't make any sense for you to dig your hole any deeper. All you gotta do is tell me what we need to know. That's all. Understand?"

"Yeah."

"Did you go to Motor Vehicles that morning?"

"Yeah."

"Did you turn your plates in that morning?"

"No."

"Why not?"

"I scored with a chick I met on line at Motor Vehicles."

"What do you mean you scored?"

"I scored. That's what I mean. I mean I fucked her and she blew me, right there at Motor Vehicles in the stairwell. After that, I didn't want to go stand on line again. My knees were weak, you know what I mean?" He smiled.

Dooley never thought he had much of an imagination, nevertheless he managed to picture the scene—to his dismay. Slob Edgar and some slobbier cheap whore in the concrete stairway. "You know her name?"

"Why? You gonna look her up?"

"Don't be ridiculous. You're smack-dab in the middle of a murder investigation, pal, and this woman can either confirm or deny the veracity of your puny alibi. Now, what's this tramp's name?"

"Maritsa something-or-other."

"Where can I find this Maritsa something-or-other?"

"I don't know her address. I have her phone number—if it's her real number." He dug through his pockets, looking for the torn slip of paper. "I think she said she lives off of Piano Street." He handed Dooley the slip. "What's wrong? You look kinda strange, cop. Your asshole talkin' to you again?"

"No, it's not that. It's this Piano Street thing. I've got an association with it." Dooley looked pained for a moment. "Did you have any customers when you opened early that morning?"

"No, not one. Nope." Edgar picked up and polished a drinking glass.

"No?" Dooley reached back and scratched his butt. "Are you sure?"

"Look, cop, I've got work to do. See?" He held his arms out to showcase the phalanx of glasses set up on the bar, all waiting for attention.

"Sure, Edgar. I'll talk to you again. Don't take any vacations, huh?"

"No, sir." Edgar smirked one last time as Dooley turned and left the bar.

Dooley made sure to stuff that phone number in his pocket with the intention of finding Maritsa, which wouldn't be too hard if the phone number proved genuine. That whole story that Edgar told seemed phony, but his asshole contradicted only parts of it. He first thought there wouldn't be much to gain from Edgar. For no reason in particular, he didn't think Tiny's Tavern had played any role in the First Lady's murder, but he was beginning to think differently now.

Dooley found himself back sitting at the counter of the Riviera, downing cup after cup of hot coffee, each sweetened with several teaspoons of sugar. Marty kept the coffee flowing as Dooley ran some scenarios through his head.

"You know, Hank, you've been stumped on a lot of cases over the years."

"Have I? Not that many."

"I would say *most* of the cases you work on never got solved."

"Are you kidding me? I thought I solved almost every case I've ever worked on."

"With all due respect, Hank, I think you're batting about .300."

"No way!" He pushed his cup forward on the counter. "I'll take more coffee."

"Think about it. The little Jackson girl that was kidnapped; the poisoning of every patron in La Putana restaurant; the guy they found stuffed head first in the storm drain; the nine old ladies, each left to die in the middle of a busy street by some bogus Boy Scout impersonator. I could go on and on."

49

"I get the point. But, those were some of the toughest, most bizarre cases this city has ever seen. It's not clear if anybody would have been able to solve them. I don't think it's fair to judge me by normal standards."

"Don't get me wrong, Hank, I'm not judging you. I don't care if you never solve any cases. No skin off my nose."

"Anyway, I solved all those other cases."

"I think you're using the word 'solve' loosely. Just because someone is arrested, interrogated and confesses doesn't necessarily mean that you have solved the case."

"Which cases do you mean?"

"I remember you, last July, sitting right on that stool, complaining about the high number of cases that were being dismissed by the courts due to lack of evidence."

"I had signed confessions for each of those cases and I had provided the prosecutors with plausible motives."

"Just because you can cook up some plausible motive doesn't mean the guy actually committed any crime. You have to figure—look, Hank, I'm not looking to argue with you. I'm just sayin'…"

"I can't figure out the angle on this First Lady murder, though. I have no motive and no good suspects. I know less about this case than I do all the others and she died in my arms, for chrissakes!" He polished off another cup of coffee. "I keep sayin' she died in my arms, but actually, she died at my feet."

"You look tired. Are you running out of gas, Hank?"

He chuckled weakly. He did feel odd. The luncheonette was strange and Dooley closed his eyes. He felt woozy and weak and he was perspiring. "I don't know if it's just being out of gas, Marty." He shook his head. "Man, if I was a car, I'd be afraid to pull into a service station. I'd be afraid of what they might find out."

"If you were a car, you'd *have* to pull into a service station. It'd be the only way to find out what you need to know." Marty's voice sounded strange to Dooley—different somehow. It sounded like his own.

"If I could pull into a service station, maybe I'd find out something." He was mumbling and slurring his words and he knew it, but at the same time, he couldn't talk clearly despite his best efforts.

The next thing he knew, he was driving out to the service station on Plano Street. He wasn't sure why. When he pulled in, Eddie was pumping blood-red, leaded gas into a flat-windshield 1965 Chevy van.

"You back again, cop? You ever get to Piano Street?"

Dooley ignored the little dig. "The guy that pumps gas for you—what's his name, again?"

"Faustino."

"Right. I need to talk to him. Is he on duty today?"

"Yeah, but he hasn't shown up yet."

"What time is he supposed to get here?"

"He was supposed to get here a couple of hours ago, actually. So I'm stuck here alone in this shitty gas station while he's probably doin' his sister."

"That's a helluva thing to say. Is she a hot tamale?"

"What?"

"Is he late a lot?"

"No, he's never late a lot. Maybe I should call." Eddie left the pump and went into the small office, where he dialed the phone. After a moment, he hung up the phone and walked back to the pumps.

"What's his address?"

"I don't think I have it. We're kind of informal around here." Eddie topped off the tank on the Chevy van, spilling some blood-red liquid on the ground, and finished the transaction with the driver.

"Then, how about his phone number?"

"I don't have that either."

"You just called him!"

"No, I didn't."

"I saw you. You just called him."

"I didn't. I called time and temperature."

"Why the hell would you do that?"

"To verify that he's late."

"This is going nowhere. Okay, Eddie, what's Faustino's last name?"

"Rickenbacher, I think." Eddie approached a new customer that had pulled up to the pumps in a black 1967 Olds Toronado. One of the pop-up head-lights was up while the other was down.

"Fill it up with Hi-Test, chief."

"Right-o, sir." Eddie dialed the Hi-Test and began pumping what looked to Dooley like coffee into the man's gas tank.

Dooley was aghast. "What the hell do you guys sell here?"

"What do you mean? It's a gas station. What do you *think* we sell?"

"That shit doesn't look like gas to me. It looks more like coffee. And that other guy you took care of, it looked like you gave him blood."

Eddie shrugged his shoulders. "I just dial up what the customer needs. I don't fill the storage tanks. The company does that. Some people need blood and some need coffee, I guess."

"What did you say Faustino's last name is? Rickenbacher?" Dooley was incredulous. "Faustino Rickenbacher? Are you sure?"

"Yep, one hundred percent."

"Spell it for me." Dooley clicked his ball point pen and copied as Eddie spelled.

"Um, let's see. I'm pretty certain it's R-I-C-K-E-N-B-A-C-H-E-R."

"Wait a second. R-I-C-K-B-A-C-H-E-R?"

"No, no. R-I-C-K-*E-N*-B-A-C-H-E-R."

Dooley scratched out what he had written and started over. "R-I-C-K-B-E-N..."

"No, Rickenbacher. R-I-C-K-E-N-B-A-C-H-E-R."

Dooley read back what he had written. "R-I-C-K-E-N-B-A-C-H-E-R."

"That's it. No, wait a second! That's not it. What was I thinking?" He smacked his forehead with the palm of his hand. "His last name's not Rickenbacher. It's Mora."

"Mora? That name sounds more appropriate for a guy named Faustino. How do you spell it?"

"Mora. M-O-R-A. Mora."

"Got it, thanks. Say, what's *your* name?"

"My last name? It's von Houteinenen."

"Von what? How do you spell that?"

The coffee-like gasoline that Eddie was pumping into the Toronado began pouring out onto the ground.

"You'd better get that, Eddie. I gotta use your phone anyway." While Eddie attended to the spill, Dooley ducked into the office and dialed headquarters.

The operator was the first to answer. "Headquarters, who do you need?"

"This is Dooley. Give me Homily." Dooley waited through some beeping and clicking noises.

"Yeah?"

"Captain? Dooley here."

"Dooley! Where the hell are you?"

"I'm heading up to Northside."

"What the hell for? I wanted you to work on the First Lady case. You're not working on any of the others are you?"

"No, I'm still on the First Lady case."

"Listen, Dooley, I want you to devote all your efforts to cracking this one. If you can't solve this one, it's back to crossing guard duty for you, Dooley. Understand? I'm not kidding. I'm going to put you at the corner of 202nd Street and 17th Avenue. I mean it!"

"I'll solve it."

"You sound pretty confident. You get some kinda break in the case?"

"I was having some coffee and I had a brainstorm. The pieces are starting to fall into place."

"What are you going to Northside for? Not another wild goose chase, I hope."

"No, this is the real thing this time."

"Get results, Hank. We need it, bad. The City needs it. The entire *world* needs it. Everything is riding on this one, Hank. Get results."

"I will. I need something, though. I need an address for a Maritsa or Faustino Mora. One or both live somewhere near Piano Street."

"Hold the line. I'll transfer you down to Records." Homily bungled the transfer and disconnected him.

Dooley walked back out of the office to Eddie, who was standing near the pumps squeezing the foam pad of a squeegee into his open mouth. The blue windshield washer fluid was tinged with dark red. "I've gotta go, Eddie."

"Good luck, cop. You'd make an awful crossing guard." Eddie was laughing as Dooley left the Sunoco station.

Chapter 8

Maritsa Mora answered the door without caution or hesitation. This was an unusual and refreshing change from the stone-cold reception he normally received. Dooley quickly looked her over. She was a little on the short side and a tad chunky, but not unpleasantly so. She wasn't a slob, just sort of comfortable with herself.

"I'm Detective Dooley, Miss Mora. I'd like to ask you some questions."

"You really a detective, Mister? You look too stupid to have passed the test. What about your badge?" She looked closely, albeit quickly, at Dooley's badge. Her expression softened for a second while she was studying it. "Okay, come in." She locked the door after he entered. "I guess you're smarter than you look. You smell like coffee, Detective. What do you want with me? Whatever it is, I'm sure I did it."

Dooley walked into the dining room area at the end of the hallway and figured he'd gone far enough inside the apartment for comfort. "Miss Mora, have you been to Motor Vehicles recently?"

Maritsa walked past him and into the tiny living room, drawing Dooley a couple more steps into the apartment. "Motor Vehicles? Yeah, I been there."

"Do you recall meeting a man there?"

"Yeah. So?"

Dooley had expected a little resistance and was surprised at her willingness to answer so frankly. "This guy, did you—how can I put this...?"

"Make it with him?" She smiled a little and looked penetratingly into Dooley's eyes.

"That's about the size of it." Dooley was a little uncomfortable with how easily she was talking about it.

"So what if I did? Is it against the law to spread your legs nowadays?"

"I'm investigating carnage not carnal knowledge, Miss Mora."

"Ooh, I bet you're real impressed with yourself for that one."

55

He snuck a look down at her thighs. She sneered at him, but he missed it. All he could see was a quick image of what she might look like with her legs spread. He recovered himself quickly and pressed on. "I am, actually. Did he talk to you about anything?"

"No, he just whipped it out and screwed me silly without saying anything. I mean, what kind of girl do you think I am, Detective Doobie?"

Dooley didn't have to think long and hard on that one. "If you must know, I think you're a slut. I think you'd screw anything as long as it paid you a compliment first. Does that sum it up?" She didn't have a quick retort. "What did he tell you, eh? Did he talk about his job or anything he was up to that day?"

"No, nothing like that. He talked about wanting to do some traveling—get away from the City, you know?" She turned around, bending a little to pick up a pack of cigarettes and matches from the cluttered coffee table.

Dooley waited until she turned back and he knew he had her attention again. While he waited, he enjoyed the generous curve of her rear end. "Did he talk about his friends? Did he have any strong political opinions? Did he mention an event of great importance?" She finally straightened up and turned back to face him. "Did he tell you that you have a nice ass?"

Maritsa smiled as she lit up her cigarette. "No."

"No, what?"

"No, he didn't say I have a nice ass." She took a deep drag and scrutinized Dooley as she blew out the smoke. "He liked my tits."

Dooley caught himself glancing down at her chest.

"You see, Detective, I wasn't wearing a bra that morning. He was captivated by my nipples." She took another drag on her cigarette. "What a coincidence!"

"What coincidence?"

"Well, I wasn't wearing a bra that morning and I'm not wearing one now." She pulled her T-shirt away from her neck and looked down to her chest. "I think that's a coincidence, don't you?"

Dooley was stupefied. He never expected this murder investigation to stall on a question about a young woman's nipples. He nervously reached for his tie, fiddling with it as if it was askew. At the same time, he locked his head and eyes above her chest.

"Hey, wait a second. Why would you think he would've complimented my ass, Detective?"

"Huh? Oh, well, no reason in particular. It was a figure of speech. I didn't..."

"Bullshit. It's that *you* like my ass, Detective. Isn't that it?" Maritsa turned and leaned over, putting her cigarette out in the ashtray on the table. "Do I have a nice ass?" She asked him, without turning, while she was still bent over.

Dooley cleared his throat, realizing he had missed a breath or two. "Well, when you stand like that and stick your hip out that way, I suppose a reasonable person might be inclined to say..."

"Come on, Sherlock. Take out that magnifying glass of yours and take a good look at my ass."

"I don't have a magnifying glass. That's not standard issue..."

"Well, you don't need a magnifying glass anyway, with your eyes being so big and round. Why don't you just come out and tell me I have a nice ass, Detective Dooley?" She looked over her shoulder at him, while she ground her hips slowly and hypnotically.

"Look, Miss Mora, I didn't come here to talk about your ass, for chrissakes."

Maritsa abandoned her pose and turned to face him, closing the gap between them. "Ha! 'Miss Mora'! How formal we are—like you're my social studies teacher or something. You're standing there with your mouth agape, turning red as a beet, staring at my tight round ass, and you call me 'Miss Mora'." She dropped her voice in a comical imitation of his when she said the last words. "Why don't you call me Maritsa? Everybody else does." The next words she whispered to him, as if they were sharing a private secret in a public place. "You can touch my ass, if you want to. I'll let you."

Dooley felt uncomfortably hot and wiped his forehead with his left palm. "Maritsa—Miss Mora, you really shouldn't do that. I'm here on official police business, you know. I'm, I'm..."

"I'll tell you what you are. You're sweating, Detective Dooley. You should take off that jacket and tie."

"Please stop undulating your hips like that."

"How do you want me to undulate my hips, Detective? Like this, maybe?"

"That's not what I meant. I don't want you to undulate your hips at all." Dooley knew with every atom in his being that he should've walked to the door and left Maritsa alone to practice her nymphomaniacal hip-dance in solitude. However, even at a distance of three feet, he could swear that he was feeling the heat of her body. He wondered if she had any blood or if it was pure estrogen coursing through her veins.

She spoke again and killed any last scrap of willpower he might have used to get away. "What's the matter, Tarzan? You don't like my ass anymore?"

"No, I like your ass. It's really a fine specimen. But, that's not the point! I have some very important questions."

"Well, if you like my ass, I bet you'll *love* my thighs. Here, let me show you," she said excitedly as she unsnapped her jeans and pushed them down her legs. When she got them to her knees, she grabbed Dooley's arm to steady herself. She peeled the jeans off first one leg, then the other. "They're brown."

"What?"

"My thighs, Detective Dummy! They're brown like coffee with cream because I'm Colombian. That's where the smoothest, best-tasting coffee comes from. My mama said I was born in a coffee field, surrounded by coffee beans. Look, Detective, see how brown and smooth they are?" She stepped back and displayed her thighs.

Dooley didn't want to look. He wanted to ask his questions and get the hell out of there. But, Maritsa was right. Her thighs were indeed just as she described—smooth and unblemished and a lovely brown color—and he *did* love them. They reminded him of coffee. She remained with her hands on her hips, wearing just the light blue snug-fitting T-shirt, white panties and black socks. "Holy Jesus."

"Maybe you don't believe they are smooth?"

"I believe they are smooth."

"Nah, I don't know, Detective Dooley. You look a little skeptical to me. Maybe you need to touch them a little. Just to remove any doubt you might have." She grabbed his tie. "Here, let me help you. You look like you can use all the help you can get." She pulled him down and forced him to his knees in front of her, placing her hand gently on the back of his head.

He looked at her as he reached out to encircle her thighs. He could see her hairs. He could smell her perfume. He was astonished at how good she felt—soft and firm. He pressed his face into her and made up his mind to ask his questions later.

Chapter 9

Maritsa rolled her naked body over and rested her cheek on Dooley's hairy chest. "Didn't you say you wanted to ask me something, Detective Dooley?"

"Huh? Oh, yeah, *that*." He sighed heavily. "Yeah, I came to your door yesterday investigating a murder, didn't I? I had a hunch you might be able to help me."

"And did I help you?"

"Me? Yes! I feel like a new man. Jesus H. Christ, Maritsa, if all the people I question were like you, I'd work for free." He reached down and scratched his knee. "Now, the investigation—that's a different story. You haven't helped that at all."

Maritsa scooted up on Dooley's chest and ran her finger over his chin and lips. "Do you still like my ass, Detective? I mean now that you and my ass know each other so well? And wasn't I right about my thighs?"

"You certainly were, Maritsa." He stroked her smooth, coffee-colored arm.

"What about my nipples?"

"What about your nipples?"

"Do you like them, too? Look how nice and dark they are." She propped herself up to display herself to better advantage. "See?" She toyed with her left nipple.

Dooley rolled his eyes. "Oh, please, Maritsa. I've already lost more than thirty-six hours. I really can't afford to lose any more time on this investigation. I need to make some progress on this case or I'll be the next crossing guard in front of Daisy Hill Elementary."

Maritsa lowered herself back down on his chest. "So what is this big, important case you came to ask me about?"

"This guy you met at Motor Vehicles…"

"*He* liked my tits."

"That's true. I recall your saying so. Anyway, do you remember about what time you hooked up with him?"

"I think so. Let's see. Motor Vehicles opens at eight. I got on line at about five after eight. Then it turned out I got on the wrong line. I didn't find that out until I got to the window and the lady told me."

"How long did that take?"

"I guess maybe forty five minutes? Something like that. So, then I had to get on the right line and by then the place was mobbed. I had to wait about an hour on that line."

"So what time did you finish up?"

"A little before ten, I guess."

"Is that when you gave the guy you met a blowjob?"

"A blowjob!" She popped up like a jack-in-the-box. "Ha! Is that what he said?"

"He didn't really specify. I thought he said that you gave him a blowjob in a stairwell at Motor Vehicles."

"No way! What do you take me for? Honey, I don't blow *anybody*. Nobody gets Maritsa's mouth, no matter how much I like 'em. And certainly not at Motor Vehicles! I'm saving that for when I get married."

"I just thought…"

"Well, *don't* think! That's not exactly an ideal romantic hideaway, you know. I took him back here. Hey, how come you're scratching your butthole? Does it itch you, baby? You want me to scratch it for you?"

"No, I don't think it would help. What was this guy's name?"

"The guy at Motor Vehicles? Ed was his name, I think."

"Did he happen to say what he does for a living?"

Maritsa pursed her brow in concentration. "No, he didn't say. But, he did say he was running late for work."

"Late? Are you sure?"

"Yeah. He said he was already a half-hour late and he shot out of here like—you know, you really shouldn't scratch your butthole like that. It can't be good for it."

"Will you forget my butthole for a minute? What time did this Ed cut out of here? Do you remember?"

"I don't know. About nine or nine-fifteen."

Dooley propped himself up. "That's not possible."

"Maybe you should see a doctor about your butthole. That's not normal. It shouldn't itch like that."

"Maritsa, you said you finished at Motor Vehicles around ten o'clock. How could...?"

"Because, Detective Dummy, you're not thinking in Maritsa-Time. That was ten o'clock on *Tuesday* and Ed left on *Wednesday*. He really liked my tits a lot. Do you like my tits, Detective?" She scooted up so that her breast was directly in front of his face. "What about this one? Isn't it nice and cute? Look, the nipple is getting hard."

"Oh, jeez, Maritsa." It was obvious the investigation would stall a little longer.

Chapter 10

Dooley dragged himself heroically up the stairs at police headquarters. He felt the way he imagined someone feels after they go fifteen rounds in a world title fight. He had sore muscles where he had forgotten he'd even had muscles. He had mustered just enough energy to get back home to his apartment, change his clothes and get to the office. He would have preferred to have stayed home and slept for a few hours or even a few days, but he knew he was badly overdue reporting in and the Captain would be upset.

He knew Homily would be expecting *something* from him after five days incommunicado—something other than just a sore back and dry testes. Something Maritsa had cried out during one of her innumerable orgasms got Dooley thinking of non-political reasons for the murder of the Mayor's wife. Because of the woman's shabbiness at the time of her death, Dooley hadn't considered money or jealousy as a motive. But, closeness to the Mayor's office meant closeness to power and, by extension, money. Once he finally managed to extricate himself from the soft and satiny clutches of Maritsa Mora, Dooley spent nearly twenty-six hours digging into the files of all the businesses that seemed to be connected—by proximity or by person—to the event. He'd found a couple of intriguing tidbits, but nothing concrete. Sometimes that's all a detective has to go on.

"Good morning, Captain."

"Dooley! Where the hell have you been? I had the harbor patrol dragging the river for your body! You didn't answer your phone. We sent a squad car around to your apartment."

"I wasn't home."

"Well, we figured that out. After a while we figured that some terrible characters had gotten ahold of you like they did poor Pfeiffer."

Dooley thought for a second that if Pfeiffer had been given the chance to meet his maker in Maritsa's bedroom rather than that dark alley, he might have done so willingly and stopped off for a box of chocolates on the way. "Captain, I've been working around the clock on this case, questioning witnesses—one key witness in particular. And I've been spending a lot of time in the Hall of Records."

Homily seemed relieved to hear it. "That's good, that's good. But you are supposed to check in twice a day. I can understand missing a time or two, but nobody's seen you for four days, Hank!"

"I'm sorry, Captain. I really couldn't check in. I was seriously compromised for most of that time. I'll tell you that there were moments when I was in no condition to report."

"I believe you, Hank. I didn't want to say, but you really look like shit. This witness must have given you a hard time."

"I haven't had any sleep. And I haven't eaten much either."

"It looks like they just sucked the life right out of you."

"No, not sucked. Everything *but* sucked."

The Captain got an eager look on his face. "Tell me, Hank, do you have something? Have you found anything out yet? The witness you mentioned, have you gotten anywhere with him? I don't think I need to tell you, the newspapers are breathing down my neck again. They think these things are easy. They think all you have to do is just walk up to a witness and get a description, match up a fingerprint and make an arrest. Arggh! Fuck 'em!"

Dooley noticed for the first time that the Captain looked haggard. "Captain, I have a theory I want to run by you. Can I sit down?"

"Sure, go ahead. Say, you really have been working hard on this case. You're shaking like a leaf."

"I'll be all right once I get some food and a good night's sleep. I think the First Lady was killed by a local merchant that had a beef with the mayor's office."

"What merchant? What was the beef?"

"Just for instance, Tiny's Tavern had a major difficulty with their liquor license and had to shell out a lot of money to fix the problem. They'd served one too many minors, it seems, and they were just about to be pad-locked the day after the murder. And the guy that works the day shift opened early that morning, which, according to people who know, is highly unusual."

"Good! Check him out. See if he's got any friends who might have— Dooley? Hank!"

Dooley snapped awake. "Huh? What is it, Captain?"

"You sort of drifted off there for a minute." Homily peered at him, closely. "You'd better go home and get some rest."

"You're right. You're right. I'll go home. That's what I'll do."

"Hey, what about that Marissa Mora or Francisco Mora lead you were following?"

"Maritsa Mora. I've been pumping her for all it's worth for days, Captain."

"Any hot tips there? Or is she holding out on you?"

"Captain, if she's holding out, it's not apparent to me. She's opened up and offered whatever she has, with little or no encouragement, I might add. Quite willing. Quite willing. If we had more help like hers..."

"Good work, Dooley. Keep it up."

"I have. Believe me, I have."

"Did you get to talk to Francisco, too?"

"Who's Francisco?"

"The brother."

"Oh, Faustino. No, I didn't. I guess I should, huh?"

He put his hand on Dooley's shoulder. "Hank, don't leave any stone unturned. You know, if you manage to solve this case, there'll be a promotion and a raise waiting for you." He smiled proudly for a second, then dropped the other shoe. "If not, you're dead meat, friend. Now, go home and get some rest. I'll see you in the morning." He patted Dooley on the back and ushered him out of the office.

Dooley nodded and shuffled down the stairs and to the parking lot. Despite his overwhelming fatigue, he needed sustenance, so instead of going straight home to bed, he stopped at the Riviera first.

"Hank! Jesus, are you all right? Where have you been? I thought I lost a customer."

There was one other patron, a shabby old guy, who sat quietly at a table, still wearing his hat and overcoat. The guy was slowly working on a spaghetti and meatballs dinner, washing it down with a cup of coffee. Dooley's heart leaped when he saw the coffee cup. "I'm still here, Marty. I need coffee. And fix me up a burger and fries, but bring me the coffee first."

"Of course, my friend."

Dooley couldn't get the sugar in the cup fast enough and he drank the sweet and hot beverage with his eyes rolled up in his head like a junkie shooting up. "Ohhh, man. Ahhh, that's so good."

He had a second cup and was feeling more himself as Marty finished frying up his burger. "Colombia must be an interesting place, Marty."

"I've never been to college. Hell, I just barely escaped high school."

"I mean the country, not the University."

"Oh, of course. Colombia is a country. I heard of it. What's so interesting about it?"

"They grow coffee beans there."

"Oh, yeah?"

"You ever meet anybody from Colombia?"

"Can't say that I have. Are they anything like Porto Ricans?"

"They've got a lot of energy. You have to have a lot of energy to make coffee beans, I guess."

A strange, abrasive voice piped up from the middle of the room. "Don't talk to me about Porto Ricans." It was the lone guy at the table, talking from under his hat. "My wife was Cuban. I'll tell you this: there's no way in hell that the Cubans didn't really want Castro."

Marty was willing to bite. "Why's that, bud?"

"'Cause those communists would have been no match for just half a dozen Cuban women, that's why."

Dooley and Marty assimilated that for a moment, then Marty broke the silence. "I had a customer from the Dominican Republic once."

"What did she order?"

"Ham and eggs I think."

"That's not very exotic."

"These women from other countries are *not* exotic, I tell ya." It was the guy with the Cuban wife talking again. "They're just far away. They're from across the sea. The Greeks call 'em Barbarians, you know. We call 'em Cubans. Same thing, if you ask me." Then he started singing, "you say ta-mayto an' I say tamotto…"

"Here's your burger, Hank. Onions with that?"

"Sure. Why not?"

"I hope you haven't got a hot date planned tonight."

"The onions? No, I've had enough 'hot date' to last me for a while."

"Ah! So *that's* why you look like the walking dead. And here I thought it was some mob guys that worked you over. Ha! You're getting' too old for playing the tomcat, Hank. Who was it? One of the girls at Dolly's Gentleman's Club? Or a suspect?"

"It was just a Colombian girl I went to question."

"Colombian! Marty, did this guy say he's got a Colombian girlfriend?"

"Yeah, he sure did, bud."

"She's not my girlfriend, pal. I just met her in the line of duty. She's a possible witness."

"A witness to what, Officer?"

"A crime."

"Which crime, Hank?"

"If you must know, Marty, it's the murder of the First Lady."

"Oh, was she there when it happened?" Marty refilled the coffee cup.

"Nope."

"Did she hear something? Does she know something?"

"Well, no. Not exactly."

"Then what is she a witness to, Hank, other than your sweaty grimace?"

"I don't know yet, but I'll find out." He took a big bite of his burger, the onions dropping out of the far end of the bun as he did so.

"Hey, Officer, you shoulda ordered the spaghetti and meatballs. It's a lot better than that lousy burger you got there."

"How's that?" Dooley wondered how a plate of spaghetti and meatballs could possibly be better than the fat, greasy burger he was chomping on right at that moment.

"It's the tomato sauce. It's good for a man's blood. Makes him more virile."

"Oh yeah? What does it do for women, pal?"

"Makes them more..." The man waved his fork around as he searched for just the right word. " ... busty." He bit into a big, round meatball.

Dooley was only half full of shit when he said that Maritsa was a possible witness. He didn't really think she knew anything of value, but he was certain that the people around her were lying about a lot of things and that they were guilty of something. As he crunched down on a large piece of gristle in his burger, he decided he'd talk to her brother, Faustino. He'd eluded being questioned thus far. Maybe he was hiding the truth, too.

The following day, he drove out to Plano Street and pulled into the service station just as a young dark-haired man was finishing with a customer.

"Fill 'er up, sir?"

"Sure. Why not?" Dooley got out and picked the squeegee out of the bucket.

"You should let me do the windshield, sir."

"That's all right. I like using a squeegee. Are you Faustino?" Dooley swiped the windshield of his sedan.

"You know me from somewhere?" Faustino dialed up the 87 octane and started pumping.

"I don't know you, but I know *of* you."

"And who are you?"

"Police, Detective Dooley. Hey! This stuff looks like real windshield washer fluid."

"It is. We're the only station in town that uses it. Everybody else cheaps-out."

"Faustino, what do you remember about last Tuesday?"

"Last Tuesday? What am I supposed to remember about last Tuesday?" The gas tank was already filled and the pump stopped after some gas splashed out onto the ground.

"Did you work last Tuesday?"

"I suppose so." His answer got no response from Dooley, so he thought about it some more. "Yes, I did work last Tuesday."

"What time?"

"From six to four. No, wait. I had to work late one day last week and I'm pretty sure it was Tuesday."

"Until what time?"

"I had to work 'til closing. The other guy that works here didn't show up that day. He usually closes up, but not Tuesday. I had to close that night. Your gas is only a dollar ten."

"Did he ever say why he didn't show up?" Dooley finished with the windshield and dropped the squeegee back in the bucket.

"No, he never did. And he was late the next day, too. I thought I was going to have to stay late again, but he showed up around eleven o'clock. Good thing too, because I had to cut out early to help my sister out."

"What'd your sister need?"

"Why do you need to know that? She didn't do anything."

"Just routine. You never know when some bit of information turns out to be important to a broad investigation like this one."

"Well, okay. You see, my sister is kinda popular—with boys, I mean."

"No kidding."

"What did you say?"

"Oh, nothing. I just said no kidding. What girl isn't, huh? Just a figure of speech. Go on."

"Well, my sister may be in the top percentile in that category. It's a long story. She's been popular with the boys since she was eleven or twelve. She's very forward. Mama kicked her out of the house last year because of it. She's been living in her own apartment for about a year now. I pay her rent for her, but now that she's almost sixteen years old…"

Letting out a noise that sounded something like 'gned', Dooley leaned on the hood of his car to keep his knees from buckling under him. Almost choking on his own saliva, he started coughing and sputtering and had a sudden urge to go to the bathroom.

"Are you okay, sir? What's the matter? You're white as a sheet!"

He finally stopped coughing long enough to answer Faustino. "I'll be all right. I'll be all right. I just—I had a reaction." He took a few deep breaths and placed his trembling right hand on his chest in a vain attempt to calm his pounding heart. "Jesus H. Christ," he panted.

"You don't look too good, mister. You're sweating!"

"Don't worry about it. What were you saying?"

"Are you sure you're okay? You're lookin' kinda greenish, now."

"Go ahead, will you!"

"Okay. So, anyway, my sister is trying to get a learner's permit. The thing is she may be precocious in some ways, but she's hapless when it comes to business matters and taking care of important stuff. She's kind of irresponsible. I have to practically force-feed her birth control pills. She forgets to take them half the time. I'm worried right now because I haven't checked in

70

on her in a few days. Hey, are you sure you're all right? You look really horrible!"

Dooley was practically doubled-over. "I did have a few more questions, but maybe I'd better come back tomorrow. You think I could do that, man?"

"I won't be on duty tomorrow. Eddie will."

"Eddie?"

"The other guy that works here. Here let me help you into your car."

"Is his last name von something-or-other?"

"Yeah, that's him. Von Houteinenen. You look strange again."

"My asshole suddenly started itching me."

"You're really a mess, aren't you?"

"No, it's a good thing."

"If you say so, sir."

Dooley pulled out of the gas station without paying for the gas and headed straight for Tiny's Tavern. It took him nearly the entire trip to recover his calm and catch his breath. Visions of paternity suits and Maritsa's birthday suit flashed before his eyes several times en route to Tiny's. He pictured her belly growing rounder. He saw images—like mini documentaries—of his sperm swimming frantically upstream to her youthful eggs. Each time he had to pull over and wait for the panic attack to subside. He knew she was a young woman, but he would have guessed her to be nineteen or twenty, especially based on how world-wise she was. He actually began to formulate an escape plan to some other city or country before he finally came to his senses. There was no reason to panic yet.

He'd expected to see Edgar behind the bar at Tiny's, but instead there was a sour-looking man, polishing glasses and smoking a cigar.

"Where's Edgar?"

"I haven't a clue."

"Isn't he supposed to be tending bar right now?"

"I don't know no Edgar. Either order a drink or beat it, fella."

"Look, you slimy shit stain, I'm not here to schmooze with Edgar. I'm investigating a murder and you're going to help, whether you like it or not. You get me?"

"Yeah, I got ya. It don't change nothin', 'cause I still don't know no Edgar. I was hired this morning when the owner called the agency, sayin' the regular guy quit."

"What agency?"

"AAA Employment Agency on Garber Street."

"What time did they call you?"

"I don' know. About ten? Maybe five minutes to ten? Listen, pal, maybe there's something you oughta know."

"What's that?"

"There's a stiff in the dumpster out back. I seen it when I broke down some cartons. Maybe it's this guy you're askin' about."

"Didn't you think to call the police, for chrissakes?"

"Sure I did. I figured that would be a bad idea, though."

"Why?"

"I didn't want no trouble. The guy was dead already anyway, so *he* wouldn't care. I need this job real bad, you know what I mean? I got rent to pay."

"What if it was *you* stuffed into a dumpster?"

The bartender smiled. "Then I wouldn't be worried about payin' my rent no more, would I?"

Back at Headquarters at quarter past five, Dooley was looking at the lab and coroner's reports that had just been placed in his hands. The body in the dumpster did turn out to be Edgar's. Dooley had waited for the reports to come back before going in to see Captain Homily. All afternoon, while he was waiting for the reports, he dug deeper into the backgrounds of the businesses that seemed to be connected to the case. He hadn't had the opportunity to re-interview any of the parties involved before Homily was at his doorstep.

"Whoa! What's all this paperwork, Hank?" There were several piles all over Dooley's desk and still more on the floor.

"I've been pulling public records on the local businesses that I believe are connected somehow to the First Lady's murder. I believe I may have had a breakthrough in this case. Interested?"

"Give it to me from the top."

Dooley took a deep breath. "All right, this is what I've ascertained so far. Wednesday morning, Edgar opens Tiny's Tavern early. The Mayor's wife gets shot. An old man, claiming to be a killer, is seen wandering around like a nut that morning. Eddie von Houteinenen shows up late for work that day at the Sunoco Station on Plano Street. His co-worker, Faustino, has a sister who did Eddie on Tuesday night and Wednesday morning. Meanwhile Edgar falsely claims to have done Faustino's sister in a stairwell at Motor Vehicles. Now Eddie has disappeared and Edgar is dead. Furthermore, Edgar seems to have been killed by, according to the lab report..." He shuffled through some paperwork. "Let's see. Here it is: 'repeated blows to the head by a squeegee'."

"A squeegee! How do they know it was a squeegee?"

"Evidently, there were bits of foam rubber imbided with motor oil and windshield washer fluid and numerous dead bugs, all of which were found embedded in Edgar's skull."

"Death by squeegee. But, what about a motive? Does anybody have one?"

"That's the interesting part. I checked with the various licensing bureaus to see who had a beef with the mayor's task forces."

"And?"

"Tiny's had to pay out a bundle in fines and kickbacks to keep their license. Nifty Oil Corporation, the owners of the service station on Plano Street that Eddie von Houteinenen works for..."

"You like saying that, don't you?"

"...anyway, they had to pay fines for rigging their pumps and overcharging their customers."

"No wonder they can afford to use real windshield washer fluid in their squeegee bucket."

"I checked, by the way, and they are the only service station in the entire city that uses real windshield washer fluid in their buckets. Everybody else uses oily water. But that's not all. The old guy I mentioned?"

"Yeah?"

"He lived in Alberghetti's rooming house for fifteen years, which the City condemned and he got put out on the street. But, that's *still* not all. Twitchell's Pharmacy, where the murder took place? They were cited nine times for violating laws in handling and improperly dispensing drugs. The old man, Kinder, complained about Twitchell's to his councilman, who started the investigation."

"So, you're telling me that *everybody* has a motive for the murder?"

Dooley sat back. "Everybody and nobody."

"Huh? What do you mean by that?"

"I checked further and found out that a lot of businesses have had similar dealings with the Mayor's office in the last year. Do you know how many?"

"How many?"

"Over thirty-three thousand."

"They can't all be guilty. What are you telling me?"

"I'm telling you that I don't think anybody had a good reason to kill the Mayor's wife. That having been said, I do think there may have been good reasons for one or more of the interested parties to kill another."

Homily stood up and paced back and forth as he ran it through his mind. "You're telling me that you think the Mayor's wife was killed by accident in the crossfire?"

"That's what I think."

"Then, who was supposed to have gotten their ticket punched?"

"We should know pretty soon. They're bringing in Eddie von Houteinenen as we speak. They picked him up at the bus station this afternoon."

Chapter 11

Twitchell tried to play it super-nonchalant, but he was apparently nervous that Dooley had come into his drug store to question him again. "You want to ask me questions? I thought you came in because this case was giving you a headache or a bellyache or something. Ha, ha! I can help you with that kind of thing. I don't know what I can help you with, otherwise."

"No, I don't need any help with any medical condition."

"Well, that's good, eh? Ha, ha."

Twitchell was busying himself with looking through prescriptions, but Dooley could tell that he was nervous and just killing time. Dooley decided to dive right in. "Twitchell, ever hear of a young woman by the name of Marthe Kinder?"

"Marthe Kinder, eh? Hmm." He rubbed his chin, thoughtfully. "No, the name doesn't ring a bell. Should I know it?"

"My asshole is itching me something fierce all of a sudden."

"Right behind you on the top shelf. Anusol and Preparation H."

"I don't have piles."

"What, then?"

"Marthe Kinder was the light of Heinrich Kinder's life."

"That's mighty sentimental, Dooley, but I really have to fill these prescriptions, you know."

"You filled a prescription for that poor girl, Marthe Kinder. You filled a prescription for her ten years ago last Wednesday. Do you remember that prescription, by any chance?"

"Ten years ago, you say? Don't be ridiculous, Dooley. How could I remember one prescription from so long ago? Please let me finish these prescriptions, now. I really don't have the time for this chit-chat." He went back to fishing through the prescriptions and looking busy.

Dooley waited a few seconds, watching Twitchell nervously fuss with the paperwork. "I'm surprised that you don't remember that prescription, because somebody else does. That somebody will never forget that prescription as long as he lives."

"Oh? It all sounds very mysterious. I suppose this somebody has some kind of photographic memory."

"I have a suggestion."

"What's that, Dooley?"

"Why don't you cut the bullshit?"

Twitchell finally stopped fidgeting with the paperwork and gave Dooley his undivided attention. "Have you ever made a mistake, Dooley? You know, I wasn't exactly number one in my graduating class. In fact, as I recall, I was never 'number one' in anything. My brother, however, was a different story. My brother, Mitchell, was the apple of my mother's eye. For her, he could do wrong. And he never *did* do wrong. My mother…"

Dooley rolled his eyes and he whined. "Oh, jeez! My asshole is driving me crazy! I told you to cut the bullshit, not serve it up with coleslaw and fries, Twitchell! You killed that poor innocent young woman, Twitchell, and you did it deliberately. You hired her to work the register and you seduced her one night at closing time, while she was counting the money in the till. Then, because you were never particular with whom you got your jollies, you gave the poor girl a dose of the clap. When she found out what horrible disease she had contracted and threatened to reveal to her distraught father who gave it to her, you prescribed her a dose of death—just to shut her up and save your reputation."

"I did not!"

"The Grand Jury cleared you for lack of evidence, but Heinrich Kinder knew the truth and he never forgave you. He kept close tabs on you for years. Always coming to you for his prescriptions, despite the fact that there were half a dozen pharmacies closer than yours to his crappy little apartment. He waited patiently until you couldn't take his hounding anymore and you tried to kill him, too! Didn't you?"

"That's not true, Dooley! You're making it all up. And you're upsetting my customers, too."

That part *was* true. There were a couple of old ladies in the drug store and they did look upset. Dooley glared at the old ladies until they demurred, then turned back to Twitchell and forged ahead. "It backfired, didn't it? You gave him poison, he turned you in and you paid hefty fines and almost lost everything. The Inspector General got a nice early Christmas present from you that year, didn't he?"

Twitchell slammed down his hand on the counter and Dooley flinched, expecting the glass to shatter. "None of this is true! You'll pay for this slanderous attack. I swear it. I have powerful friends in high places, cop. I'll have your hide for this. And I'll stuff your skin so I can use it to display trusses and adult diapers in the window for everyone to gawk at. Ha, ha!"

The old ladies, shocked at this unprecedented display of raw emotion at the pharmacy counter, scurried out of the store as fast as their osteoporotic legs would take them.

Dooley was unperturbed by Twitchell's threat and went on without missing a beat. "Kinder never gave up. The emotional strain almost killed him, but he kept at it, year after grueling year. Everybody thought he was so very old. Ha! I looked him up. He's only fifty-seven years old. Fifty-seven, Twitchell! That's how hard this ordeal has been for him."

Twitchell was shocked. "That's impossible! That can't be true."

"Ah, but it is. He's got the appearance of a man twice his age. That's what the loss of a loved one—a child—can do to you. But, you wouldn't know about that, would you? You've never loved anybody in your whole life, have you? Have you, Twitchell?"

"What's all this leading to, Dooley? Surely you can't arrest a man for someone else's prematurely wrinkled face."

"No, you can't. But you can arrest a man for murder."

"But, the Grand Jury found no grounds for a case, remember?"

"I'm not talking about Marthe Kinder. I'm talking about the Mayor's wife."

"Ha! You saw me yourself, unloading the truck when she got shot! You're nuts, Dooley. I had no motive to kill that woman. Get the hell outta my store, before I call your superiors and have you brought before a disciplinary board."

"I must admit, Twitchell, although I had my doubts while I was chatting with you, I never really seriously suspected you. That is until we found the bartender at Tiny's, across the street, stuffed into his own dumpster."

"Are you going to blame me for that, too?"

"I don't have to. Edgar's death note blames you."

"What are you talking about? What the hell is a 'death note'?"

"Edgar suspected that you'd double-cross him. So he left a note, detailing your partnership and placed it in an envelope, marking it: "in the event of my death". We found that note, Twitchell, neatly typed out. You and he were partners in a plot to kill Heinrich Kinder. You couldn't kill him with drugs. Kinder made sure of that by filing that complaint and repeatedly coming back to your pharmacy. Naturally, you'd be the first and only suspect in the event of a drug-related death. So you hired Edgar. The shot could be fired from the roof over the tavern, which affords a perfect view of this side of the street through the elm trees. Problem was that Edgar knew he couldn't hit the broad side of a barn. So he subcontracted his old army buddy, "Steady Eddie" von Houteinenen, an expert marksman and the meaner of the two Eds. And if you think solving this case was hard, learning to spell Eddie's last name was ten times harder."

"I congratulate you."

"Thank you. Everything was set. The old man, Kinder, took his morning walk to pick up the paper and buy his egg on a roll, like he did every morning around a quarter to ten. He was sure to pass here around nine-fifty or nine fifty-five, as he always did. People would think you were just loading boxes from the van, but you'd be out here to give the signal when Kinder was approaching. You can't see up the avenue from the roof of the tavern. Edgar opened early, which provided timely access to the roof for Eddie. But, "Steady Eddie" was late. You couldn't have known it at the time, but he had for weeks been trying to figure out a way to score with his co-worker's sister, Maritsa. He'd heard some pretty enticing stories about her from her brother, who couldn't stop her from bedding every schmuck that crossed her path. But Eddie couldn't figure out how to hook up with her without the brother knowing. He'd heard that one morning—the morning before the job, it turned out—she'd be alone at Motor Vehicles downtown and he'd be free to approach her where her brother could not run into them. The problem was that Maritsa turned out hotter than even Eddie could manage. He spent all night and most of the next morning of that fateful day with her and could just barely drag himself away from her and stagger out of her apartment. Once he left Maritsa, he thought all was well."

"Well, was it?"

"No. It wasn't. He arrived late. When Eddie failed to show up on time, Edgar panicked. He didn't want to lose out on the payoff you had promised and couldn't trust that you wouldn't back out of the deal entirely, so he jumped the gun and pulled the trigger himself. But, if you recall, I said Edgar couldn't hit the broad side of a barn. He shot at Kinder, but missed so badly that he hit the Mayor's wife standing in the alley, instead. Eddie showed up a couple of minutes later, but too late. Kinder didn't even have a clue anything was going on. He went on to the Three Guys Luncheonette and got his egg on a roll as usual."

"You really believe this saga? What a disaster! When they make a movie out of it, they'll have to get Irwin Allen to direct it."

"When you saw what happened, you told Edgar the deal was off. Edgar was willing to live with that and go back to tending bar. He wasn't a killer and he liked tending bar well enough. He could live with that, but Eddie? Eddie was a different story. He wanted that money more than anything. He despised his job, his co-workers, his customers and his gas station attendant's uniform, so he had made these big plans for an escape. He told Maritsa, the girl he picked up at Motor Vehicles, that he was going to skip town and take her away with him. She didn't pay too much attention to what Eddie told her, but she did remember his telling her that he wanted to travel. When Edgar wouldn't pay off, Eddie became enraged and blamed Edgar for not waiting for him to take the shot at Kinder. He thought he was going to lose the chance to run away with his little sexpot."

"Poor Eddie."

"Don't feel too bad for Eddie. This bungled job didn't cheat him of his chance at running away with Maritsa. She wouldn't have run away with him anyway. She didn't want him anymore than she wanted m—um, anymore than she wanted any other man she could screw for a couple or three days. And anyway, Maritsa's brother stepped into the equation last night, whisking her away from that apartment after the neighbors told him of strange men coming and going and spending the night in her apartment during the past few days. To protect his sister from harm, Faustino has put her in the care of a widowed uncle, who lives with his three teenage sons on 121st Street. They'll be able to take care of her, keep her out of trouble and make sure all her needs are met."

"Well, that sets my heart to rest."

"Save your sarcasm. You're going to need it. As bad as Eddie's heartbreak was over the loss of the money, he was even more distraught over his lost chance at Maritsa. He couldn't believe he'd missed out by a whisker on such a hot piece of ass. Having had a few days to stew about his bad luck, Eddie beat his old army buddy to death with a squeegee last night. Eddie should have beat himself to death, because it was his getting that crack at Maritsa in the first place that led to him blowing his part of the job, scotching the big payoff, and preventing his running away with her. In effect, it was all his fault. End of story."

Twitchell took a long time to respond, standing stock still for seconds. "Well, who would ever dream that William Shakespeare is alive and well and working as a detective in our fair City? Unbelievable. Unbelievable. What about the "Steady Eddie" guy? He couldn't have corroborated this gothic tale of yours."

Dooley smiled. "Oh Eddie von Houteinenen? Eddie tried to beat it out of town on a Trailways bus this morning, but we nabbed him and brought him downtown for questioning."

"And?"

"Well, unfortunately, he sorta died during the interview."

Twitchell turned red. "What?!"

"Yeah, he went nuts and thrashed about and hit his head and kinda choked to death. Just between you and me, I don't think he would've survived a long road trip with Maritsa anyway. Yeah, he's no longer with us. But, before he croaked, he left us a present. He managed to scrawl his signature on a typed confession. So, when I say it was unfortunate that he died, I meant it was unfortunate for you."

Twitchell had gone from red to pasty-white at this last revelation. "This is a frame. You guys killed the only people who could have exonerated me. You'll burn in hell for this, Dooley. You'll fry like a cheap eggroll for all eternity. Satan will turn up the heat and your skin will look like the skin of an eggroll and every nerve in your body will scream out in unbearable agony!"

"Sorry you feel that way, Twitchell. Let's go, I have a warrant for your arrest. You've filled your last prescription."

"Wait!"

"What is it, Twitchell?"

"I'm not going anywhere with you unless you stop scratching your ass."

Chapter 12

"Papers, papers, papers." Dooley was muttering to himself as he finished up some standard forms pertaining to the regrettable outcome of the von Houteinenen questioning. Whenever a suspect dies in police custody there are endless forms to complete. This is done so that an accurate record is kept of the officer's version of events.

"Hi, Hank!"

"Hi, Perk. You're working late, too?"

"Nah, we were playing a few hands of pinochle in Capelli's office. I lost my stake."

"You'll get it back. I have to finish up these damn forms. That's the one drawback to losing a suspect here in the office."

"It was worth it, though, wasn't it?"

"I suppose so."

"I gotta hand it to you, Hank, you really pulled a rabbit out of the hat on this case. I could've sworn you were headin' for crossing guard duty this time. Tell me, how the hell did you keep a straight face when you were laying it all out for Twitchell?"

"I'll be honest with you, I didn't feel like laughing at all. All that time I thought my asshole was going to turn inside out. I couldn't believe how itchy it was."

"Ha! You and that asshole of yours—I didn't know it works on you, too. If I had known, I could've stepped in and done the deed, maybe saved you some grief. Though, like I said, I might've cracked up right in his face."

"You deserve half the credit, Perkins. I couldn't have made it stick without your help."

"You did most of the work. I only contributed the typewriter. And I got that replaced already."

Dooley was surprised. "How'd you manage that so fast? Usually they make you jump through hoops when you break a machine."

83

"I didn't claim it as broken. I claimed that it was lost or stolen while moving from room 208 last week. I got the new typewriter this morning. If I was going to claim it as broken, I would've had to clean it before handing it in. I didn't want to do that, so I tossed it in the dumpster—blood and all—and claimed it as stolen."

"I'm going to do that next time."

"Hi, boys. That was mighty fine work today, from both of you." Homily patted Perkins on the shoulder.

"Thanks, Captain. Hey, Captain, why didn't you let us question Twitchell, too?"

"Too high profile, Perk. He owns an established neighborhood business. Everybody knows him. Not to mention, I wanted the honors myself. I didn't want to leave it to a couple of flunkies who might screw it up." He laughed. "Plus, I promised the Mayor I'd handle it personally. That's the real reason."

Perkins sighed as he rose to his feet and stretched his spine. "Well, I'm tired. I'd better go. Billy's got little league tomorrow and I promised him I wouldn't miss another game." He wearily left the office.

"See you tomorrow, Perk."

"It's too bad we couldn't interview the girl. She might've provided some very interesting information."

"Captain, I think it was wise of the legal team to protect her. After all, we don't need her testimony and she's young and emotionally unstable. Who knows what things she might have said in her crazy sexual haze. She would have discredited her own testimony, no doubt. I think it's best."

"I suppose you're right. We don't need that kind of witness. A simple statement from her was sufficient. You're heading home now?"

"I thought I'd stop for some coffee before I go home."

Part II
<u>Assisted Suicide</u>

Chapter 13

"Another cup of coffee, Hank?"

"Sure, why not? I've already got the shakes. Might as well become completely spastic."

"You could switch to Sanka."

Dooley's eyes went wide. "Hank Dooley and Sanka? I might as well wear a girdle and high heels. That would really wash me up if the criminal element in this town found out I was drinking decaffeinated coffee. It's bad enough I have to drink it black. I hate it black, but I can't take the chance that someone might see me put milk in my coffee. That's why I load it down with tons of sugar."

Marty poured the coffee. "I always wondered about that. I just figured you have a sweet tooth."

"It's a wonder I have any teeth at all, with all the sugar I take in." He upended the sugar dispenser. "That's another reason I end up staggering out of here like I'm being butt-fucked on a rowboat. My blood sugar is so low after breakfast here that I'm weak as a kitten and have the shakes."

"Why don't you just drink less coffee? You don't really need eight or ten cups, you know."

"You're starting to sound like my mother."

"Must be that you bring out the motherly instincts in me."

Dooley got up from the stool. "I'm done. What's the damage?"

"Three-twenty."

Dooley plunked down a five-spot. "Here, keep the change."

"See ya, Hank."

A middle-aged man walked in just as Dooley turned to leave. "Are you Detective Dooley?"

"Yeah, why?"

"Hank Dooley?"

Dooley sized him up for a second. "Who are you?"

"I'm supposed to give you this." The man presented Dooley with a Hush Puppies shoebox.

Dooley accepted it. "What's this? Is it Christmas already?" As soon as Dooley had taken the box, the man hustled out the door. "Hey, you! Where ya going? Come back here!" Dooley's request for the man to stay fell on deaf ears. He didn't even hesitate as he left the Riviera and darted down the street. Dooley shook the box gently and tested the weight of it. "Sounds pretty heavy."

"What did he give you, Hank?"

"Let's see what's inside." He opened the lid and peeked inside. "Oh, jeez!"

"What is it, Hank, a sculpture? If it's a bomb, throw it out into the street, will ya'? The last thing I need is to blow up."

Dooley looked a little upset and wore an expression of disgust on his face. "I'll tell you later. I've gotta take it downtown." With that, he rushed out the door and to his car. On the trip to Headquarters, Dooley glanced repeatedly at the box, feeling a little spooked and afraid the contents would somehow jump out of the box at him. While he waited for a red light to change, he pushed the box to the far end of the passenger seat and placed a small duffel bag on top of it.

Once he got downtown, he turned the box over to the lab to analyze the contents and file a report, which he requested be rushed to him in the Captain's office. While he waited for the report, Dooley paid a visit to Homily to give him an account of the strange encounter.

"You didn't recognize the guy? Could he have been mob-connected?"

"He didn't look or act the part, Captain. He was really ordinary. I don't even know if I could describe him, other than to say he was middle-aged, white, clean-shaven, with an average height and build."

"That describes three hundred thousand men in this City, including you and me. Can you think of any reason why he might have given you the object?"

"Other than the two or three puns I came up with on the drive over here? No, none."

Just then, a young man entered the office, carrying an inter-office envelope. "Here you go, Captain Homily. Fresh off the presses."

"Thank you, Andrew. Tell the lab boys thanks for me, will you?" Captain Homily took the envelope from the messenger, removed the report and looked it over it as he walked back to his desk. Andrew withdrew as quickly as he had entered. "Well, Hank, looks like the lab boys confirmed what you thought."

"It was a woman's foot in that box?"

"Yep, a woman's foot." He closed the folder and placed it on his desk. "Well, I don't know too many men that paint their toenails."

"I know a few that do."

Homily picked up the folder and looked at it again. "It says here that it belonged to a woman in her twenties, about 5'5" and 125 pounds. It was, as we suspected, her right foot. The foot was very fresh. Hmm. They even have a checkbox for that. They've got 'Very fresh', 'Fresh', 'Turned', 'Rotten' and 'Skeletal'."

"Could they figure out how it was severed?"

Homily's eyes scanned the sheet. "Ah, here, they did! The pattern on the bones and soft tissue indicate that a Sawzall was used."

"A Sawzall? Is that some kind of medical equipment?"

"It's an electric reciprocating saw. Building contractors use it."

"What do you mean? Like a lathe?"

"No, not like a lathe. A lathe has a continuously rotating blade. A reciprocating saw has a short blade that sticks straight out from a hand-held unit and the blade moves in and out like a piston. Zzj, zzj, zzj." He demonstrated the motion with his right hand.

"I can't picture it. Any fingerprints?"

"It was a foot, Dooley. It has toes."

"I mean *on* the foot—you know, from the person who sawed it off."

"You can't pull fingerprints off of someone else's foot."

"What about those black granules in the box? Do they know what they are?

"The lab says some were mouse droppings. There were also some chocolate sprinkles with traces of icing. So, I guess we're looking for a contractor who likes donuts."

"What contractor doesn't? What if this lunatic doesn't actually own the saw, Captain? Maybe they rented it."

"That's a possibility. A rented Sawzall. See if anyplace rented one recently. And I'm not talking about having rented one to a mouse either!"

"Gotcha. I'll get working on it. Do you want me to work with Perkins on this?"

"I can't really spare Perkins on this one. He's working on the Brewster case."

"Which one is that?"

"Brewster is the seven hundred pound guy that was found dead in the women's restroom at the Museum of Modern Art."

"Ah, of course. I remember that case."

"I thought you might. Record-holder as the heaviest man ever murdered in this City."

"I thought he killed himself."

"He was hanged from a pipe and nowhere near anything he could have jumped off of. In addition, both his arms were lopped off and shoved down the back of his trousers. He couldn't have done that himself."

"No, I suppose not." Dooley got up to leave the office. "All right, then. Alone it is. Gimme the file and I'll get on it, Captain."

"Be careful with this nut, Hank. If he's willing to sever a foot, who knows what he's willing to cut off in order to fully express himself."

"Right." Dooley unconsciously held the file in front of his crotch as he turned to walk out.

Chapter 14

Dooley spent a couple of days slogging through the phone book, calling places that sell and/or rent tools, specifically trying to find sales and rentals of Sawzalls over the last three days. He visited dozens of locations and interviewed the counter clerks, compiling as much information as he could. From the sheer numbers alone, this investigation was proving to be arduous in the extreme. He talked to more than one hundred people, many of whom were dull-witted and unhelpful. Those that possessed sharper faculties tended to be distrustful and unhelpful.

The largest and most successful chain of lumber yards in the City was Woody's. They had eight locations around town, all of which rented power tools. Dooley had been to four Woody's lumber yards that morning. None of them had provided a promising lead. The next one up was the Woody's in Rosterdam on 34th Avenue. He parked his car around the block from the entrance and walked around the back of the yard toward the front of the store.

On his way, he stumbled over a small boy who had rounded the corner, running at full speed and paying no attention to his surroundings. "Whoa! Hey there, little buddy!" The boy looked stunned and disoriented—not from the force of the impact, but by the surprise of it. "Here, sonny, you dropped something." Dooley bent down and picked up an object that he noticed had fallen out of the boy's hand.

"That's mine!"

"I'm not trying to take it from you, son. I'm handing it to you, see?"

"That's my lucky rabbit's foot."

"Hey, I used to have one of those. It was a key chain with a rabbit's foot attached. I'm not sure that it ever brought me any luck, though."

"Mine brings me luck all the time," the kid boasted.

"Well, maybe because I touched it, it'll bring me some, too."

"I don't like you. You're a *mean* man!"

Dooley was genuinely shocked. "Why'd you say that, kid?"

"You *look* mean! You have a mean, old face!" The kid scowled at him.

"Wonderful. Aren't you the little darling. I bet your mother is a real bit—ah, forget it, kid." As a conciliatory gesture, Dooley tried patting the boy on the shoulder as he passed, but the boy ducked the touch and ran off.

Shaking his head, Dooley walked on and turned the corner to the entrance to the lumber yard. He walked past the cardboard cutout of the plank with a smiling face and straight to the back to where Woody's rental counters are all located—right next to the restrooms. Dooley was met by a gangly guy that was all nose and jawbone and elbows. "Hey, pal, you guys rent Sawzalls, don't you?"

"Yes, we do. We have…"

"Save it. I'm not looking to rent one. I'm looking for someone who may have rented one from you in the last couple of days."

"What business is it of yours?"

"I'm a Detective. Here's my badge and ID."

"A Sawzall, eh?" He took out the blue book and turned to the Sawzall section. "Let's see. Hmm. Yep, someone rented it on Monday and returned it yesterday."

"You have the name and address?"

"Sure we do. We never let a tool get out of here without proper credentials. Here's all the information, Detective." He turned the book around toward Dooley and pointed to the relevant line. "Yeah, we had to charge him the extra fee on that one."

"What extra fee?"

"Part of the deposit—or in this case it was *all* of the deposit—doesn't get refunded back."

"Why was that?"

He stepped back to the shelves behind the cage door and pulled a Sawzall off the shelf. "We tell the customer that they have to bring the unit back in approximately the same condition that they received it. Well, this thing's all caked in blood." He plunked it down on the counter.

"Blood, eh?" Dooley got excited. Sure enough, the unit was a mess.

"The idiot must have ignored the safety instructions. We give 'em a sheet that has all the safety warnings for the particular unit. The customer has to sign the book that he received and read the copy we gave him. Here's his signature. He signed it, all right. We tell 'em it's real important to follow safety precautions. With something like a Sawzall you can cut off a finger in a second or two.

"How about a foot?"

The guy thought for a second. "That would take longer. Got an itch, Detective?"

Dooley was perplexed. "Yeah, I do, but I don't know why—especially so early in the investigation. I'll need to take these items as evidence, of course. Can you get me a garbage bag for the Sawzall?"

"What do I do if someone wants to rent it."

"Pull one off the shelf."

Dooley was astonished at his sudden turn of fortune. In one five-minute stretch he had gone from having no leads to a unit that had been signed out of a Woody's and returned to them, caked in blood. He took the evidence downtown and turned it over to the lab, then stopped in at his office to check for messages. Perkins was at his desk, eating a banana and looking at a file.

"Hey, Hank."

"Don't talk with your mouth full. Didn't your mother teach you that?"

"My momma didn't teach me as much as *your* momma taught me."

"What are you doing here, anyway? I thought you were out on that fat guy's murder case."

"Suicide."

"Suicide? I thought Homily said that…"

"Yeah, yeah, I know. The arms, right? Suicide, not murder."

"Right, the arms. That and the fact that there was nothing he could've jumped off."

"Well, it turns out that the cleaning woman came in to clean up the washroom and she moved a broken stool we think that he might have used to jump from. She also picked up his arms and stuffed them into his pants just to get them out of her way so she could mop the floor. So, it looks like it was suicide after all. On another note, you're back pretty quick yourself. What gives?"

"I just dropped off a rental Sawzall that was caked in blood. The lab says they'll have a report to me by two o'clock. As soon as they confirm that it's the same blood type as the foot, I'll head back out and pinch the guy that rented it. I've got his name and address and his signature, so it looks like a tidy package."

"Boy, that was lucky! You haven't gotten too many of them lately. The guy didn't even wash the saw off before he returned it?"

"Nope. It's like he cut off the foot, got in his car and returned the saw. You should've seen the mess."

"What a jerk, huh? It's great to get an easy one once in a while, isn't it?"

"You said it, brother. Hey, Perk, I was going to ask you: How does a guy get to be seven hundred pounds?"

"I don't know. I guess he eats three times more than anybody else does."

"Or mostly cakes and pies, eh?"

"Maybe his mom was a good cook."

"Is she still alive? She would had to have cooked a lot of food to get him to seven hundred pounds."

"We couldn't find any living parents."

"Maybe that's what killed her."

"What do you mean?"

"That she died of exhaustion from endless cooking." They both laughed at the thought of this mountain of flesh wearing out his poor mother.

"Hey Hank, she probably she probably died right there at the stove, with a wooden spoon still in her hand."

"Yeah, stirring the sauce for that pig of a son, with her last dying breath. Hey, what size pants did he wear?"

"I don't know. That's a good question. I'll check the report."

"Speaking of pants, I know you said he didn't stuff his own arms down his pants."

"Right, the cleaning woman did that."

"Right, that's fine. But, how did he lop them off in the first place? Have you figured that out yet?"

Perkins paused. "No, come to think of it. We haven't addressed that angle yet."

"You might want to look at that before you close out the report."

"Gee, thanks, Hank. It still might only turn out to be a red herring, but we'll look at it, for sure. Thanks, man."

"Don't mention it."

The phone rang with the distinctive two-ring bursts indicating a call from within the building. "Perkins here. Yeah, he's here. Okay. The lab says they're done, Hank."

"Come down with me. We'll see what they came up with. The fat guy can wait."

Chapter 15

Dooley walked up the four steps to the door of the small bungalow. There was no doorbell, so he knocked. A man in his early thirties opened the door. "Are you Felix Jiminez?"

"Some people are under that impression. Why would you care who I am?"

"I'm here to arrest you, Felix." Dooley displayed his badge.

"Me? For what?!"

"Mayhem."

Jiminez chuckled. "What the hell?"

"It's not funny, Felix. Mayhem is very serious business."

"I'm sure you're right, Detective Dooley. The thing is, I don't even know what mayhem is. You know, you hear these words all your life and you don't really know what they mean. Mayhem is one of them." He chuckled again.

"We may charge you with something else eventually, but right now, I figured mayhem is good enough and seemed appropriate under the circumstances."

"I don't want to give you the wrong impression, Detective. I honestly don't mind you arresting me—really, I don't—but, couldn't you at least tell me what mayhem is? I mean, it's only fair. Don't you think?"

Dooley was only a little annoyed. Felix had a point. "Okay. Mayhem is statute 140.7, section D of the city penal code."

"That's not what I meant. You know that. Look, if you're not going to tell me, can I at least look it up in my dictionary?"

"All right, I'll tell you. As a matter of fact, I'll do one better than that. I'll show you. Here, look at this picture. Recognize anything?"

Felix pulled a pair of reading glasses out of his shirt pocket and put them on. "Yeah, that's my wife's foot! How did you get it?"

96

"What do you mean, 'how did we get it'? You know perfectly well how we got it, Felix. You sent it to us in a box."

Felix looked askance at Dooley. "And why would I do such a strange thing?" He handed the photo back.

"Because you're a sick bastard, maybe? I don't know why and I don't care. I'm not a shrink, Felix. I'm a cop. I only know that you did it and I'm taking you in."

"I'll go with you, Detective, because it seems important to you, but I'm telling you now that I didn't do it. You're going to see that, in time."

"Come on, Felix. Let's go."

Felix hesitated and looked back inside. "Can I change my shirt, first? This one has grease spots on it. See?" He pulled out his shirtfront to make the splotch easier to see.

Dooley could easily see the stains. "We won't mind how you look."

"That may be, but *I* do. We're not going to go anyplace fancy, are we?"

"For chrissakes, Felix, I didn't come here to pick you up for a night on the town. I'm taking you to Headquarters to be questioned."

"All right. I just don't want to be embarrassed, that's all." Felix closed the door behind him and locked it. "Hey, Detective?"

"What is it, now?"

"What about the rest of my wife?"

"That was going to be one of *my* questions."

Dooley questioned Felix Jiminez for a day and a half with the assistance of Perkins and Sergeant Marmot. They kept at him, day and night, not letting him sleep or eat. They asked him about every private detail of his life—right down to his bowel movements and masturbatory habits. They learned a lot about Felix's home life, his upbringing, his likes and dislikes, his family, and his relationship with his wife, who no longer lived with him. He was very cooperative and earnest. He was constantly fidgeting with his shirt, worried about the grease spots, despite being reassured that he was—at least in his attire—an above-average suspect. They had also conducted a painstaking search of Felix's house and property, which turned up absolutely nothing at all that would incriminate him. The big problem was that it was starting to look like he was not necessarily the culprit.

Exhausted and frazzled from the relentless barrage of questions, Dooley decided to get himself a nice, hot meal and some coffee. Leaving Felix in the capable hands of his colleagues, he drove out to Lingstrome Avenue and the Riviera Luncheonette.

"Ham and eggs, Hank?"

"Sure, Marty."

"Hey, I was reading about that sicko that cut off his wife's foot and sent it to you. That musta been one hell of an arrest, huh?" He plunked down a cup of coffee to get Dooley started.

"How's that?"

"Well, the guy's totally wacko, right? Did he have body parts all over the house? Heads in the fridge and all that?"

"No, nothing like that."

"No? I don't get it. The newspapers painted this loony as the most de-mented and perverted creature on the East Coast."

"I don't really know what to say. The guy seems perfectly normal to me. No body parts, no weird ticks. He's got some quirks, but nothing you'd associ-ate with psychotic behavior."

"Well, like what? Come on, Hank. Gimme the lowdown on this nut." Marty's eyes were wide with anticipation as he waited to hear all the horri-ble, twisted details.

Dooley took out his notebook. "Let's see. He has a modest campaign button collection, going back to "I Like Ike". He likes Mantovani records. He eats Rice Crispies and TV Dinners. He drinks Shasta sodas. He jerks off to Oui magazine."

"*I* jerk off to Oui magazine! That's no fun. He sounds perfectly normal." Marty was truly deflated.

"I know. That's the problem. I need more coffee, Marty."

"Where are the horrible tools of his sadistic acts? Where is his torture chamber? He has to have one somewhere. What about the owner—I guess I should say *former* owner of the foot?" Marty refilled the cup.

"He says she left him late last year for some other man—he doesn't know who—and that he hasn't seen her since and doesn't know where she lives. We're looking for her now."

"It should be a cinch to find her."

"How's that?"

"Just look for a woman wearing one shoe." Marty finished cooking Dooley's breakfast and served it up. "Here's your ham and eggs."

"It's not that simple. She might be dead, you know."

"Just look for a corpse with one shoe. More coffee?"

Dooley pushed the cup forward. "Do you have to ask?"

"Hey. You Hank Doody?" It was a boy around the age of ten standing inside the door of the Riviera.

"The name's Dooley. What do you want, kid?"

"I'm supposed to give you this package." He presented it to Dooley.

"Who gave this to you?"

The boy shrugged. "Just some man. He gave me five bucks to give this to you."

"What did this guy look like?" The boy got nervous at Dooley's question and suddenly darted back out the door and took off down the avenue. "Hey, kid! Come back here! Damn!" He got up and went out the door after him, but, by the time he looked down the block, the boy had gone too far to be chased.

"You're getting very popular these days, Hank. I wish people gave me presents."

"Oh yeah? And tell me what would you do with a foot?"

99

Marty thought for a second. "Well, just think, if you could get two more, you'd have a yard. I always wanted a yard. Ha, ha!"

"Forget about Felix. *You're* demented."

"Well?"

"Well, what?"

"Are you going to open it?"

"You want me to open it in here?"

"Why not?"

Dooley gestured with a sweep of his arm. "What about your customers?" There were three others in the place, eating toast, sipping coffee and reading the paper.

"Whatever it is, Hank, they've seen worse. Ever seen my scrapple?"

Dooley elected to bring the box downtown to open it in Homily's office. First, however, he finished his breakfast in the usual leisurely fashion. The presence of the unopened box on the counter was the source of tremendous frustration to Marty, who had hoped to see first-hand what new part this evil fiend had removed from Mrs. Jiminez's body. On the way back to the office, Dooley examined the box. It was an old, striped hatbox this time and it weighed less than the first box had. This one made no thumping sounds when shaken.

Homily was at his desk when Dooley walked in. "Captain, some kid handed me a second box this morning. I thought you might want to be present when it's opened."

Homily cleared a space on his desk to accommodate the box. "Good thinking, Dooley. Let's see." He cut the scotch tape holding the box closed and lifted the lid, the two men peering inside as it revealed its contents. "Okay, let's see what we've got this time." He pulled out the mass of hair and held it aloft. "It's a wig."

Dooley was disappointed. "Anything else in there?"

Homily checked the box, just to be sure. "No, just the wig."

"Well, ain't that a kick in the ass?"

100

They examined the wig carefully, hoping to spot some kind of clue or at least some distinguishing characteristic. "That a good quality wig. That's no dime store wig. Whoever dreamed up this gag spared no expense."

Homily ran the hair through his fingers. "They could've washed it. It feels a little greasy. There's no label on it. Nothing in the hat box. Send it down to the lab and see what they can come up with."

Dooley took the wig back and dropped it in the box. "Captain, I wanted to talk to you about this guy, Felix Jiminez, that we've got in Room C."

"You still working on him? I thought you already got him to confess."

"Yeah, we did—a couple of times, actually."

"Then why the long face?"

"I don't know. I just don't like it. I'm not too sure he's guilty."

"What does guilt have to do with anything?"

"It wouldn't make a difference normally. The thing is, I kinda like the guy."

"Oh, come *on*, Hank! Are you going soft on me? You've arrested a lot of likable folks over the years. What, are you sweet on him or something?"

"No, really. Most of the time we had him down there we were swapping stories about this, that and the other thing. The way he talked about his wife—I don't know—I just don't think he'd cut her foot off."

Homily sighed loudly. "Her foot was cut off with a Sawzall and Felipe…"

"Felix."

"Okay, Felix rented a clean Sawzall and returned it caked in blood." Homily was ticking off the items on his fingers as he spoke. "The blood type was the same type as the foot. He himself identified the foot as his wife's. What more do you want? The guys at the tool rental counter identified his picture as the man who checked out the Sawzall. Nail him, Hank. I don't care if he's the coolest cat on the continent. He's guilty enough and I have to satisfy the Mayor's office. The newspapers are breathing down our necks again. They want justice and I've got to give it to them and nothing else matters one bit. He's a good suspect and he'll be convicted and everybody will be happy. Don't worry about him. He'll accept his fate eventually.

They always do, you know. It might take him a few years, but sooner or later he'll get used to the idea that he's going to die in the gas chamber. And when he does, he'll feel much better about the whole rotten deal."

"I'm not as sure as you are. We don't have the body. He says he hasn't seen her in months. He said he had the Sawzall for two days and did a household project with it. We saw what he had cut with it. He's putting an exhaust fan in his bathroom. Someone could have swiped the Sawzall, used it and returned it while Felix was at work on Tuesday. That's a possibility." He looked at Homily, who was sucking his teeth and smirking. "You're skeptical, Captain."

"You're really digging for something to get this guy off the hook, aren't you? You feel pretty strongly about this?"

"Yes."

"I'll give you a couple of days. No more than that, though. The papers have been full of this sordid tale all week. We need a pigeon."

"I'll get one—the right one."

Chapter 16

Dooley got the address of Jiminez's mother-in-law and drove out to 112th Street to pay a call. He was hoping to extract some piece of information that might lead to her daughter's whereabouts. Perhaps she'd know a favorite hangout or the name of a friend who had seen her out and about with some-one recently. It's unpredictable what people know or don't know and in the jargon of Police Headquarters: a golden nugget can come from a rhino's ass.

Rosalie Jiminez's maiden name was Mendez. Felix had supplied his mother-in-law's address. He told Dooley that she was in her mid-fifties and spoke virtually no English, but that she was law-abiding and would proba-bly cooperate fully and unhesitatingly with any request for information about her daughter. Mrs. Mendez lived alone in a three-story walk-up in Kensington, the City's largest Puerto Rican neighborhood. She was a widow, her husband having died of a heart attack six or seven years ago.

After ringing the bell, Dooley was greeted by a handsome older woman, wearing a green polo shirt and a loose-fitting, wildly-patterned skirt and drying her hands on a dish towel. "Are you Mrs. Mendez?"

"Si. Mendez."

"I'm Detective Dooley, with the police department." The woman's eyes got very round as soon as she heard the word 'police'. "Please don't panic Mrs. Mendez. Calmo, calmo yourself, por favor." He showed her his badge to set her mind at rest, but his credentials, if anything, made her even more agi-tated.

"But, you policia. No criminal. I hard work." Mrs. Mendez was hyperventi-lating. "Ay, madre mia!" She clasped her hands together and pressed them to her chest, her eyes gazing upward and searching for salvation.

"Oh, jeez. Calmo, Mrs. Mendez. No peligrosa." He'd anticipated a struggle to get information because of the language barrier, but Dooley had declined to take along an interpreter because he thought it would take too long. He had picked up some Spanish over the years and figured he could fudge it wherever necessary. Now that Mrs. Mendez was in a panic and screaming in that echoing hallway, he didn't know what to say to her. There seemed no way of calming the woman and she was totally distraught.

"No jail para mi. No jail. No arresta, por favor, I do what you want." She suddenly got an expression of hope in her desperate eyes. "You want sexo? I do sexo para ti." She grabbed his arms and, searching his face for encouragement, forced a hopeful little smile to her lips.

"No! No, sexo, Mrs. Mendez. I want your daughter, Rosalie Jiminez."

She paused for a second to assimilate what he said. "You want sexo Rosalia?"

"Huh? No, no! No sexo. Where is Rosalie? Uh, donde esta Rosalie?"

When she realized that he did not want sex with Rosalie, the poor woman went back into total panic again. "No arresta Rosalia! Rosalia no es un criminal. Rosalia es una buena chica. Por favor, no arresta Rosalia." Tears welled up in her eyes as she begged him. Then she stepped out of her doorway and put her hands on Dooley's forearms, pulling him closer to her. "I do sexo, you no arresta, okay?" She pulled her polo shirt over her head, revealing a generous bosom in a dark red bra, which Dooley could not help but notice was working to its capacity, and a round belly, hanging over the waistline of her skirt. Mrs. Mendez didn't hesitate a second and quickly reached back to unhook the bra. "Aqui, Detectivo, ahora, I do sexo."

Dooley tried to grab the straps of her bra to keep them on her shoulders, but the woman was strong and determined. "No, please, Mrs. Mendez. Stop." He looked nervously around the hallway. None of the doors to the other apartments showed any signs of life, but he was scared they would be caught nevertheless. "Mrs. Mendez, please put your bra back on."

Then, after she had won the battle of the bra and had tossed it aside in the hallway, she stood there with her big brown nipples on display and began working on removing Dooley's sports jacket and shirt.

"No, Mrs. Mendez." Dooley was whispering, but could still hear every sound echoing throughout the building.

"Si, si. I do sexo good. No arresta Rosalia. Okay?" She had his shirt open and was rubbing his chest, paying a lot of attention to his nipples. Her hands were warm and strong and her massage was surprisingly effective. Her insistent touch was breaking down Dooley's weak defenses.

Still, he was conscious enough of their dangerous exposure in the dingy hallway to recommend a change of venue. "Mrs. Mendez, the neighbors! Stop it." She had his pants unfastened now and wasted no time in fishing around in his fly. He grabbed her wrist with his left hand and gestured toward the door of her apartment with his right. "Look, let's at least go inside and work it out there, eh? Come on. I could lose-o my job-o if anybody sees this." He tried to remove her hand from his pants, but she had a firm grip on him.

"Si, si, go apartamento. I do sexo good, you no arresta mia Rosalia. Vamos." She pulled Dooley inside by his member. He went inside willingly, shuffling his feet awkwardly.

Chapter 17

At four o'clock, Dooley was back at his desk and still digesting what had occurred that afternoon. He had intended to talk to Mrs. Mendez for information about her daughter and to let her know the awful thing that had happened to her foot. Instead, he found that talking to her was impossible. Every time he began to address police business, she would frantically engage him in another sexual act in a misguided effort to placate him and protect her precious daughter from arrest. He couldn't even bring up the subject of the foot, though he had attempted twice, with unintentionally orgasmic results. Of course, he found out nothing that would be useful in tracking down Rosalie Jiminez. The only thing he learned was that her mother loved her very much and would go to great lengths to protect her from the clutches of the law.

He sat at his desk, feeling somewhat guilty that he didn't have the will to tell her of her daughter's mutilation. At the same time, he had enjoyed his two hours with Mrs. Mendez very much. He left the poor woman, promising her truthfully that he would not arrest her daughter.

Dooley's guilt-ridden daydream was interrupted by Perkins, who was returning from a late lunch break.

"Hi, Hank. Any luck? Did you get anywhere with her?"

"What's *that* supposed to mean?"

"Take it easy, buddy. I didn't mean anything weird. Just wondering how it's goin'—you know, looking for Felix's wife. That's all."

"Oh, of course. Sorry, Perk."

"What's the matter with you? You seem itchy or something. Did you speak to the mother-in-law?"

Dooley wasn't sure how to answer that question. "Kind of."

"What does that mean? 'Kind of'?"

"Nothing. Why are you asking me all these questions, huh? Don't you have an investigation of your own to take care of?"

"Damn! What's eating you, Hank?"

"Nothing! I just don't feel that I should be standing around answering end-less questions from you. No big deal, but I don't think I should have to ac-count to you for all my time, that's all."

"All right, Hank. Take it easy. I understand." He leaned over and patted Dooley on the shoulder. "You've had a tough afternoon. Don't worry about it. I understand."

Dooley calmed considerably. "Thanks, Perk." He sighed heavily, and they sat in silence for a few seconds.

"So, how *did* it go? Did you get anywhere with her?"

"Oh, jeez!" Dooley rolled his eyes. "Why don't you let it drop, already?"

Perkins looked intently at Dooley, who could not meet the gaze. "What's going on here, Hank? There's something you're not telling me, isn't there?"

"There's nothing. So drop it, will ya, please?"

"No, I want to know what it is. You look guilty about something. You didn't kill the old broad, did you?"

"No, for chrissakes! That's horrible."

"Did you beat her up a little or something?"

"No, no, no. Nothing like that."

"What do you mean 'nothing like that'? I was right. There was something, wasn't there?" Perkins was smiling. He knew Dooley was hiding some-thing.

"I didn't hurt her. I hardly even got to *talk* to her."

"She gave you the slip?"

Dooley chuckled. "I wish."

"What do mean by that? Hey, am I going to have to pay her a visit to find out what's going on here?"

"All right! All right, I'll tell you. I've got to tell somebody, so it might as well be you. But, listen, you have to promise not to tell anyone else. I mean it. Do you promise?"

"Sounds pretty serious, Hank. Okay, I promise."

Dooley took a breath and tried to formulate how he was going to say it. "Mrs. Mendez was convinced that I was there to arrest her daughter. So, she pleaded with me not to."

"Well, didn't you tell her the truth?"

"I tried."

"What do you mean, you tried?"

"I started to tell her, but she couldn't understand me, I guess. She hardly spoke any English at all. Just a few words."

"So, did she get hysterical or something?"

"Kinda. She—look, you gotta promise you won't tell anyone."

"I promised that already. Did she jump out a window? What?"

"She started saying—begging me—that if she had sex with me that I wouldn't try to arrest her daughter." Dooley was just barely able to get the words out.

Perkins eyes got round as saucers. "And you agreed?"

"No! Well, not at first. I told her I was not trying to arrest her daughter. I told her to put her clothes back on. I had a hold of her bra straps, trying to pull them back up, but she started in on my shirt and then my pants. Finally, I managed to coax her out of the hallway and into the apartment."

"Oh, shit!" Perkins doubled over with laughter.

"It's not funny! I was scared. You can get written up for stuff like that."

"Ha, ha! Oh, man, I can picture the whole thing! So, you did it with her?"

Dooley shrugged his shoulders. "I had to. I couldn't stop her, for chrissakes. She was quick and strong and to be honest with you…"

"Hank, she's almost old enough to be your mother!"

"Remember, you promised."

"Okay, Hank. Oh, man!" He composed himself. "So?"

"So, what?"

"How was it, man?"

"That's the embarrassing part."

"It was good, wasn't it? Ha! You *liked* it!"

Dooley smiled and nodded.

Captain Homily walked in, holding a folder. "What was good, Perkins?"

Perkins and Dooley shot upright at the sound of his voice. "Hi, Captain!"

"So, fellas, what was good? What did you like?"

Dooley gave Perkins a warning glance, then replied. "Oh, nothing. We were just reminiscing. Fudgcicles were good. Remember Fudgcicles? Whatcha got, Captain?"

Homily gave the two the once over, not buying the Fudgcicle story, but decided to drop it. He held up the file folder. "It's the lab report."

"On the wig?"

"That's just it, Dooley. There wasn't a wig in that box."

"What do you mean? Of course there was a wig. We both saw it." Homily shook his head 'no'. Dooley didn't want to consider the alternative. "If it wasn't a wig, it could only have been..."

"That's right, Hank. It was Rosalie Jiminez's scalp."

Perkins lost his lunch.

Chapter 18

"Hank, Hank, Hank, Hank, Hank. You seem glum, today, Hank. What's the matter? You don't like my corned beef hash and eggs?"

"No, it's not your hash, Marty."

"What, then? You're not your usual sprightly self."

"It's this case I'm on. It's a depressing investigation. Can I get more coffee?"

Marty poured. "You're hitting the java pretty hard today, Hank. I lost count after your eleventh cup, but you must be on number fifteen or sixteen at least. What's so depressing about the investigation? Did you find anything out yet?"

"No, we haven't turned up a single clue really. We have the murder weapon, but the lab boys can't establish that she was cut up in her husband's house. The husband says he hasn't seen her in months, and I believe him when he says it. The problem is that we're probably going to have to pin it on him regardless of the evidence." He chugged down his coffee.

"It's not the first time you've pinned a crime on an innocent man, and it sure won't be your last. Don't get upset about it." He poured another cup.

"You're right, of course. I like this guy, Felix, but mainly what really bothered me was the scalp in the box. Just a little too grim, you know? And her poor mother, so desperate to make sure no one arrested her daughter—as if we were looking for the girl so we could arrest her. Ha! Poor woman. This coffee is good. Ahh. Pour me another, will ya?"

"Okay, if you're sure." He poured again. "Ah, just forget about it, Hank. Don't get wrapped up emotionally with these victims. It's just your job. You think I get emotionally involved with my customers?"

"You married one of them, didn't you?"

"Yeah, that's true. I married *two* of them, in fact. Arlene was my second wife." He hesitated. "I think. I can't remember anymore. They all blur together after a while."

"Well, I feel kinda close to Mrs. Mendez. I got to know her pretty well in the five or so hours I spent with her."

"Did you have to tell her about the scalp?"

"No, we didn't know it was a scalp until after that. I think that would've changed the personal dynamic between us, if she had known. I didn't really get a chance to tell her much of anything during the visit."

"Just think of it this way: She must have been very grateful that someone like you was willing to spend so much time with her for her daughter's sake. It must have been tough. She must be very worried—her being a widow and all. You must have helped put her mind to rest a little, huh?"

"I don't know. I hope she's grateful for all I did while I was there."

"Hank, you're looking kinda sweaty. Maybe you've had one too many cups. Your hands are trembling. Hank? Hank!"

Suddenly a woman appeared before Dooley's eyes. He had trouble focusing on her, but he could see that she was primly dressed in a powder blue skirt and jacket and wore a white pillbox hat with a short veil over her forehead and white gloves. She looked like she was dressed for church.

"Detective Dooley, I presume?"

"I'm Dooley. Don't tell me. You've got a package for me, right?"

"How did you know that, Detective Dooley?"

"I'm psychic today. Don't go anywhere. Let's see what's in the box, shall we? A little smaller than the previous two, eh?" He opened the lid and looked inside. "Ah, just what I needed—two lips. That's just wonderful."

"Hank, can you close up the box, please? Think of my customers."

Dooley grabbed the woman by her arm. "Come with me, lady. We have some questions to ask you downtown."

Dooley drove her downtown in his sedan. She sat in the passenger seat and made no move to escape. The box was on the seat between them. It was a cheap white paperboard box, such as you would get from an Italian bakery, except it wasn't tied up with the traditional red and white string. It was held closed, instead, by a piece of Scotch Tape. They didn't speak on the way downtown and the woman stared straight ahead the entire time, which was not very long because Dooley made every single traffic light along the way.

Once they had reached police headquarters, he escorted the woman to interview room 9, just down the hall from the morgue. He then summoned Perkins to the room by interoffice phone. Directing the woman to sit, he opened a closet and removed a large tape recorder and placed it on the table. "Okay, ma'am, we'll be recording the interview on this Concord 444 reel-to-reel tape recorder so that no mistake is made and the interview will be preserved in the best quality high fidelity sound possible and you'll be impressed with the results. This machine was manufactured in Japan." Within seconds, Perkins entered the interview room and took a seat in front of the machine. "Sergeant Perkins here will be assisting me in this interview, ma'am. He'll operate the tape machine."

"Hello, Sergeant. That's quite a machine you have there."

"Thank you, ma'am. It's very heavy. See these lights here? Isn't that cool?"

Dooley intended to lead the interview, and once Perkins had switched on the tape recorder, he began to address the woman. "In the squad car on the way down here you waived your rights to be represented with a cup of coffee, is that correct?"

"Yes, that's correct, Detective."

At that point, Perkins interrupted Dooley. "Then let's begin, ma'am. State your name and address for the record—or in this case, tape."

"My name is Mrs. Helen Drucker and I live at 89 Fuller Avenue, apartment D-2."

"Mrs. Drucker, you gave Detective Dooley here a box—this box, in fact. Is that correct?"

"Yes, that's right."

"Did you know the contents of the box before this afternoon?"

"No, I did not. I was told what was in the box, but that turned out to be a fib."

"What were you told was in this box, Mrs. Drucker?"

"I was told that six seven-layer cookies were in this box. As you can plainly see, this was an untruth."

"Who gave you this box to give to Detective Dooley?"

"A man."

"What man? Do you know this man?"

"No, he is a perfect stranger to me, Sergeant."

Dooley cut in and addressed Mrs. Drucker harshly. "Why'd you accept a box from a man you don't even know?"

"Simply told, because he paid me to do it. He told me where you'd be at that time and he handed me the box and a ten-dollar bill. And that's all there was to it. Despite my perfectly respectable appearance, I would do anything for a ten-dollar bill."

Perkins resumed questioning the woman. "What did this man look like, Mrs. Drucker?"

"He was very fat. That was why I didn't question when he said the box contained six seven-layered cookies."

"How fat was this man? How much do you think he weighed?"

"Oh, I haven't a clue. I'm no good at guessing people's weight. Suffice it to say he was quite large—*quite* large. Why, he could barely walk."

"How did he get in touch with you?"

"He accosted me as I was leaving the ladies' room."

"Where was this ladies' room, ma'am?"

"Why, at the Museum of Modern Art, of course."

"Of course. Mrs. Drucker, was this man someone that the health and fitness experts might call 'enormously fat'?"

She thought for a moment about that one before finally answering Perkins. "Yes, he was, Sergeant."

"Did he waddle?"

"I believe he did."

"Do you recall if he jiggled when he waddled?"

"Perk, what the hell kind of questions are these? 'Did he jiggle when he waddled?' I got a box of lips, my friend! We need answers! A man's life depends on it, and more importantly, the Captain's job depends on it!"

"I know that, Hank. Just bear with me a little longer. Now, where were we? Oh, yes. Did he jiggle when he waddled?"

"I'm no expert, mind you, but I'm fairly certain that he did."

"Was he a white guy, about thirty-five years old? Black hair, long and stringy?"

"Yes, that's right."

Perkins and Dooley looked at each other. They both thought the same thing. Perkins broke the silence. "What do you think—coincidence?"

Dooley turned back to her. "Mrs. Drucker, could this man have weighed as much as seven hundred pounds?"

"Oh, my word, no!" She pondered for a moment, putting her finger to her lips. "Well, now, wait a moment. Let me think. Seven hundred pounds, you say? Yes, certainly he could."   '

"When did this man give you this box?"

"Oh, last week, I believe. Let's see now, I went to the museum on Wednesday. Yes, last Wednesday is when he gave me the box.

"You've had this box since last week?" Perkins took the lips out of the box to examine them, turning them in his hand. "These lips look fresh. Did you put it in the fridge or something?"

"Yes, I did."

Dooley jumped in aggressively. "How'd you know to do that? You knew what was in the box, didn't you?"

"No, I did not, Detective! He told me to keep it cold. So, I did."

"Did he say why he wanted the box kept cold?"

"Yes, he told me there were fancy tulips from Belgium in the box and he didn't want to risk their spoiling. His exact words were, 'these are fancy tulips from Belgium in this box and I don't want to risk their spoiling.'"

"I thought you said that he told you they were seven-layered cookies? Now you say he told you they were tulips."

"I said nothing of the sort, cop."

"They would have been pretty small tulips, don't you think? I mean, how could tulips fit in a box this small?"

"Hank, I saw small tulips on TV last night. They were about this long." Perkins held up his fingers, spaced about three inches apart.

"Mrs. Drucker, did he say why he wanted you to deliver this box of tulips to me? I mean, didn't you think it was a strange request? How often does a seven hundred pound man give tulips to a cop?"

"He offered an explanation to me that seemed perfectly logical, Detective. He said he couldn't walk this far." Suddenly, she burst out laughing and covered her mouth as she giggled.

Dooley was stunned. "Why are you laughing?"

"Because you are sitting there, sporting an erection, Detective."

"You are wrong, Mrs. Drucker. I'm not." Dooley really thought he wasn't.

"Oh, you *are*, though. You must like my bosom, Detective Dooley. You keep staring at it."

"Perkins, make her stop." Perkins was preoccupied with the volume control knobs on the tape recorder and didn't respond. "Perkins!"

"I have two breasts, Detective Dooley." She pointed to each one in turn. "One and two. See?"

"She's right, Hank. You like her bosom. There was some question about it at first, but there's no doubt about it anymore. We have it here on tape. It's been recorded for posterity on Mylar."

"That's not true! None of this is true! You like her better than you like me. That's mean, so I won't listen to you anymore. And anyway, it's not my erection. I'm just holding it for a friend. It's what you might call a loaner. A loaner boner."

Perkins watched the machine as the tape was running out, picked up the microphone and spoke directly into it. "Hank! Can you hear me, Hank?"

"Hank? Hank! Can you hear me, Hank?"

"I won't listen to you anymore!"

"Hank, wake up, will ya? I gotta clean up and go home."

"Marty! Oh, shit! I thought I was downtown at headquarters. I was questioning the woman that brought me that box of lips."

"What box of lips?"

"Then I was staring at her chest and she knew it. She caught me, but I couldn't stop staring."

"Dreaming of a broad? Was she a hot tomato?"

"She was middle-aged and very prim, as a matter of fact. Kinda like a Sunday school teacher."

"Boy, you *must* be hard up."

"I'm not hard up!"

"Hank, if you're not hard up, then why are you passing out at the counter of a luncheonette. You should at least be passing out in a *bar*. That's pretty sad, if you ask me."

Dooley rubbed his face to get some circulation back. "Nobody asked you. Give me one more cup of coffee. I feel I'm on the verge of some major breakthrough."

"You're on the verge of some major break*down* is more like it. Get the hell outta here, Hank. Go home."

"All right, I'm going. I'm going. Boy, do I feel weird."

He didn't go home, however. He felt strangely enervated by his dream vision, so he went back to headquarters instead. He combed the files in the Records room, working on a hunch before heading up to his office. On the way, he passed Homily and Perkins in the Captain's office, so he stopped in.

"Where have you been, Hank? We called your house, but there was no answer. You look odd."

"I was eating, Captain. Why? Is something up?"

"I'd say so. Perkins here got a box. Hank, you didn't get that way from eating, did you?"

Dooley ignored the question. "You got a box, Perk?"

"Yeah, a woman named Collins brought it to me while I was eating lunch at the Chesterfield Lounge."

"What did you get in the box?" Dooley looked back and forth between the two, waiting for a reply. Neither wanted to say.

Finally Homily opened his mouth to speak. He gulped and had trouble forming his words before finally blurting them out. "It's Rosalie Jiminez's ass, Hank."

Dooley thought about the ramifications of what he had just heard. "I don't suppose there's any chance that this woman is still alive at this point."

"I wouldn't think so." Both Homily and Perkins shook their heads.

Dooley thought about it for a second or two in the silence. "I mean, there's an outside chance you could live without your feet, but how can you live without your scalp and your lips and your ass?"

"No, that would be tough. We're looking for a murderer now, Hank—plain and simple—not just a nut or a prankster. Do you have anything at all, Hank? *Anything* we can use? The evening paper published an Extra about the ass Perkins got. We've got to crack this thing fast! Wait a minute. What do you mean 'lips'?" He looked back and forth between Perkins and Dooley. "Did we get lips, too? I don't recall hearing about this."

"No—well, not really, but—I don't know what it's worth, Captain…"

"What? What do you have? Tell me."

117

"I'm almost embarrassed to say."

"Go ahead. I'll take anything at this point."

"Well, okay. I had a dream while I was at the luncheonette. In a way, it was more like a hallucination than a dream, brought on by drinking sixteen cups of coffee. I entered a dream state. Suddenly a woman entered and brought me another box and then I was back here and we were questioning her—Perkins and me—except the woman's name was Drucker in my dream and not Collins. So, anyway, in this dream, she says the guy who gave her the box was that seven-hundred pound guy that hanged himself in the museum."

The Captain waited for more. "That's it?"

"No, there was more in the dream that had to do with breasts, but I'm not sure how that would help us on this case. She caught me staring at them and she pointed to them and counted them like this: one, two. Oh, and in the dream she says she lives on Fuller Avenue."

"Look, Hank, when I said 'anything', I didn't really mean…"

"Captain, I checked just now in Records. Luther Brewster, the seven hundred-pound man, had an uncle that lives on Fuller Avenue. And, get this—his name is Dexter Rucker. D. Rucker. Get it? Drucker! Like the woman in my dream!"

Homily stared for a long time at him. His face betrayed no emotion the entire time. Dooley started feeling uneasy until the moment the Captain spoke. "I love it! Go for it. Whatever you need. Team-up with Perkins if you want, but crack this case! Now, get going!" Homily was practically pushing the two of them out the door, but stopped them abruptly for one last question. "And let me know if Dexter Rucker has breasts."

Chapter 19

Dexter Rucker was a white-haired older man, quite average in his appearance. What was remarkable was that he gave Perkins and Dooley no hassles when they knocked on his door. It was a pleasant change of pace for them. The apartment smelled stale, as you would expect from a man living alone.

"You fellas came here to talk about my poor nephew, Luther?"

"That's right Mr. Rucker." Dooley checked. Mr. Rucker did not have breasts.

"The one I feel sorry for is Melvin."

"Who's Melvin?"

"His brother, of course."

Perkins and Dooley shared a glance. "We didn't know about a brother. That changes things a bit."

"They were very close, you know."

"Mr. Rucker—can we call you Dexter?"

"Sure."

"Mr. Rucker, can you tell us anything about your nephews?"

"Of course I can. Like what sort of thing do you want to know?"

"Did they have similar interests? Did they always get along? That sort of thing."

"I'd say no, they did not have similar interests. Luther was into science. He liked anatomy. He wanted to become a surgeon. He never did, though."

"Why didn't he?"

"He was too dumb, Sergeant Perkins. I suggested he try being a tree surgeon instead."

"Why a tree surgeon?"

"I'm retired now 'cause of my back, but I ran a gardening and landscaping business and I could've used a tree surgeon, you know? He didn't like that idea much."

"How'd he react when you suggested it?"

"He said, 'trees are shit'. Those were his exact words. I'll never forget it. 'Trees are shit,' he said to me. Can you imagine?"

"What did he have against trees?"

"Beats me. I like trees, myself. Even the worst trees I'm kind of indifferent to. I don't know what his problem was with trees."

"What did you do then?"

"Well, I told him, 'donuts are shit!' Boy, did *that* make him mad. Luther's fond of donuts, you know."

"So am I."

"A lot of us are fond of donuts, Sergeant Perkins, but not like my nephew is. Believe me."

Dooley threw his two cents in. "I'm like that about Ring Dings and to a lesser extent, Yodels."

Rucker smirked and shook his head. "Not like my nephew. You should ask the people at the donut shop about Luther. They knew him much better than I ever did. I think it's a Donut Depot over on either Aqua Boulevard or Garrison Street. I can't recall which."

"We'll check it out. You said Luther was interested in science. What about Melvin?"

"He was a different sort of person. He was a huge sports fan—especially the decathlon. Any time there was any mention of the decathlon in the papers or during the Olympics, Melvin went crazy. Boy, did he love the decathlon. Couldn't get enough of it."

"What do you think he loved about the decathlon, Mr. Rucker?"

"Beats me. I think the decathlon is shit. I tell you what I like. I like watching the little girlies on ice skates. That's my favorite sport."

Dooley and Perkins took their leave of the old man after thanking him for his time and help, whereupon, they set off to visit the Donut Depot on Garrison Street. There was a cheap-looking young woman behind the counter.

"Is the owner around, Miss?"

"Yeah, he's in the back. Who wants 'im?"

"Tell him it's Detective Dooley and Sergeant Perkins—police."

"What's a matter? He do sumpin' wrong?"

"We want to ask him some questions. Will you just get him for us, please, young lady? We want to ask *him* the questions, not you."

"Aren' *you* darling." She sneered, then disappeared into the back with a quick and athletic step. Her light blue waitress uniform, cut a few inches above the knee, showed her curves to great advantage.

"She has a lot of attitude."

"Yeah, but she's got killer legs and a nice ass, eh?"

"True. You know, you don't talk like a married man, Perk."

"Hank, whether I'm married or not, that girl has a nice ass. Anyway, what's a married man supposed to talk like?"

"I don't know, but my father never talked like that."

"Not in front of you, he didn't. But, I bet you get him in front of his buddies at the bakery and he'd be talking about how far she could..."

Just then, a shoddy specimen of manhood came out of the back room, with the counter girl trailing behind him and peeking over his sloped shoulder. "How can I help you gentlemen?" He spoke through flabby red lips, which were surrounded by pale gray skin.

"You're the owner?"

"That's me." He had an annoying nasal quality to his voice. "My name is Les Lee."

"Well, Leslie..."

"Lester."

"I thought you said…"

"My name is Lester."

"Leslie Lester?"

"Nope."

The counter girl, standing behind Lee, failed to suppress a laugh and it came out as a snort.

"What the hell are you laughing at?"

"Don't berate Dawn like that, Officer."

"Hank, just forget about this screwball's name. We can get it from down-town."

"You're right." He turned back to Lee. "Okay, pal, my name's Dooley and this is Sergeant Perkins. And those really are our names. We're investigating the case involving Mr. Luther Brewster."

"Oh, the guy that hung himself!"

"Hanged. Yeah, that's right."

"Hey, how'd he manage to tear his own arms off? You got the inside scoop on that? Somebody I know who works for the Daily Bulletin says you guys tore 'em off so you could fit him into the coroner's wagon. Is that true?"

"Not exactly. Actually, we came here to ask *you* some questions. Do you mind very much if we do that?"

"Guess not, Sergeant. Were they torn off or cut off? A customer told me…"

Dooley didn't like Lee much from the start, but now he had a quick fantasy of tearing *his* arms off and stuffing him into a coroner's wagon. Instead of acting on it, he pressed on with the questioning. "This Brewster, he was a customer here, wasn't he?"

"Ha! Are you kidding me? If he could've eaten the *ovens*, I think he would've. He must've spent three or four hundred a week here. Just in donuts!"

The counter girl interjected. "Five hundred."

The owner looked over his shoulder at her. "*Five* hundred?"

"Yeah, easy. You don' know, 'cause you didn' wait on him. I did."

"Five hundred, Detective."

"So he was what you might call a good customer, eh?"

"No, Sergeant, he's what you might call the best customer of all time."

Dooley was jotting down in his notebook. "How many donuts does five hundred dollars translate to?"

"Tisk! Do the math, Detective!"

"I'm trying to do the math, Mr. Lester. How much is that, Perkins?"

Perkins looked up into the heavens at an imaginary chalkboard. "Five hundred? Each donut costs what—um—forty divided by five hundred—uh, that's um…"

"That'd be about nine-hundred fifty donuts, dependin' on what type he ordered."

Dooley and Perkins looked at the girl and then at each other. Both were impressed. "Did he buy them for somebody else?"

Lee found that quite amusing. "Ha! He ate them himself, Detective. Have you ever *seen* this guy?"

"Yeah, we saw him."

"Then you should know better than to ask such a dumb question. Funny, I just thought of something. His brother would come in with him sometimes, but he very rarely bought a donut for himself."

"What do you mean? He mooched off his brother?"

"No, he didn't like sweets or cakes. He wasn't fond of donuts."

"Was his brother a health nut? We heard he was a nut about the decathlon."

"Melvin? He was in worse shape than Luther! He just didn't like sweets and cakes, is all."

"When you say he was in worse shape than Luther, do you mean that he was even fatter?"

"No, I wouldn't say he was fatter, necessarily. I think they were probably about the same, give or take fifty pounds."

"Do you know if Melvin was older or younger than Luther?"

"That's really splitting hairs, isn't it, Detective?

"What do you mean, 'splitting hairs'?"

"I mean, what difference does a few minutes make?"

"Well, I don't understand. What are we talking about here?"

"What Mr. Lee is tryin' tah tell ya', Mr. Detective, is that Luther an' Melvin wuz twins."

"Say, you're pretty damn smart. You're almost as smart as you are pretty. What are you doing tomorrow night, Dawn?"

"Fuhget it, cop. I only date beer-swillin', pot-smokin' losers. You just don' measure up in my book."

"I think she just complimented you, Perk."

"I'm not so sure about that."

"Come on. We've got work to do." Dooley grabbed Perkins by the arm and dragged him out the door of the Donut Depot. "We've got to talk to this twin brother, Melvin. I'll bet you dollars to donuts that he's got some part in this case."

"I have to have that girl, Hank."

"That dirt bag? Are you nuts?"

"You don't know, because you're not married. You don't know what it's like."

"What what's like? You've got a solid marriage, you dolt. Your wife loves you."

"My wife? Ha! She doesn't understand me."

"Nobody understands you—least of all, you! Now get your mind out of the gutter and back on this case. We're cops, Perkins. We can't go around compromising our integrity, sleeping with every bimbo that comes down the pike."

Perkins seemed to come to his senses. "Of course you're right, Hank." He put his hand on Dooley's shoulder. "Thank you. I can always count on you to be a shining example of what a cop can be if he's willing to take the hard road."

Chapter 20

"Who is it?"

"It's the police. Open the door, Brewster."

"Show your badges, first."

Dooley and Perkins did as required, holding them up to the peephole. "I'm Detective Dooley and this is Sergeant Perkins. Are you gonna open up now?"

"Okay." Brewster unlocked the three locks and opened up. He was a mountain of flesh—the largest living human being either man had ever seen in person.

"Do you know why Sergeant Perkins and I have come here, Brewster?"

"Are you going to tell me? Or do I have to guess? You know, my crystal ball is on the fritz." Brewster started walking into his apartment toward the living room. Both Dooley and Perkins were astonished at how much room he took up in the hallway. He practically scraped both walls.

"Are you telling us you don't know about your brother?"

"I know my brother exists, of course, but I suspect that you are here to talk about something other than his mere existence. So, what about my brother?"

"You don't read the papers?"

"My brother was in the papers? What did he do, swim the English Channel?"

Perkins noticed Dooley reacting to something, though he couldn't tell what. He got close as they followed Brewster and whispered in Dooley's ear. "What's the matter, Hank?"

Dooley waved him off. "I'll tell you later." Then he addressed Brewster again. "Have you spoken to your brother recently?"

Brewster reached the living room and laboriously squatted on a large reinforced metal chair. It was one of those heavy steel chairs made for public buildings, but the two officers were still surprised when it didn't crush down like an aluminum soda can under Brewster's gargantuan bulk.

"I haven't spoken to him in awhile and certainly not this week. Is he in trouble with the law?"

"When was the last time you spoke to your brother?"

"Let's see. We got together on Saturday for coffee and pie."

"Where was that? What diner?"

"Um, I don't really remember the name of the place. It was somewhere near the bus terminal. He knows it. Ask him. Do you need to use the bathroom, Detective?"

"Why did you ask that?"

"No reason, really. It's just that you—well, you're scratching your ass, so I thought, maybe…"

"No, Brewster, I don't need to use the bathroom. It just so happens that my asshole is a funny thing."

"Look, Detective, I'm certain your asshole should have its own TV show on ABC, but I think we ought to get back to the subject of my brother, don't you?"

"Interesting you should say that, because in a sense my asshole *is* about your brother."

Brewster stared at Dooley for a long time. "How did you become a detective? Are they hiring out of the psycho ward, nowadays?" He turned to Perkins. "Is your partner cuckoo?"

"Hank Dooley's not crazy, Mr. Brewster. In fact, he's a fine detective. And one of the things that makes Hank Dooley a fine detective is Hank Dooley's asshole."

"Is that so? I hope you're not going to tell me next that you have first-hand experience of Detective Dooley's asshole."

"I will not say that. However, it is a fact that if his asshole itches him, then something is definitely amiss."

127

"You bet it is, Sergeant. But, then, if he'd wipe his ass properly, maybe nothing would be amiss." Brewster crossed his arms as much as he could across his giant fat chest.

Dooley interrupted their exchange. "Funny, you talking about wiping your ass. I should think that you'd be the last person to want to bring that subject up."

Brewster uncrossed his arms and leaned forward a little, putting his hands on his shapeless knees. "What's *that* supposed to mean?"

Dooley felt a little bubble of fear at the thought of this unmanageable mountain of humanity possibly rising from his chair and advancing on him, but he soldiered on anyway. "Oh, nothing. It's just that looking at you…"

Perkins shared Dooley's bubble of fear and didn't relish the thought that he'd be crushed and smothered in this apartment on this day. "Hey, Hank."

Dooley ignored his partner. "It's just that looking at you, I wonder if you've been able to even *reach* the crack of your own ass in the last bunch of years, let alone wipe it."

"Hank." Perkins tapped Dooley on the arm, but was ignored.

"I don't have to remain here taking this shit from you. Who do you think you are, anyway? You stand there scratching your ass and insulting me. I won't stand for this." He slowly got up and ponderously advanced on them. His face was a splotchy red and a heavy sweat had broken out on his forehead and upper lip.

Perkins and Dooley backed down the hallway as Dooley continued the taunting. "Oh? What are you gonna do? You could hardly get out of that steel-reinforced chair of yours!" They managed to get out the door and back into the hallway and to relative safety as Brewster reached them.

He was bellowing now, at the top of his lungs. "You lousy son of a bitch! Keep backing up, just like a weasely coward. I hope you know where the unemployment office is, Detective, because if I have any say about it, you'll be visiting it soon enough!" With that, he slammed the door extremely hard.

"What the hell is the matter with you?"

"Nothing, Perk. Let's get back downtown. I ordered a tap on his phone while we were back at headquarters. I want to see if he places any calls."

"Are you thinking he's going to report you?"

"No, I want to see if he calls his brother."

"What?"

"Didn't you notice that he seemed pretty eager to get rid of us?"

"Yeah, of course he was. But, you were making fun of him and goading him, so—*oh*! I see what you mean. He went right along with it and he never did find out why we were asking about his brother."

"Think about it. If I knocked on your door and started asking about your twin brother and when was the last time you saw him, would you care if I was scratching my ass? Or would you be more concerned about your brother?"

"My brother? It would be a toss-up. But, what do you think it means? Do you think he's involved somehow?"

"I'm not sure yet, but I have a theory that's based on that weird dream I had. Let's go back downtown."

They drove back to headquarters and darted up the stairs to the communications room, running into Captain Homily on the way.

"Hey, you two! Any progress on that Rosalie Jiminez case?"

"I don't know, Captain. We're not working on that case right at the moment. We're checking Brewster's phone calls."

"Brewster? Who's Brewster?"

"The seven hundred pound fat suicide's seven hundred-fifty pound twin brother."

"But, that's *your* case, Perkins. Wait a minute, Dooley! I told you that you could use Perkins, not the other way around."

"They may be related somehow."

"How? What does one case have to do with the other?"

"We'll see. We're working on the connection. There were chocolate sprinkles on the coffee table in Brewster's living room."

"So?"

"This Luther Brewster was a donut fanatic."

"This doesn't have to do with that dream you told me about, does it, Hank?"

"It does. I really think it must have meant something."

"What the hell could it mean? I think all it means that you've got problems." Homily stopped himself. "No, maybe that's not true. I do remember you said she made a point of counting her breasts."

"Yeah."

"And you said she counted two, correct? And now it turns out that you're dealing with twin brothers." Homily rubbed his forehead as he pondered the situation. "I don't know what to make of this shit. Look, if this is anything like your asshole, maybe there's something to it. I trust your asshole implicitly. We all do. Why not your caffeine-induced visions, too? Oh, what the hell. Stick with it, I guess."

Dooley was relieved, especially since he had completely lost interest in the Jiminez case anyway. "Let's get up to Communications, then."

"Boys, what do you suppose you'll find out from Brewster's phone calls?"

"I think it's not so much the phone calls he makes, but the one he *doesn't* make that will tell us what we want to know."

"Perkins, you're his partner. Do you know what he's talking about?"

"Yeah, I do. Hank's theory, backed up by his telltale itch, is that Brewster knows more about his brother than he let on. He claimed to know nothing about Luther. If that's so, he ought to try calling his brother."

"How could he not know about his brother? It's been in the papers and you guys would've told him, right?"

"Except neither Perk nor I told him and he claimed to have no knowledge of his brother's whereabouts."

"Good work, guys. Excellent. But, I still don't get how Brewster is tied in with the Rosalie Jiminez case."

"Yeah, Hank, the only connection right now is your dream."

"I said there were chocolate sprinkles on the coffee table in Brewster's apartment. There were sprinkles in the box with Rosalie Jiminez's foot. And the lab reported that Sawzall had traces of chocolate frosting on the blade." They arrived at the communications room.

"Hi guys. Hi Captain."

"Hi, Ashby. We're here about Dooley's tap. Anything on that Brewster line?"

"Yeah, Captain, we got some action. He just placed a call a little while ago, as a matter of fact."

"Do you have the number?" Dooley stepped forward.

"Sure do. Here it is."

Homily tried to peek over the top of the paper. "Well, Hank, is it the brother's phone number?"

Chapter 21

"You again? I don't think I have any obligation to talk to you again. Why don't you go shakedown some poor dumb pusher or something and just leave me alone. I've got enough to handle at the moment."

On the way to Brewster's apartment, Perkins and Dooley had stopped in at the donut shop and bought a powdered jelly donut for each of them, which they were munching on when they knocked on the door.

"Look, Brewster, I'm sorry about yesterday." Dooley employed his most contrite tone. "I realize I said some things that were out of line and unprofessional and, as a result, we didn't even get done what we came here to do in the first place. If you'd just forget that unfortunate sparring we did yesterday and just let us in, I'm sure we can take care of business without any static. It'd be really big of you, Brewster." Brewster didn't budge nor did he say anything. "Come on, man. Let's let bygones be bygones, huh? Be a sport. Let's get this thing over with." Dooley took another bite out of his donut and chewed as he waited for Brewster's response. The white powder was all over Dooley's lips.

Brewster mulled it over for a minute, looking very uncomfortable and staring at the donuts before condescending to Dooley's pleading. "Well, okay. But, no harsh words, please. I've had a tough couple of days." He swallowed hard.

Dooley feigned great concern. "Oh, what about?"

"Stop playing your little game, Detective. My brother dying, of course."

"So, you *do* know that he died? I thought you hadn't heard anything about him or from him?"

"Yeah, that's right, but after you left here yesterday I suddenly realized you hadn't told me what was going on with him. So I called my uncle and he'd read about it in the paper. How come you didn't call me down to identify the body? Isn't that what you usually do in these cases?"

"That all depends on circumstances."

"I don't understand how you police work. I've certainly never seen the likes of you on the television."

"That stuff on TV is just a bunch of juvenile fantasies, Brewster. This is reality. Can we come in? I don't like talking official business out here in the hall."

"Sure, come in." They followed in his wake as he navigated his apartment like a great ocean liner in the confines of a canal.

"So, your uncle knew all about it and he never called you to see how you were doing?"

"He's not that kind of uncle."

"No, I suppose not. You don't mind that we have these donuts, do you? We didn't get a chance to eat any breakfast. We just barely had the chance to grab these. There was a place on the way over here—what was the name of that place, Perk?"

"Um, I think it was called Donut something, Hank. Yeah, that's it, Donut Depot."

"Hey, Brewster, your brother liked donuts a lot. Isn't that right?"

"Why, yes, he did. He, um—I always told him to go easy on those things. Ever since we were young, I always said they were a heart attack in every box—all that sugar and fat—terrible for you, especially those cream and jelly-filled ones. Oops, sorry." Brewster drooled copiously down his chin at the instant he'd said 'jelly-filled'.

"That's all right, Brewster. I salivate a lot when I talk about food. Especially fresh baked cakes and pies and donuts and danish and a delicious tangy apple turnover, with that brown sugar and maybe some of that white sugar frosting dripped on the top. Boy, when I think of the aroma of a donut shop—the sugar and doughy goodness and chocolate and that powdered sugar, I can't help myself. I'm like Pavlov's dog! You know what I mean? Just thinking about that soft and chewy quality of a really good donut, fresh from the oven gets me going and I can hardly stop salivating."

"Yes!" Brewster looked a little crazed and his cheeks had acquired a hot-looking blush. He was swallowing as fast as he could.

"But, from what I've heard, you abhorred those donuts and pastries, huh? I imagine you were a lot healthier than your brother. Don't you think so?"

"Yes—uh, yes. I was, as a matter of fact."

133

"Well, that's a good thing. You know what? All that talk about donuts got me thinking. These donuts, as delicious as they are, are hardly a full meal. I'm still not completely satisfied. Are you, Perk?"

"No, come to think of it. I guess I could eat more."

"I was thinking that I was feeling kind of hungry myself, Detective."

"Really? What a coincidence!"

"Hey, Hank, I remember seeing a nifty little bakery on the corner. We passed it on the way here."

"Say, why don't we continue this conversation down the street?"

"That sounds good to me. We should try it out. Maybe they've got some fresh donuts or pastries, huh?"

Brewster became giddy with excitement. "Yeah, yeah! I'll get my coat and—wait a second. I don't think I should. I mean, I just remembered I'm not fond of donuts." He almost choked on that sentence. "I don't know what I was thinking. You two better go ahead without me."

"Oh, no! I wouldn't think of it." He scratched his chin for a moment. "Hey, maybe we should do this instead. There's an all-you-can-eat rib place not far from here. You ever hear of it? I'm sure you must have, since you're so into healthy stuff like meat. What was the name of that place? It's right under the highway, not too far from here. Do you know the place?"

"I, uh, can't remember the name, but I know the place you're talking about."

"Yeah, they've got these gigantic meaty ribs and this delicious hot barbecue sauce. The meat is so well cooked that it's literally falling off the bone. Sizzling, savory slabs of sinewy sensuality."

"Well said, Hank. That's what I could really go for, right about now—a rack of thick and meaty ribs, fresh off the flamin' grill. Doesn't that sound great, Brewster?"

"Yeah, Brewster, what do you say to that?"

Brewster had gone from looking like he was going to have a culinary orgasm to looking like he had just swallowed a cupful of rotten cat meat. "M-m-meat, eh? Well, it sure sounds, um, great, but I really should be, um…"

"Oh, come on, Brewster. What else do you have to do? Dooley and I will treat. Let's get some ribs, huh?"

"That's very nice of you guys, but, I'd better not."

"Well, maybe next time. We'd better get going and leave you alone since you're in mourning. We've bothered you long enough, I think."

"Don't worry about it. I'm glad to be of service."

"Good luck to you, big fella."

"Yeah, see ya' round, Brewster."

The pair passed out of the apartment and back into the hallway.

Perkins spoke quietly. "What do you think? I see your asshole is itching you again."

"I'm sure of it. He's Luther Brewster."

"I noticed how he stared at our donuts when we walked in. You were sure right about him."

"We need proof, though. Let's get back to headquarters."

They sped back to headquarters and to the communications room, where Ashby was eating a chicken salad sandwich.

"Hi, Ashby. Sorry to interrupt your lunch."

"Oh, don't worry about it. I never get a regular lunch anyway."

"What do you have on Brewster? Anything?"

"Yeah, he placed two calls shortly after noon. One to this number, here." He handed a slip to Dooley while he read a second one. "And this one to the Avalon Wholesale Baking Company on 3rd Street."

"Play that one, Ashby."

Ashby rewound the tape to a designated number on the tape counter. They all listened as the recording began with Brewster dialing the phone. After the phone rang three times, a woman's voice could be heard.

"Hello, Avalon Baking, how can I direct your call?"

"I want to order some donuts, please."

"Hold the line, please."

There was some clicking and silence before another woman's voice came on.

"Hello, you want to place an order, sir?"

"Yes, please."

"What company, please?"

"I'm not with a company."

"I'm sorry, sir, we don't sell individual products. We only sell wholesale, in large quantities."

"I know that."

"Are you looking to cater an event?"

"No, I just want to buy some donuts."

"Well, I'm sorry, sir, but we only sell donuts by the gross. That's one hundred forty-four donuts for a minimum order."

"Can I get them delivered?"

"You want to buy one hundred forty-four donuts?"

"No. I want to buy four hundred and thirty-two. They're going to have to last me a few days."

"You're not buying these for a luncheonette or restaurant?"

She sounded incredulous. None of the men listening to the call could blame her.

"No, I'm not, miss. What's the matter with you people?
Can't a man buy some donuts, for Pete's sake?"

The recording continued on, but Dooley cut in. "I've heard enough."

"You were right, Hank. I just want to know one thing?"

"What's that, Perk?"

"Where can I get an asshole like yours?"

"Ha ha. Sometimes I'm not sure if it's a blessing or a curse. It can be pretty annoying, you know."

"What's the big deal? I'm surrounded by annoying assholes most of the time, anyway."

"Let's go talk to Luther."

When they showed up at Brewster's door at half-past three, Brewster opened the door wearing a surprised and dismayed expression on his face.

"Detective! What are you doing back here?"

"What's the matter, Melvin Brewster? You don't look happy to see us again."

"No, no. It's not that. No, I, uh…"

"Well, no matter. It doesn't really matter if *Melvin* Brewster isn't happy to see us, because we didn't come to talk to *Melvin* Brewster. We came to talk to *Luther* Brewster. Isn't that right, Perk?"

"Yep. We kinda think Luther's home, right now."

"What's that supposed to mean, Sergeant?"

"Come on, Brewster. I know Luther Brewster is here because Avalon Bakery is going to deliver four hundred thirty-two donuts to him here, by five o'clock tonight."

"You tapped my phone." Brewster looked sad.

"You want to tell us what's going on?"

137

Brewster took a deep breath and let it out slowly. "Where do I start?" He lumbered over to his reinforced chair and sat down heavily. "Detective, the Brewsters are a very proud family. We come from quite a distinguished lineage. Our family can trace its roots back to all the most important events any person can recall from their fifth grade history class. If it was something to brag about, a Brewster was there. We are a very distinguished clan—very old and *very* proper. You wouldn't have a clue about such a lineage and all that goes along with belonging to an old and proper family and having to uphold a standard. You two couldn't possibly know what that means. We Brewsters would look at someone like you, Detective Dooley or you, Sergeant Perkins, and we see pigs."

"Most people do."

"I don't mean pigs as in police. I mean low-down, scum-sucking swine." He held up his hand. "Now, before you get sore because I called you both low-down, scum-sucking swine, you have to understand that there is also a down side to the equation. When you are part of a family like the Brewsters, there cannot be a quote-unquote *normal* childhood. When Mel and I were boys, we were never allowed to play with the other children. No child was good enough to play with a Brewster. We weren't even allowed to touch other children for fear of contamination. We were told that if we touched other children, we would become just like them. That struck fear in our young hearts. We couldn't imagine anything worse than that. Can you imagine what it's like to be better than everyone you know and to live in terror of becoming one of them?"

"As a matter of fact..."

"Mel and I became outcasts and laughing stocks. The other children would tease us relentlessly. I recall them threatening to touch us if we didn't do what they wanted us to do for their amusement."

"Like what, for instance?"

"One time, one of the meanest boys, Billy Martin, ordered me to lie on my back and kick my legs and wave my fists and wail like a little baby."

"And you did it?"

"I had to do it. He said he was going to touch me otherwise. That wasn't the only problem we had at school. Mother dressed us every day like little fops. We wore satin pants and silly hats, with our hair hanging down in ringlets, while all the other boys dressed like cowboys and pirates and explorers. And there we were in our short pants and stockings. I honestly don't know how we got through tenth and eleventh grades. It got to the point that there was nothing for us to live for. No girl wanted us. No boy would even talk to us. We had nothing until we discovered food."

"Food. Uh huh." Dooley stole a glance at Perkins, who rolled his eyes slightly at Brewster's saga.

"Food, Detective, had been there since the beginning. We took it for granted all that time and hadn't noticed that it had been our one truly loyal companion all along. It had never plotted against us, deliberately humiliated us, cheated us or threatened us. Once we discovered it, food became our best friend. It quickly evolved into our lover, our confidant and, ironically, our nemesis. We couldn't play tag or baseball to save our lives, but we could eat anyone under the table."

He shifted in his seat and Perkins jumped slightly, expecting the creaking chair to snap under the pressure. When it didn't snap and he was finished shifting his bulk, Brewster continued his tale of woe. "I was drawn to cakes and pies and cookies, but donuts were my drug of choice. I call it a drug because that's exactly what it became. I started using donuts, occasionally at first. Then, over time and without my awareness, the habit grew until it became more a way of life than a food. Melvin was that way about sausages and greasy fried food, mayonnaise and heavy biscuits. He justified it all by drinking Diet Rite Cola, eventually switching to Tab. I preferred Fresca. But, he was hooked as much as I was and we were both on the slippery slope. Father and Mother pretended to not notice that we were gaining weight. They had blinders on because they didn't want to admit that a Brewster could have an emotional or psychological problem. Eventually, though, the result of our addiction became so pronounced that even they could not ignore it. I was over five hundred pounds by the time Mother suggested that I might not really want to eat my twenty third apple turnover one morning after breakfast. I agreed with her and had a cheese danish instead. Father never said a word to either Mel or me about our eating. He just held it all in until that fateful afternoon at the Frisky Chicken Diner on East End Avenue."

Perkins interjected at that point, mainly to keep himself awake. "What did he do that afternoon, Luther?"

"Two things bothered Father that day. Mel had run the diner out of fried chicken and I cleaned them out of all their baked goods. The second thing was, uh—I don't remember what the second thing was anymore. I'm certain it was important, though."

"Oh, jeez! What did he do, Luther?"

"Father ran away. He ditched us at the diner."

"So what? It sounds like he was a non-factor, anyway."

"Brewster, would you take it as an insult if I suggested to you that you should get to the point?"

"No, of course not. I appreciate your bluntness, Detective. I really do. Life can be very cruel to overweight people, Detective, very cruel."

"You say you admire my bluntness, Luther, so I'll be blunt. You're *not* overweight."

"Huh? I'm not?"

"You're not what most people would call overweight."

"No?" Brewster was bewildered at Dooley's assertion.

"No, you're not what most people call overweight. You, my copious friend, are what most people would call an enormous fat blob!"

"I should have expected as much, coming from a cop. You see, that's the kind of attitude that makes it so difficult for people like me and my poor, deceased brother."

"Aren't you blaming the victims, Brewster?"

"How am I blaming the victims? My brother and I..."

"Are *not* the victims. *We* are the victims, Brewster. The people that have to sit next to people like you on the subway or bus or an airplane are the victims. The victims are the people who have to pay more to eat at a buffet because you ate up all their profits. The victims are the people who have to smell your rank backside as you struggle to get your mammoth bulk up a flight of stairs ahead of them."

"My brother and I are the victims of your prejudice and loathing and discrimination. That's what led Mel to hang himself. He couldn't stand the cruel taunting and brutal insults anymore. He didn't want to hear anymore the sniggering of the waiters at the Frisky Chicken when he ordered his fifth Fried Chicken-in-a-Basket entrée. He was running out of money, too. It's expensive to eat that much meat, you know. He was in a panic, facing a future without the funds to support his habit. He had already run through his inheritance. Within the last few weeks, he had begun to rifle through dumpsters, looking for sausages and ribs."

"So, you're confirming that he killed himself?"

"Yes, Detective, he killed himself."

"His arms were cut off. How do you explain that?"

"I cut them off for him."

"He wanted you to cut his arms off?"

"No, Detective, he didn't know about it."

"Then, why the hell did you cut his arms off?"

"It was the only thing I could think of at the time to make it appear that he had been murdered. I didn't have much time and I didn't want the world to think that a Brewster had stooped so low that he was forced to take his own life. That's why I did it. Despite my plus-size physique, I'm still a Brewster. We Brewsters have pride, you know. I can't have the Brewster name dragged through the mud."

"No, of course not. So, you saved the Brewster name from the mud and dragged it through the shit instead."

Perkins jumped in at this point. "Speaking of shit, why'd he pick the women's room at the Museum of Modern Art to end it all? Was he some kind of perv?"

"That was uncalled for, Sergeant. No, I'll tell you why. He'd been depressed—more than depressed, really. I would say he was despondent. I was worried he might do something rash, so I'd been sticking to him, not letting him out of my sight. I guess it was the only place he could think of to duck out on me. We were looking at Wayne Thiebaud's *Cakes* painting together, which is my favorite, by the way. I was standing there, transfixed, when I suddenly realized that he had slipped away from me. By the time I had located him, he had cut the rope off that horrid iron sculpture in the Post-Modernist room, dragged a guard's stool into the bathroom and hanged himself."

"Who suggested that you two go to the museum to look at that painting?"

"He did. I think he knew I would be so captivated by it that he would be able to sneak off—at least long enough to do what he needed to do. Anyway, when I saw what he had done, I cut his arms off."

"Naturally. What did you use to do that?"

"The guard's stool broke under my brother's weight, so I used the jagged plywood seat. It took a lot of sawing, but it did the trick."

"Why are you impersonating your brother?"

"To protect his reputation. It's a selfless act on my part."

"What about Rosalie Jiminez?"

"Who's that?"

"Let's cut the bullshit, Brewster. Rosalie Jiminez is the woman you cut up into pieces, sending those pieces to me in boxes, that's who."

"I don't know what you're talking about. Honest. I haven't done anything like that. That's sick, Detective."

"You mean to say that you didn't send us a foot, a scalp, an ass, and perhaps a pair of lips?"

"That's disgusting. I would never do anything like that."

"You cut your brother's arms off with the seat of a broken stool. Why wouldn't you slice up Rosalie Jiminez with a Sawzall?"

"That's awful. I loved my brother and my family. That's why I dismembered him. I don't even know this Rosalie Jiminez. And what's a Sawzall?"

"What does your A-hole tell you, Hank?"

"Nothing. Maybe Felix was our man, after all?"

"That's too bad. I know you liked him a lot, Hank."

"That's right, I did. But we need to wrap that case up, fast. I've been dragging my heels on it for days. I can't keep the Captain at bay much longer and I have no idea where to turn next."

Dooley thought for a moment, but it was Perkins who came up with a plan. "Listen, Mr. Brewster, you wouldn't be interested in stepping in and in effect take the rap for this other case, would you?"

"Hey, that's a nifty idea, Perk! Look, Luther, we can make it worth your while. We can swing it so you get a really good lawyer and maybe even beat the rap. What do you say?"

"You mean confess to this sicko butchery case? I'm sorry, fellas, that doesn't seem..."

"Listen, it makes no difference to us whether you are convicted or not, as long as we get the arrest. Come on, Brewster, be a pal."

"I don't know. I'd like to accommodate you guys and help you out of a jam, but it doesn't seem quite right. I'm afraid I'll have to say no. Hey, why don't you catch the person who actually committed that crime? Wouldn't that be better?"

"It's not that easy, Brewster. You can't go and catch a criminal, just like that." Dooley snapped his finger. "It takes a lot of work and a lot of time. And time is what we really don't have lots of. What if we treat you to dinner? Still not interested?"

Brewster shook his head.

"That's okay. We'll be okay without your help. We'll need to talk to Felix again, Perk. Well, Mr. Brewster, you take care of yourself." They rose to depart.

"Wait! You guys aren't going to arrest me?"

"For what? You said your brother killed himself, right?"

"I did cut his arms off, you know, to make it appear to have been a murder. Isn't that a crime?"

"Yeah, I guess so. But, we've got bigger fish to fry right now, Luther."

"Bigger even than me?"

They all shared a laugh.

Chapter 22

"But, I don't understand. You yourself said you thought I was innocent of this terrible deed. Isn't that right, Sergeant Perkins? You were there. You heard him say it."

"Felix, listen to Hank. He's not actually saying you did it. He's just saying that you're going to have to stand trial for it. That's two different things."

"I did say that you seemed innocent, Felix. But, unfortunately, we have no choice. We haven't been able to dig up any good suspects and we're plumb out of time on this thing."

"What about this connection between the man who was murdered at the museum and my wife's murder? You said..."

"You told him about that?"

"Yeah, I'm sorry, Hank. I mentioned it to him when we let him go the other day. You seemed pretty certain, so I didn't see any harm in it."

"Felix, that was just a hallucination I had after I drank sixteen cups of coffee. It turned out to be fruitful in one regard—we solved that other case. I know that doesn't help you at all and I feel bad about that. Really I do, Felix. Don't cry. Please, Felix, it makes us feel bad."

"But, I didn't do it!"

"Somebody did it."

"Yeah, but not me. Did you check out any leads? What about the possibility that she was having an affair?"

"We haven't gotten very far on those leads. I really didn't have a lot of time to check out any leads. Look, Felix, please just take the rap, will you? I promise we'll put in a good word for you. Maybe we can bungle the handling of the evidence somehow and you can get acquitted. What do you think of that idea, huh?" Felix continued to sob, dabbing his eyes with a handkerchief. "Perk, can you talk some sense into him? Maybe he'll listen to you."

"We desperately need an arrest, Felix. You could say we over-committed ourselves, and without a..."

Suddenly, the door burst open and Captain Homily, smiling from ear to ear, poked his head in the room. "Boys! Listen up!"

"Hi, Captain."

"I have great news. You can send Mr. Jiminez home, boys. Detective Marmot just made an arrest—a real suspect, too! The tool-rental guy confessed to killing and butchering Rosalie Jiminez. Do you remember him, Dooley? He's that guy you talked to at the Woody's where that Sawzall was rented. They found whatever parts were left of Mrs. Jiminez in the guy's fridge. Oh, hello, Mr. Jiminez."

Felix wiped his eyes and sniffled. "Hi, Captain. Do you know *why* he did it? Did he tell you?"

"Mr. Jiminez, evidently your wife had been having an affair with him ever since you had her return a pipe cutter that you had rented from him a year ago. It seems that after a few months she got tired of him and wanted to break it off. They fought and that's when he killed her. The next day, he got himself a night job, moonlighting at the Dandy Deals appliance store up the street from Woody's. He bought a locker-style freezer with his employee discount so he could stash her body. He saved her body for months in the freezer until he had the chance to frame you. It was simple for him to falsify the rental book and use the extra day to cut up your wife." He turned to Dooley. "And while you were dreaming about some middle-aged woman's breasts and going around scratching you're A-hole, Marmot did some good old-fashioned police work and caught the son of a bitch." He smiled and waved. "See ya 'round, boys." He breezed out as quickly as he had breezed in.

"What the hell are you crying about now, Felix? You're off the hook, for chrissakes."

"My poor wife, all sliced up like car parts in a junkyard. It's so terrible. And her poor mother. Oh, my God! How will I be able to tell her? She'll never understand it all."

Dooley popped up out of his chair. "Hey! I could try to tell her for you, Felix."

"But, how can you do that? My mother-in-law speaks no English."

"Give me a day or two. I'll see what I can do for her. Leave it to a professional, Felix. This is not a job for a son-in-law to handle."

Part III
Mergers and Acquisitions

Chapter 23

The weeks and months tend to fly by in the foggy haze of the grinding routine of police work. The cycles of crime—investigate—arrest—testify overlap each other so that it becomes difficult to remember which case you are investigating and which crime you are accusing someone of. Some cops take money; some take booze; some take it out on their wives. In order to cope with the stress and the confusion, they all take something. Hank Dooley takes coffee.

In the three days since the Rosalie Jiminez and Luther Brewster cases were wrapped up, Dooley had been navigating the rapids of a river consisting of sex and coffee, roiled up into a frothy, heady mixture. The soon-to-be-bereaved mother needed to assert her life force in her struggle with menopause. Dooley felt the need to prove his potency after young Marmot easily solved his seemingly unsolvable case. Once the two had worked out their needs, they bid each other 'adios'. Mrs. Mendez put her can of Café Bustello back up in the cupboard, hit the showers and went back to her life.

Dooley went back to the Riviera.

"Here you go, Hank."

"Smells good. Did you just brew a fresh pot?" Dooley sniffed deeply as he dumped a carload of sugar in the cup.

"I thought you were going to cut back on this stuff? Didn't you say something like that a couple of weeks ago?"

"I did, but I got a headache and felt drowsy. It got so bad that, on the second day, I fell asleep during an interrogation of a suspect in that mob rubout case. It was so egregious that the Captain played the videotape of it afterward for the entire department. In the tape you can see the suspect get up, walk right over to me, shake me by the shoulder a few times, and, when he couldn't rouse me, he puts his jacket back on, calmly walks right out the door and gets on a plane to Venezuela."

"That's tough."

"That was pretty embarrassing. I can't have that happen all the time, so fill 'er up!"

"You're done already?"

"Wait a second, wait a second, man. What the hell is this?" Dooley peered into his cup and rotated it slowly.

Marty tried to see over the edge of the cup. "What is what?"

"This doughy stuff in the bottom of my cup."

Marty snatched the cup from Dooley's hand. "Oh, sorry, Hank. Don't worry. I'll give you another cup."

"Jeez! Last week it was a dead deep-fried roach in my French fries. I hope at least that it was a French roach. What's it gonna be next week? A rat in my Reuben sandwich?"

Marty looked very grave. "Don't joke about that, Hank. A woman *did* have a rat sandwich, day before yesterday. It's not funny. I didn't notice that the damn thing got heat stroke and keeled over onto my grill while I was finishing up her meatloaf sandwich. It was about the same size and color as her meatloaf and I was in a hurry, so, naturally I just served it up, you know…"

"It's a good thing a rat doesn't look like two eggs, sunny side up, eh?"

"Yeah, but you'd be surprised at all the things that *do* look like egg. I'm telling you…"

"No, don't tell me! Maybe we oughtta talk about something else, huh?"

"Here's your new cup. I won't charge you for the coffee this time, okay? Save yourself a quarter."

"I appreciate that."

A man suddenly burst into the Riviera, short of breath and excited. "Dooley! Dooley! I been lookin' all over fer you."

"What's the matter, Pepperino?"

"Captain wants all us back at the office fer a big pow-wow."

Dooley pointed to the cup. "I just got a fresh cup of coffee. Can it wait a few minutes?"

Pepperino shook his head, still gasping for breath. "Captain says every-body—right now!"

"Sounds pretty important, Hank. Maybe you should go?"

"But, my coffee…"

"Dooley, word's out that it's a full-blown war between the two main mob families."

"Who'd you hear *that* from?"

"You haven't heard? It's been the talk of the office for days."

"Well, I've been working hard on wrapping up some loose ends in the Rosalie Jiminez case, you know. What kicked off this war?"

"Don't know all the details, but I *do* know that the Feci family torched the Spazzatura's headquarters."

Dooley continued sipping his coffee as he listened. "Did they get Giancarlo Spazzatura?"

"Don't know any more details. Let's go, Dooley!"

Dooley finished the coffee. "Okay, I'm ready."

Chapter 24

Dooley and Pepperino walked into Squad Room J. The room was packed with every plain-clothes detective the City currently had on payroll who wasn't also up on charges. Captain Homily stood at the front of the room. "Well, look what the cat dragged in. It's about time, Dooley. Peppy, didn't you tell him to get his ass down here right away?"

"I sure did, Captain. Took me a while to find him. That's why we're late, sir." Pepperino and Dooley sidled in and took places on the side of the room, since there were no available seats.

"Do you realize we've all been waiting for you so we could start? I thought you'd be at that horrible luncheonette, hooked up to an I.V. drip, with a pot of coffee at the other end of the tube. Where were you?"

"That's where I was, Captain."

"Well, let's get started. I don't know what you've all been told, but this is what we do know. Looks like the Fecis have launched an all-out war against the Spazzaturas. It seems they set fire to the Spazzatura's headquarters right before sunrise. They also blew up the Spazzatura Lanes Bowling Alley and Family Fun Center on Holland Street and they got the manager and gave him the notorious Faccia di Feci."

Pepperino raised his hand and piped up. "What's that, Captain?"

"I forgot, some of you youngsters don't know about that. Tell him, Dooley."

"The Faccia di Feci is the trademark of the Feci family. If you ever see a man with the Faccia di Feci you never forget it—ever. It's unspeakable horror." There was a general hum of low murmuring around the room.

Pepperino still didn't quite grasp it. "Is this guy dead?"

"No way. It's not that easy. I'm sure he *wishes* he was dead. Some of the recipients of the Faccia di Feci kill themselves afterward. They can't take it. Then they have a closed-casket funeral, of course."

Homily let the buzz continue for a few seconds, then cut it short. "All right, everybody, let's settle down. Come on, fellas. O'Brien! Don't tip your chair back like that. You'll fall and hit your head. Come on, both feet on the floor

151

and face front. So, fellas, we've got the first campaign in an all-out war. The papers have already picked up the ball and are running with it, so we've got to stop this war—or, at the very least, hush it up so the papers can't make us look so bad."

A voice came from the corner of the room. "I vote to cover it up, sir!" This comment was followed by several assenting voices.

Pepperino raised his hand again. "How do we do that, Captain?"

There was laughter around the room.

"You're pretty new, Pepperoni…"

"Pepperino, sir." There was more snickering around the room.

"Yeah. Well, you're still wet behind the ears. What I mean is that you guys need to find alternate explanations for the things that happen in this turf war. If you can't pin it on someone other than a Feci or a Spazzatura, explain it away as an unfortunate accident. You understand? Just plain stupidity or operator error will explain most things. I've got the lab boys on board, so we're all on the same page in this all-out campaign against bad press."

Dooley noticed that Pepperino still looked lost. "Give him an example, Captain."

"All right. The bowling alley, for instance. You can explain that as carelessness instead of a bombing. See?"

"How could it be carelessness, sir?"

"Look, some guy's smoking a cigarette while they lacquer the lanes, causing an explosion. See how much better that sounds than there's an all-out gang war that will destroy millions of dollars of property, kill hundreds of people—some of them innocent bystanders—and cost the taxpayers millions of dollars in police overtime?"

Pepperino was still concerned. "But, what about the Feci di Ficcio? You can't explain that away, sir."

"No, so don't talk about it to anyone. All right, fellas, hit the streets and stop this thing cold in its tracks."

Dooley remained behind and approached Homily. "Uh, Captain, can I talk to you over here?" He drew Homily over to the blackboard, next to the

American flag. "How do you really expect us to stop this war? We can't even catch loiterers, let alone professional mobsters."

Homily smiled broadly. "Are you kidding me, Hank? I just want you guys to shovel up the body parts and file a report. That's all. These families have been warring on and off since the 1920's. We're not going to be able to stop them or even slow them up. Just don't get caught in the crossfire. And anyway, I'm not too sure we *should* stop them."

"What do you mean?"

"Just that I'm inclined to think that this latest flare-up might be just the ticket. I think this town would be better off with the Fecis in charge. I've heard that their recent change from the old guard was a good thing."

"How was it good?"

"Oh, I don't know any specifics, but I just heard that it was good, that's all. You know, good for the City."

Dooley surreptitiously scratched his butt. "Gotcha, Captain. You want me to start on something in particular? I mean, we should put someone behind bars for this shit."

"Yeah, why don't you work on the bowling alley job and see what happens?"

"Good, I know just who to start with."

Dooley immediately thought of a woman he had known for a long time who might have heard something through the grapevine. In years past, she had been a moll for a big wheel in the rackets. He went to visit her at her current place of employment, Dolly's Gentlemen's Club on 53rd Street.

Dooley entered the club through its main entrance, located in the alley behind Petwick Stamps and Coins. It was as he remembered— warm and quiet like a library. Immediately, a slovenly-looking woman approached him. She was sporting dyed-red hair and wearing a tarty dress. Dooley recognized her right away. "Hi, toots. Is Shirley around?"

"Shirley? Who wants to know?"

Dooley was taken aback. "What do you mean: 'who wants to know?' It's me—Hank Dooley!"

"Hank Dooley? Oh, my god. Hank Dooley! Jeez, I never woulda known. What happened to you? You look like—well, let's just say you used to be kinda good-looking, you know what I mean? But, now—jeez! You look like your own father, for chrissakes."

Dooley shook off her comments and wasn't offended. He knew he didn't take the best of care of himself, working late hours and eating at the Riviera must have left their marks. Besides, the woman in front of him showed the ravages of time, too. "Hey, Libby, none of us still look the way we did years ago. It's a tough city to live in. It ages us fast and then it finishes us off and sends us on our way. The years have been tough on you, too, if you want the truth."

"I'm not Libby. I'm her mom, Maisy!"

That one *did* hit Dooley hard. "Oh, I see. Well, Maisy, how are you doing?"

"Ah, you know how it is in this business, Hank. Someone like me knows the ins and outs as well as anybody, so I just take it as it comes."

"I guess I do. So, is Shirley around?"

"Sure, I'll get her for you" Maisy shrieked out into the quiet gloom. "Shirl! There's a man here to see you! She'll be out in just a sec, hon. Why not park yourself here on this die-van?"

"Thanks, Maisy. Look, I hope you didn't take offense. You know, I didn't mean anything when I said…"

Maisy patted his arm, reassuringly. "Ah, forget it, Hank. I don't mind, honest. At least I'm actually the age I look." She sashayed down the hall and disappeared behind a curtain.

Dooley waited a few minutes, looking at the framed artwork hanging on the walls. The walls themselves were covered in the same velvet-patterned grotesque wallpaper that had always been there. The frames for the paintings were all of ornately carved gold leaf. The pictures depicted voluptuous unclad women in rather immodest poses, surrounded by lustful satyrs and mischievous cupids.

"Somebody wants me?" Shirley peered hard at Dooley for a second until she recognized him. "Hank? Is that you?"

Dooley turned toward the door to the back and looked at the woman that stood there in the gloom. She was holding the heavy curtains apart. Even in the murky light he could see that her face was thick with make-up.

"Yep, it's me, Hank. Shirley."

"Hi, Shirley."

Shirley advanced, holding her hands outstretched. "Gee, are you all right? Are you on the skids, honey? I thought you were working as a cop or something. What happened?"

"I *am* a cop. Nothing's happened, Shirley. As a matter of fact I'm a full-fledged Detective now."

"Oh! I'm sorry. I thought—aw, never mind what I thought. What brings you here Detective Hank?"

"The Spazzatura Lanes Bowling Alley and Family Fun Center brings me here."

"I should've guessed it. You realize we don't have much to do with family fun here, Hank." She opened an oriental box on the sideboard and pulled out a cigarette.

"I know that, Shirley. But, I also know that you used to…"

"Look, Hank, I kinda like living, you know what I mean?" When he didn't move to light her cigarette, she quit waiting and lit it herself with the Art Deco lighter next to the box.

"You know me, Shirl. Whatever you tell me stays with me."

She thought about it for a while. "Promise?"

"Cross my heart. You're Luigi Feci's sister-in-law. You used to date that skinny guy—what's his name?"

"Polpo Feci."

"That's him, Polpo, The Octopus Feci. See what you can come up with. Keep your ears open. Listen to the buzz."

"I haven't seen Polpo in fifteen years. I've been divorced from Gianni Feci for ten years. I'm out of that racket now, Hank. I'll be perfectly frank with

155

you. This club doesn't get much buzz anymore, if you catch my drift. The gents that come through that door are all retired now. Most of those guys have one foot in the grave when they come calling, and some of them put the other foot in while they're here. Pronto Ambulance Service parks one of their ambulances in the alley every Saturday night."

"Well, if you do hear anything, give me a call. Give me a call just for old times sake, eh, Shirl?"

"What do you mean, 'for old times sake'? You make it sound like we were an item or something." She laughed a husky smoker's laugh.

"We weren't? I thought…"

"You tried to cop a feel a couple of times when I was dancin' at the Round Bottom Club, but that's about all. You were rip-roarin' drunk most of the time. We used to undress you and put you to bed after you'd pass out on the dance floor at my feet. That was before you swore off spirits and took up coffee."

"Those were the good old days, eh?" She stared at him with an odd expression. "Well, anyway, see what you can come up with. And thank you, Shirley."

"Don't mention it. And listen Hank, try to take better care of yourself, huh? Check into some clinic or something."

"I'll see about that."

He thought he could hear tittering behind him as he went out the door.

Chapter 25

"Here's your coffee, Hank."

"Thanks." He loaded it with sugar and took a sip. "Oh, that's good. What's the lunch special today?"

"Fried clams. Comes with fries and coleslaw and a lettuce leaf. Fried chicken-in-a-basket. Comes with fries and coleslaw and a lettuce leaf."

"Do you think all this fried food can make a person look older?"

"Older? Fried food? Nah! We give you a lettuce leaf to combat any possible ill effects from the fried stuff. I don't think there's much to worry about, though. I eat fried food all the time and I don't look older, do I?"

"Well, I don't know how old you are."

"Take a guess. Come on."

"I don't know. I'm not real good at this. I'd say you look about—oh, let's say fifty-five, maybe fifty-eight?

"Damn, Hank! You are no good at this. I'm only forty-eight."

"I'm sorry, Marty. I warned you. Maybe I should order something else, then. Do you have anything that's not fried?"

"Sure! All the stuff on the menu that's grilled isn't fried. The pies are baked."

"Yeah, but you smear grease on the grill when you cook that stuff. Anything other than pies that's baked?"

"Nobody wants that stuff, Hank. They come in here for tasty food that they can't get at home. Nobody's gonna pay me for a bland meal. They want grease and salt and sugar. They want to feel loved."

"You think people equate grease and salt and sugar with love? How does that work?"

"When mankind was a brutal ape, living in a cave, sitting around and scratching his ass—oh, sorry, Hank. I didn't mean…"

"Forget it."

"It was just a figure of speech, you know. I was just…"

"It's okay, just go on, will you?"

"Anyway, this primitive lunkhead couldn't scrounge up a square meal to save his life. Whenever he could get his massive jaws around a rich piece of fatty Mastodon meat or a sweet honeycomb, he'd give some to his young to make 'em grow big and strong like him. It was an act of love. So, here we are, thousands of years later, still equating grease and sugar with love. It's in the genes. And if we can't get any love any other way, we eat out. You understand?"

"Hmm. I guess I'll have the fried clams, then."

"Good choice. If you're worried about your health, clams have all kinds of vitamin complexes and minerals. Sea turtles eat clams all the time and they live to be over a hundred years old."

"Sea turtles don't eat French fries or coleslaw. And I betcha they don't eat *fried* clams."

Marty dumped a plastic bag full of snow-encrusted lumps into the deep fat fryer and placed a sheet of paper liner in a grungy old basket. "So, you working on that mob war, Hank?"

"Why'd you ask?"

Marty refilled the coffee cup. "Have you ever noticed those fellas that sit at the table by the air conditioner unit? They come in here every Tuesday and Friday. The one guy has the dark blue hat with the feather in the band. Ring a bell? One of the guys is real greasy-looking."

"I don't know. I never noticed. My back's to them, I guess."

"You never noticed them? They're here every Tuesday and Friday. You sure you don't know who I'm talking about?"

"Marty, I don't know them! Just get to the point!"

"Okay. Anyway, the greasy-looking guy is Antonio Feci."

"*The* Antonio Feci? Tony Feci?!"

"Yes, the Antonio Feci. Tony Feci."

"Fat Tony? What's he doing eating here?"

"What's that supposed to mean? He likes the food here, not to mention the service."

"You ever hear any of what they talk about?"

"No, they clam up when I come around with food or take their plates. I never hear anything but small talk. Hey! Why don't you plant a bug under the table? You could record everything they say."

"That's a great idea. You got any tartar sauce for the clams?"

"What do you think we are, the Waldorf? Here, Hank, here's some mayo. Look, it even has a little greenish chunk in it. You can make believe it's tartar sauce."

Dooley ate the clams without tartar sauce.

That afternoon, he filed the paperwork for audio surveillance at the Riviera. He figured one microphone, placed under the table where the top attaches to the stanchion, would suffice. An hour later, Captain Homily dropped by Dooley's office.

"Dooley, you put in a request for a bug for a table at the Riviera luncheonette? What's that all about? You wanna hear yourself talk?"

"Fat Tony Feci eats there a couple of times a week with some of his cronies. I bet you didn't know that."

"No, I didn't. It's funny you never mentioned it before."

"Oh, well, it's just that I was waiting for when it would pay the biggest dividend, you know?"

"I'll approve it. Let me know what you get from it. I want to be there to hear the tapes."

"I sure will, Captain."

Homily took a peek down the hall way in both directions and came close to Dooley's desk. "Look, Hank, I didn't come down here for this crap. I came down here to ask you a favor."

"What do you need, Captain?"

"I've been getting threats ever since I launched this investigation into the gang war. They're not real threats and they're not to be taken seriously. I don't care about myself, anyway. This kind of shit comes with the territory, so to speak. But, my kid sister Abby got this note slipped under her door."

Dooley took the note from him and read from it. "Let's see. 'Tell your hot shot brother to cool it or we'll cool you—permanent.' Signed, 'A Friend'." He looked up from the note and took a deep breath. "Whew. Well, it certainly seems they mean business!" He looked back at the note. "They misspelled permanent. They left out the second 'n'. What it actually says is: 'Tell your hot shot brother to cool it or we'll cool you—permanet.'" He handed Homily the note.

Homily looked at it. Then Dooley snatched it back.

"Not only that, Captain, but they misspelled 'friend'. You see? They reversed the 'e' and the 'i'. How would you pronounce that? Fraynd? Frined?"

"I don't know. It worries me, Hank. I'm asking you for help."

Dooley patted him on the shoulder. "Oh, come on. Don't worry about it, Captain. What difference could it make how they spelled 'friend'?"

"I'm not worried about the spelling so much as the gist. Basically, they are threatening Abby's life in this note."

"Are they? I didn't catch that when I read it aloud." He took the note back from Homily and read it again—to himself this time. "Yeah, you're right."

"You live near enough to her, Dooley. Could you keep an eye on her in the evenings, when she gets home from work?"

"Sure I could. No problem. Are you going to tell her that someone will be hanging around? Or what?"

"That's just it. I don't really want her to know I'm doing this. I'd rather she just think you happen to be passing by. Play it— you know— real casual and nonchalant. If she knew I had you do it, she'd get pissed off and she'd

160

look for ways to escape detection. She never really lost that rebellious streak she had, you know what I mean?"

"Sure, Captain. I'll be real unobtrusive. She won't even know I'm there. Don't worry about it."

"You don't have a dog or something that you could just happen to be walking down her street, do you?"

"No. No dog or cat."

"A cat wouldn't fit the bill anyway. You can't very well take a cat for a walk."

"Don't worry, Captain. I'll make it look totally natural. If she even notices me—and that's a big 'if'—I'll have a foolproof cover story. She won't suspect a thing."

"Thanks, Hank. Listen, not a word to anyone else about this, Hank. You know I wouldn't trust anyone else with this. We go way back, you and me."

"Sure, Captain. When do I start? Should I start tonight?"

"Yes. She leaves work around half-past five and takes the Seventh Avenue bus to East 47th Street and walks from there. Sometimes she stops at Mandlebaum's grocery store on the way."

"She'll never know anyone is keeping an eye on her, Captain."

"I knew I could count on you."

Chapter 26

"Detective Dooley! Well, fancy meeting you here. What are you doing in my neighborhood?"

"Why, Miss Homily! Uh, I—I just happen to be walking around, uh—around the neighborhood, I mean."

Abby Homily cocked her head and displayed a crooked smile. "You just happened to be walking around *my* neighborhood? You aren't keeping an eye on me, are you?"

"No! No, there's no reason for you to think that. It's just that I live near here, you know. I've been walking more because my diet consists of a lot of fried food and I thought a walk would rejuvenate me."

"Funny, I don't ever remember seeing you around here before. Hmm, I got a note from the Spazzaturas and you happen by."

"Yeah, what a coincidence, right? I'll tell you the truth. It's no accident that I'm here. I was questioning a suspect about a series of bank robberies. They live here, right in this building as a matter of fact." He cocked his thumb over his shoulder at the handsome brownstone behind him.

"A suspect? That's the Widow Thompson's house. You questioned her?"

"Not this house." He turned and pointed to the house next to it. "The one over there, with the flowers in the window."

"The Assistant District Attorney lives in that house."

"Yeah, it turns out he has an airtight alibi for most of the robberies. Listen, Miss Homily, you said the Spazzaturas. You seemed certain about that. How can you be sure it was from the Spazzaturas and not the Fecis?"

"Oh, well, I suppose it could have been from the Fecis. I don't know. They didn't sign their name to it, as you must know. Besides, what difference does it make? They're all the same anyway, those swarthy Italians, aren't they?"

"Maybe you're right. You don't look too worried to me, Miss Homily."

"Don't you think this is a little ridiculous?"

"Since when is getting a death threat from the mob ridiculous?"

"No, silly, you calling me 'Miss Homily'. Why don't you just go ahead and call me Abby? If you're going to keep an eye on me, we might as well be on a first-name basis, don't you think? I mean, this is not exactly official business, is it? As you said, you're just taking a walk down my street and interrogating my neighbors."

"No, it's not official. I'm sorry, I just feel kinda funny, you being the Captain's sister. I've always called you Miss Homily."

Abby stared at Dooley and got a distant look. "I remember. I remember when I was just a little girl and my mother took me to the old stationhouse for the first time. I think my brother had forgotten either his lunch or his nightstick that day—I can't recall which. I was in the sixth grade and I remember I had no school because it was a Jewish holiday. So, Mother brought me along. That's when I saw you for the first time. Big, strong Officer Dooley, all buttoned up in his blue uniform, ready to go out on patrol and save the world from the bad guys."

Dooley smiled at that time that had passed. "You were just a little girl. The Captain was still a patrolman then, like me."

"You called me Miss Homily when my brother introduced me to you. Just like today. I had a big crush on you, Detective Dooley. My mother thought you were very handsome."

Dooley shifted on his feet. "Ha! That was a long time ago, Miss—I mean Abby. You're not a twelve-year old girl anymore."

"So, you noticed. No, I'm not twelve years old anymore. I *am* still a girl, though, Detective. And the twenty years since that day have not been too unkind to me, have they? What does your detective's gaze detect?" She took a half step back and swiveled for him.

The charm of the move was not lost on him, though it wasn't necessary since he had already determined that the previous twenty years had, in fact, been kind to her. "I'm not sure what you mean, Miss Homily."

She closed the gap between them and yanked his tie. "Don't be dense."

"I have to be dense. You're the Captain's kid sister."

"Okay, have it your way for now. I'll see you later, Detective Dooley."
With that, she sauntered off, down the street to her home.

With Abby safely deposited at her home, Dooley went to the Riviera to see
if he had been able to get anything recorded that afternoon. He had the
technicians set up the machine in such a way that Marty would be able to
just throw a switch from behind the counter and it would begin operating
immediately, actually recording sound after about twenty to thirty seconds.

"Hi, Marty. Were they here this afternoon?"

"Sure were–like clockwork. I told you they would be. I did like you showed
me, Hank. As soon as they walked in, I turned the machine on and left it on
the whole time."

"Did it work?"

He followed Dooley to the back room, behind the air conditioning unit,
where the Concord reel-to-reel tape recorder was stashed under a Flotta
tomato sauce carton. "I don't know if you got any sound, but the tape sure
advanced. It was right near the end by the time I shut it off."

"Then I'm sure it did. I left all the settings the same as when we tested it. It
sounded okay then."

"Yeah, and you could hear us pretty clear—even when we whispered. Are
you gonna play it here?"

"Nah, I'll just rewind it and put a fresh reel on and take this one back to the
office. I would like a cup of coffee, though." He turned the machine on and
rewound the tape.

"Of course."

"I saw the Captain's sister today."

"I didn't remember that he had a sister. I've only seen him a couple of times
since he was a beat cop."

Dooley sat there silently gulping down his coffee.

"So, what about the Captain's sister?"

"Oh, nothing. I just saw her, you know, for the first time in about twenty
years, that's all."

"Is she his younger sister?"

"Yeah, she's around thirteen years younger than him, I think." He gulped down some coffee as the reels of the machine spun wildly.

"That'd make her thirty or thirty-five, huh?"

"Thirty-two." Once the tape finished rewinding, Dooley threaded a new reel on the machine and set the controls, placing the Flotta carton over it again.

"Thirteen years different, huh? Sounds like one of those accidental pregnancies. Is she married?"

"No, she lives alone. Can I get more coffee, Marty? Unless she was married and is separated. I don't think so, though."

"She turned out good lookin', eh?"

"Why'd you say that?"

"Because you're talking about her. Are you thinking of making a play for her? I wonder how would the Captain like that?"

"I wasn't. Believe me."

"Then, what? Don't tell me she made a play for you!"

"Kind of. She was teasing me a little."

"Ho, ho, ho! That could be awkward! The Captain's little sister! Is she in your line of work, or what?"

"She's not in the crime industry. She studied business and finance in college and I think she's working as a consultant for some big firm downtown. No, I know what you're thinking. It wouldn't be a good match. It's tough being a cop's wife, Marty. If they don't have it in the blood, they just don't understand what it's like to deal with the criminal mind. Those marriages can be very rocky. That's one of the main reasons I never wanted to settle down."

"Her brother's a cop, Hank. She's gotten exposed to it through him. It's in the family."

"I suppose so. But, she's a lot younger than me, Marty."

"That didn't stop Onassis, did it?"

"I'm no Aristotle Onassis. Thanks for the coffee, I'll see you later."

Dooley took his first tape down to Headquarters to listen to it. Homily wasn't in his office, so Dooley decided to start listening to it without him. He picked up a spare machine from Communications and lugged it to his office. He met Perkins as he passed the vending machines in the hallway.

"Hey, Perk, I've got my first tape from the Riviera Luncheonette here. I recorded a meeting with some Feci gorillas. Wanna listen to it with me?"

"Yeah, I sure do. I'll be right there."

Dooley cleared a space on his cluttered desk for the tape recorder, threaded the tape and was warming up the machine by the time Perkins had gotten his cigarettes from the machine.

"How'd you get this recording, Hank?"

"I have a mic under the table and the recorder is hidden under a carton in the back room. The technicians rigged up a switch under the pie display on the counter. When the Fecis walked in, Marty, the owner, flipped the switch and started the recording."

"Is this Marty guy reliable?

"Perfectly."

"Hey, Hank, what about that little side work Homily asked you to do? You know, in your neighborhood?"

"I didn't know you knew about it. I thought it was top-secret."

"Ha! Are you kidding me? *Everybody* knows about it. Some of us volunteered for it, but the Captain wouldn't have it. For some reason, he only wanted you for the job. We haven't found out why she's been assigned a bodyguard yet. Care to spill the beans?"

"I was told it's secret. Why would you guys volunteer for it? Seems like a thankless job. You don't get paid any extra for it."

"Oh, come on, Hank. She's pretty easy on the eyes and she's the Captain's sister. Cops aren't above being brown-noses."

"How do you know what she looks like?"

"Homily's got a picture of her on his bookshelf. You must've seen it. She's on some kinda camping trip or something. She's wearing shorts and a striped shirt. Not bad."

"That's her?"

"You didn't know?"

"No, I didn't. I just did it because—I don't know. I remember her from the old precinct days. The last time I saw her, she was twelve or thirteen years old. She certainly seems to have turned out okay, though."

"Okay? Most of the guys in the division would give a week's pay for a crack at her."

"Does she sleep around? She didn't strike me as the type."

"No, just the opposite. Word is she's locked up like a fortress. One of the guys upstairs—Mallory, I think—said he met her at one of those luncheons at City Hall last year when he was doing security there. He came on to her full throttle, but she told him she was saving herself for one special man."

"That sounds like one of those lines they use just to get rid of you."

"Mallory said that he thought she was on the level. And you know Mallory. He's *always* on the make, so he should know. That guy can smell one molecule of bullshit from a mile away. His nose is just like your asshole. Yep, hard as it is to believe in this day and age, I think she might be a real old-fashioned girl."

"Why would everybody want this assignment then?"

"She's the Captain's sister. And because if they *did* get to screw her, it'd be a huge feather in their cap."

"Yeah, but if the Captain got wind of it..."

"That's true, but they're not thinking with their heads."

Just then, Captain Homily poked his head in the office. "Hi, fellas. Hank, can I have a brief word with you?"

167

Dooley stepped out into the hall, just outside the door. "What is it, Captain?"

"That little matter you're handling for me, how's it going?"

"I've been checking on her since Tuesday."

"You don't think she suspects that you're checking on her, do you?"

He thought about telling him the truth, but he suspected that she wouldn't want him to. "Nah, I doubt it. She's been acting really normal."

Homily seemed puzzled. "Really? Hmm." Then he collected himself and changed his attitude to seem pleased at what Dooley just said. "Well, I suppose that's good. She doesn't want me watching over her, you know. She's proud. Ever since Mother died, I've been a sort of parent to her. But, she's all grown up now, a professional woman in a traditionally male occupation, and she doesn't need a big brother anymore. You understand, don't you?"

"Sure, Captain."

Homily put his hand on Dooley's shoulder. "Thanks for doing this for me. You know, Hank, you're the only one for this job. It turns out no one else would do. Go figure."

"I have the first tape from the luncheonette ready to listen to."

"That's okay, Hank. You go ahead without me. I've got a meeting with the Chief in ten minutes." He chuckled and walked down the hall.

Dooley was still shaking his head as he walked back into his office.

"Was that about his sister?"

"Yeah." He pressed the 'play' button. "All right, let's hear what we've got."

The recording started with the sounds of Dooley blowing into the microphone and saying, "testing, one, two, testing. Let's see if it worked." This was followed by the sounds of people walking and chairs scraping against the floor.

"Aghh. My fuckin' feet are killin' me in these shoes."

168

"It's not the shoes, Tony. It's you. You're too fuckin' fat. You're putting too much stress on your feet. If you'd drop a hundred pounds, you'd see a big difference."

"I'm not fat. I got big bones."

"Hey, I got your big bone right here."

This was followed by hearty laughter.

"Hey, Bertie, what's the matter? You haven't said one word since we got in the car."

"I ain't doin' too good."

"Why, what's the matter?"

"It's Angela. She found out she's got the cancer."

The others all spoke at once.

"Oh, that's terrible."

"Maybe we should send flowers, huh?"

"So, what is it, serious? I mean, can they do an operation or something?"

"That's just it. They can't do nothin'."

"So, how long she got?"

"Six months at the most. I'm real depressed."

"What about your wife? How does she feel?"

"Who knows how my wife feels? I don' give a shit how my wife feels."

"That's pretty cold, Bertie. Put yourself in her place, man. Imagine how you would feel if you had cancer."

"Angela is Bertie's mistress, you asshole, not his wife. Carla is his wife."

"Oh! Okay, now I understand. I'm sorry, Bertie."

"Don't worry about it."

"Hi fellas. What's it gonna be today?"

It was Marty's familiar voice.

"Tony, go 'head."

"I guess I'll have the clam chowder."

"Okay, one bowl of clam chowder."

"That's the white one, right? Not the red one. 'Cause that red shit gives me heartburn. I don' want that."

"It's the New England clam chowder. It's white."

"Good. I'll take a bowl of that. Does it got lots of clam in it?"

"Yeah, lots of big chunks of clam."

"Okay, I'll have a bowl of that. And a glass of tomato juice."

"Tomato juice. Okay. The tomato juice is red, you know. Is that gonna be all right?"

"Yeah, sure. I'd worry if the tomato juice wasn' red, you know what I mean?"

"Anything else?"

"He's asking you, Tony."

"Huh? What?"

"Anything else for you?"

"Anything else? Like what?"

"Maybe coffee?"

"I ordered a fuckin' tomato juice, didn' I?"

"So you did. How about you? What'll it be?"

"Bertie, you go ahead. I'm not sure what I want yet."

"Gimme a Denver omelet, white toast and a cup of coffee."

"All right."

"And bring me a glass of water. I gotta take a pill."

"I'll bring that right away. And how about you?"

"I'll have a tuna salad sandwich..."

"Dooley, can you fast forward a little? Jesus Christ! I started to doze off there for a second!"

"Sure, sure." Dooley advanced the tape, then pressed play. "Let's see, now."

> *"You know what, Marty? I don't want no clam chowder. I changed my mind. Bring me a egg salad sandwich on a kaiser. Extra mayo."*
>
> *"No clam chowder. Egg salad extra mayo on kaiser roll."*
>
> *"And there better not be none of those crunchy things."*
>
> *"Crunchy things? You mean celery?"*
>
> *"No, you fuckin' dope! Those crunchy things! You know!"*
>
> *"I think he means eggshells."*
>
> *"Yeah, that's it! No eggshells, Marty."*
>
> *"Egg salad, hold the eggshells..."*

"God *damn*, Hank! Can you fast-forward some more, please! This is torture."

"Okay. Let's go about a hundred on the counter."

"So, your plan went off without a hitch."

"Hey, this sounds like something! Lemme rewind a bit."

"Yeah, sounds like you may have struck gold."

Dooley rewound the tape a little and pressed play again.

> *"I called the place up on the phone and told 'em it was her birthday and they had it all set by the time we got there. She was completely surprised."*
>
> *"So, your plan went off without a hitch."*
>
> *"Did she cry?"*
>
> *"She always cries. She cries at weddin's, funerals. She cries when she watches the Beverly Hillbillies, fer chrissakes!"*

"She must be fun at parties. Maybe we should fast-forward a bit more."

Dooley advanced the tape and resumed playback.

> *"If I went bald, I'd just go bald."*
>
> *"You wouldn't get a toupe?"*
>
> *"No, because I'll tell ya', they never get the hair color the same. Everybody can tell your wearin' a toupe."*
>
> *"Tony's right. I had this jerk who ran the Sunoco station where I took my car and he had this big head of hair that was red-brown. But underneath that he had a different brown. You could tell."*

"Lemme advance the tape a little more." Dooley spun the reels forward quite a distance. "Okay, let's see."

> *"... come back and remove the bodies?"*

"What do they do with the bodies? I mean how do they get rid of them so that it's not a problem?"

"Yeah, they start stinkin' right away."

"Okay, fellas. Here's your omelet. Here you are. There you go. Let's move this ketchup over. There you are. Okay, anything else, gentlemen? More coffee for you?"

"Sure, more coffee."

Dooley perked up. "Ah! A man after my own heart."

"I'll bring more coffee and I'll refill your waters."

"So, anyway, what wuz you sayin' about getting' rid of the bodies?"

"Oh, yeah. So, since I'm payin' good money for his services, I expect good service. So I says to him if he don' dispose of the bodies, I'm gonna dispose of his body."

"What'd he do then?"

"Well, after shittin' his pants, he suddenly realizes, oh yeah, it's part of the contract. So, no more mice."

"Mice!? I thought he was talking about a hit or something."

"I think I've heard enough, Hank."

"Wait, Perk. Listen to some more with me. I'm sure we got something valuable on here somewhere." Perkins agreed to listen to more of the recording. There followed several minutes of the sounds of forks, spoons and knives clinking and scraping against bowls and plates, glasses and cups being placed down on the table and someone clearing their throat. The recording was excellent and Dooley noticed the clarity of the sound of the traffic coming into the Riviera from outside on Lingstrome Avenue.

"Hank, how much longer is this tape?"

"The entire side of this tape runs two hours at this speed."

The tape continued to provide the sounds of the men eating their lunch. There was no talking.

173

"The reason I ask is that maybe we should fast-forward past some more of this."

"I think you're right." Dooley fast-forwarded the tape a considerable distance. Again there were the same sounds of the men eating, without exchanging a word. "Let me try a little further."

Still, there were only the sounds of the men eating.

"Jesus Christ, these guys eat like monks. Fast-forward some more. Go a *lot* farther this time."

Dooley repeated the process, with exactly the same result. "I'll go forward about twenty minutes worth." He let the tape advance a long time, then stopped it and pressed play. Keeping his fingers crossed, they listened some more. Again there were sounds of the street and the sounds of the men eating.

> *"I get these pimples on my neck."*

"Is there anything worthwhile on this tape at all?"

"I don't know. I didn't listen to it, Perk."

"Don't get mad at me, Hank. I just asked a question, that's all. Take it easy."

"I'm sorry. I'm a little frustrated. I thought I'd hit the jackpot."

"Look, try going forward one more time. If there's nothing, I've got other things I need to do."

Dooley sighed and repeated the steps and advanced past at least ten minutes worth of tape before stopping it. "Okay, maybe here."

> *"Move your foot. You keep kickin' me and it's annoying the hell outta me."*
>
> *"I gotta take a dump. I need more coffee when he comes around."*
>
> *"Did you see the game yesterday? Those umps fuckin' suck. They missed three calls that shoulda gone the other way."*

"Those games are fixed. I bet ya'"

"You splattered grease on your shirt."

"Where? Shit! I just bought this shirt, too. It figures."

"Did you see Louie's new Lincoln? He was drivin' it around, showin' it off all day yesterday."

"I'd never buy a Lincoln Continental. I've always pre-ferred Imperials and I always get the best service at Lombardi Chrysler-Plymouth."

"You can't match the service you get at an Imperial dealer. That's 'cause Lombardi's not a filthy Jew."

"Yeah, the Hebes love them Lincolns and Caddies."

"They're talking about cars, for chrissakes! This is totally worthless. The tape's almost finished and these spaghetti benders have spent the whole time stuffing their faces and chatting like a bunch of washerwomen. It was such a good setup, too. God dammit!"

"Are you going to listen to the rest?"

"No. I guess there's no point."

"Sorry, Hank. You win some and you lose some." Perkins left the office.

Dooley sat for a while, depressed and frustrated by the lack of substance on the tape, then he took a deep breath and listened to some more.

Chapter 27

"Well, Detective Dooley! Nice to see you again. Tell me, is this another wild coincidence? Or are you torturing poor old Mrs. Oppenheimer for a confession on a drug-trafficking charge?"

"What would you have me say, Miss Homily?"

"Actually, I think I rather like this little arrangement of ours. I'd much rather go on acting surprised that you just happen to be on my block. It's more fun that way. Would that be all right with you, Detective?"

"Sure, if it makes you happy. Oh, and while I just happen to be here on your block, I might as well ask you if you've received any other letters like that first one."

"I haven't gotten any others—at least up until this morning."

"That's certainly a relief."

"That's not to say that I haven't gotten one since I left for work this morning. One might have come during the day. You never know. These mobsters are a very stealthy bunch, as I'm sure you know. They strike in the dead of night, when you least expect it. Then, they strike in the bright of day, when you least expect it."

"That's true."

"Have you ever noticed that they never seem to strike at twilight?"

"That's probably when they're doing their laundry."

"Can I confess something, Detective Dooley?" She paused to make certain she had his rapt attention. "I am petrified with fear and terror."

Dooley laughed. "You look panic-stricken to me."

"No, really. I may have received another threatening letter. I just don't know at this point, and there's only one way to determine whether or not I got one."

"What way is that?"

"You'll have to walk with me to my door so we can see for sure if anyone has made any more threats."

"Should we go to your door, then? I'd hate for you to pass out from fright, right here in the middle of the block."

They started walking together, down the tree-lined street. Abby stuck her arm through his. "Detective, speaking of vast experience, have you been able to make any progress on this supposed mob war you are trying to forestall?"

"*Supposed* mob war? I thought it was a certainty. It's funny you should ask, though. It's turning out to be a tough process. For one thing, we're not even too sure who we're dealing with. The entire organization is shrouded in secrecy, of course. Sure, we know a few of the important figures on both sides of the war, but to be honest with you, Abby, we don't even know who the Big Boss is in the Feci organization anymore. We haven't known for several years now. We think if we can find that out, at least, we might be able to find some way to end this senseless violence and destruction."

"And what if you don't?"

"I guess it'll tear apart the very fabric of this city, plunging us into a veritable Dark Age of fear and despair."

"The Dark Ages! I recall that during the Dark Ages, the lamp of learning was not lit." She spoke the sentence as if reciting from a textbook.

"Do you have any idea how terrible the Dark Ages were?"

"Yes. I'd have to become a nun and you would shave your head and become a monk. That would be awful."

"Do you know how many tourist dollars we would lose if this City dissolved into chaos and anarchy?"

"I think I do, actually. Do you, Detective Dooley?"

"I have no idea. I work for the Police Department, not the Chamber of Commerce."

"Seriously, though, are you sure that the outcome of this mob war will be a bad thing?"

"What do you mean?"

"Isn't it possible that bringing the organized crime in this City under the control of one family, lead by a cool-headed, business-minded leader could be a *good* thing for everybody? I mean, after all, there really hasn't been any harm to the general public in this supposed mob war so far, has there?"

"That's true. So far, the bowling alley and the men killed in it were the only victims of the war. It turns out the Spazzatura's Headquarters fire was an accident and not a part of this war. Some idiot left a hot plate on all night and the cord got too hot." Dooley stopped. "This is your building, isn't it?"

"Good guess, Detective. Why don't you come inside?"

"Oh, no, I couldn't impose. I really should get going."

"Come on, Detective. It's dinner time and I'll bet you haven't eaten yet. Am I right?"

"Well, no, I…"

"I knew it. Come inside for a bit and I'll whip up something delicious just for the two of us. I have a couple of t-bone steaks in the freezer. Would you like that?"

"Well, I, um—that does sound good right about now, but I really should get along. I'll take a rain check."

"Well, why don't you just come up for a minute, just to see the place?" She looked at him, expectantly.

"I'm not sure I should, Abby. I have this investigation I'm working on, you know."

"I'll put on a pot of coffee."

"Okay, you've convinced me."

"There, it's settled, then. Let me just grab my mail and we'll go right up." She dug out her keys from her handbag and opened the mailbox. "Are you sure? I could cook up a couple of steaks, Detective Dooley. It wouldn't be a bother at all. What do you say?"

"I'll be honest, I can't remember the last time I had a good steak. In fact, I can't remember the last time I had a home-cooked meal. But, I really can't stay long. Thank you, though."

"You've been missing out, Detective. You have to allow me..." Abby stopped as she flipped through her letters and bills.

"You know, cops don't always get the chance to—Abby? What's the matter?"

"It's—it's another one of those letters. I'm almost afraid to open it."

"Here, let me see it." Dooley examined the letter carefully. Let's see what it says, huh?" He opened the envelope and unfolded the paper. Abby clutched his arm as Dooley read from the letter: 'Your hot-shot brother thinks he can keep ignoring us. If he does, he won't have a kid sister no more. This is the second warning. You won't get a third.' It's signed, 'A Friend'. Hmm."

"Oh, Detective! Do you think they really mean it? I mean, would they actually...?"

"Wait, there's a P.S. down at the bottom: 'P.S. We really mean it.' They do sound serious, Abby."

"How can there be such evil cruelty in the world? Can you tell anything from the letter, Detective?"

"I think it should have been proofread. They spelled warning as 'wanring' and they misspelled friend again."

"I mean are there any clues?"

"I suppose what I just said is a clue and I'm sure there'll be others. But, I don't want you worrying your pretty little head about that. That's police stuff. Your brother and I will worry about that." He patted her upper arm and gave it a little reassuring squeeze. The reassuring squeeze must have done the trick. She didn't look scared.

As they walked up the stairs, Dooley wrestled with guilt over his desire to stare at Abby's ass. As she walked up ahead of him, it was, of course, right smack in his face. Being a man of limited honor, he lost his wrestling match with himself and stared at her ass and her legs— what he could see of them below her hemline—and kicked himself for considering her in such a crudely sexual manner. She was, after all, the Captain's kid sister. He felt ugly and brutish acting this way. She did have a nice figure, though, and a guilty pleasure is a pleasure after all.

"You live here long?"

179

"Five years. The landlord is good. He's very responsive and accommodating. That's really important to me. That's how I am with my clients and that's what I expect from others. The place is in good shape. As a matter of fact, the building's owner is someone who does business with my company. Small world, huh? I get to use the little backyard when I want." She opened the door and they entered. It opened right into the living room. There was a small dining area directly to the left and the kitchen was to the right of that.

"Nice place." Dooley looked around at the layout and furnishings, which were attractive and cozy more than they were fancy.

"Did you mean what you said, Detective?"

"Yeah, it's a lot nicer than I pictured."

"I don't mean about my place, silly! You said I had a 'pretty little head'. Do you think my head is pretty?"

Dooley felt his blood pressure rise. He knew now that he had walked right into a trap. "It was an expression—I guess I just—well, it *is* kinda pretty. I suppose I did mean it. I didn't say it on purpose, Abby. It just sort of slipped out. I mean, I don't really know what your head looks like anyway, because you have all that hair covering it, you know? Look, if preparing coffee for me is a big bother, I can just run down to the luncheonette. I really don't..."

"Don't be ridiculous, Detective Dooley. Making coffee for the man who is risking himself by standing guard for my life is the least thing I can do. I'll get the coffee brewing and it'll be ready in a jiffy." She went into the little kitchen and quickly set up the percolator, then started gathering cups and saucers and silverware. "Detective, you mentioned my hair. Have you had the chance to thoroughly examine it?"

"Examine it? For what?"

"For evidence."

"Evidence of what?"

"Prettiness, of course." She laughed, almost a giggle. "Seriously, I thought I caught you examining it when we were outside on the street. Maybe you thought there was something illegal going on with it."

"You're pulling my leg. I really didn't, um—I just was noticing it, that's all. It looked shiny and soft. If some people think it's a crime to have such hair, I don't know." He could've kicked himself for being so forward.

"I was thinking, Detective Dooley, I wondered if you might be available for extra guard duty *after* hours?"

"What do you mean?"

"I was planning on going out to a night club with a couple of friends this Friday night and I thought that you might want to keep an eye on things. You know, just to make sure I'm completely safe. Would you be able to swing it?"

"I don't know. I probably could."

"It would be wonderful if you could do it, especially since I got this new letter that seems so threatening and terrifying."

"It would be a good idea to play it safe, I suppose. I don't see any reason why I couldn't. What time would this be?"

"Oh, I thought about eight o'clock would be fine. It'll be dinner and drinks and dancing. It'll probably be a late night, Detective Dooley. Will you be up to it?"

Dooley got a flash of jealousy when she said there would be dancing. He didn't think she meant male companionship when she'd said 'a couple of friends'. He didn't relish the idea of standing around, watching some guy feel her up on the dance floor. "Maybe I shouldn't tag along this time. I'd probably just get in the way and ruin everybody's good time."

"Nonsense! It's a great night club and besides, I really wouldn't feel safe there without you to protect me." She approached him and grabbed his lapel. "What if something evil should happen? You'd never be able to forgive yourself."

Dooley didn't want to do it, but he felt her warm knee bump against his as she held onto him and that melted his resolve. "Maybe you're right. I suppose I should come along, just as insurance."

"Fantastic! It'll be perfect! Oh, the coffee is ready." She dashed off back into the kitchen. "You need to make sure you dress to fit in. We can't take the chance of one of those gangsters recognizing you, Detective Dooley."

She brought the whole set-up in on a large tray and set it down on the coffee table. "You'll need to wear your best. It's an upscale place we're going to."

"I have something that should fit the bill. I'm not a total disaster just because I'm a bachelor, you know." He loaded his coffee with sugar and gulped it down, thinking what a total disaster he was.

"That's fine. I bet you'll look great. Maybe you'll make my friends feel frumpy, eh?"

"I doubt that very much." He didn't have a snazzy sports coat or a turtle-neck shirt, but he figured he had a couple of days to scrounge them up. He thought immediately of asking one of the young guys who work down in Property for a few pointers. "Can I have another cup?"

"Oh, certainly. No need to be so formal. After all, we've known each other for quite a long time." She poured him another cup. "I tell you what. Why don't you come by around quarter to eight on Friday night? That will give us more than enough time to get to the Private Junction by eight-fifteen."

"The Private Junction on Bragg Avenue? Out by the airport?"

"That's the one. You know it?"

"Yeah, I know it. That place is run by the Mob. Nunzio Feci manages the Private Junction."

"I've been there before. It seems like a nice operation to me. All the best people go there. It's a real top spot for dinner and drinks. They have live entertainment three nights a week—top quality talent, too." She sipped her coffee. "It's all very swank."

"If you say so, Miss Homily. I still have my doubts."

"About what?"

"We've been assuming the threatening letters were written by the Spazzaturas, but what if they were written by the Fecis? You see what I mean? You could be walking into a very dangerous situation."

"Now you see why I wanted you along, Detective Dooley? I'm absolutely certain I'll be perfectly safe with you there." She put her hand gently on his knee. "You're already strategizing and sizing up the situation. You certainly know your business."

"All the same, I wish you and your friends would go to a movie downtown and dinner at O'Malley's, or something."

"Oh, Detective!" She slapped his knee, playfully. "You'll see. You'll have a great time there. I promise." She poured more coffee for him. "You certainly like coffee, don't you?"

"I bleed dark brown."

"Is that why your hair hasn't gone all gray yet? My brother is only a year or two older than you and he's mostly gray now."

"I don't have the worries he does."

"He sits behind a desk all day, while you are out there risking your life. I would think *you* should have the gray hair, not him."

"I don't risk my life every day. My job is easy by comparison. He's under a lot of pressure all the time. He's got the Commissioner and the Mayor breathing down his neck every day. No, I don't envy his position at all. It's a tough job, being in the middle like that. Plus, he's gotta deal with clods like me."

"Don't be absurd. It's nice that you respect him and recognize what he has to deal with, Detective Dooley, but I think you're the one who should be honored."

"Oh, come on. I don't do anything special, Abby. I just roust a bunch of lowlifes and file reports. Anybody could do that. I don't have the Captain's ability to deal with the political side of our profession. That's what makes him special. Sucking up to the big boys. Sorry, I didn't mean to make it sound quite that way."

"Don't sell yourself short, Detective. I hear about what you do and how much you risk every day. I read about the cases you solve and the treacherous characters you bring to justice. I also know that you're fighting an uphill battle."

"What do you mean?"

"I know how much the police are feared and despised and misunderstood. I know how people stonewall you and mislead you. I think it's remarkable that you can solve any crimes at all, considering all that is aligned against you. You are a true hero, Hank Dooley. You're one of the most unpopular people in this City. Wherever you go, ugliness and brutality can't be far behind. Yet, there you are, in the face of adversity, bringing order and justice to a cruel and brutal town."

"You should write for television." He laughed with embarrassment, but secretly agreed with her.

"I mean it. I wish I could bring order to this City's chaos. I'm working on it, but I have a long way to go before I can hold my head up with pride in public like you can."

"A long way to go? What are you working on, Abby?"

She gave a nervous little laugh. "Oh, I didn't mean anything by it. That was just me being silly. I just meant that I want to make a difference in the world. That's all I meant. More coffee?"

"Yes, please."

"Is everything all right? You seem uncomfortable, all of a sudden."

"Sure, everything's fine. I just had an itch. That's all. I'm probably itching to get back to work. I probably should go after this cup."

"If you don't, I'll need to make another pot. You've drunk the entire carafe."

"I'm sorry, Miss Homily. I'm beginning to think I'm addicted to the stuff."

"Don't apologize. There's no need. There are a lot worse things than an addiction to coffee. I think addictions to drugs or gambling or booze are all worse addictions to have. Though, they create the greatest economic opportunities. But, they can destroy a person. At least a person can function with a coffee addiction."

"Just barely sometimes. I drink so much coffee that I have blackouts and experience visions. Gee, look at the time. I'd better get going. You probably need to unwind from your day's work and here you are, poor woman, entertaining me."

"I'll see you on Friday night, Detective."

"You'll probably see me before then if you look over your shoulder. I'll take that letter downtown and have it analyzed." They walked to the door together and Dooley opened it to leave.

"I must say, Detective, I'm sure glad to have me looking after—I mean, *you* looking after me. Ha, ha! That was funny, wasn't it? No, but seriously, it's given us a chance to finally connect after all these years. I think it was worth it, don't you?"

Dooley wasn't sure what her question meant, so he thanked her for the coffee, bid her adieu and trotted down the stairs to the street.

Chapter 28

Dooley lived for a couple of days in dread of Friday night. He was not a nightclub kind of guy and knew he would feel old and out of place hanging around Abby and her friends. She was a smart dresser and no doubt her friends were going to be trendy and obnoxious professionals. Another concern was economic. The Private Junction was a ritzy and expensive club. Hank Dooley was not a ritzy man. He was already planning on working it into an expense voucher so he wouldn't feel the pinch too badly. He also vowed not to drink. He didn't want to spend money on booze and he was afraid he might say something to one of Abby's know-it-all, la-di-da friends that he would regret.

In preparation for the big night, at the urging of the guys in Property, he went to The Gent, which is a men's clothing store on 41st Street that caters to the hip, middle-aged crowd. He told the salesman, George, where he was going and that he would be there with people ten years his junior. George knew exactly what he needed, right down to the socks, so Dooley felt reassured when he left the store. At least his clothing wouldn't look stupid even if *he* did. One of the things that George sold him was a trimmer for nose and ear hairs. Attention to the little details like ear hairs proved to Dooley that George was the right man to be trusted with this crucial task.

Then, something happened that ate up much of his mind and energy. Dooley began to speculate that Abby Homily might really be interested in him in a serious way. The thought panicked him and he began to work on it in his mind to the exclusion of everything else. He started replaying snippets of conversation and recollecting expressions and gestures, alternately trying to prove and disprove this crazy notion that a respectable citizen could have serious designs on him.

When he had exhausted all that he could recall of their meager interactions, he started running scenarios of what might occur on Friday night. They played like short films in his mind whenever he was not otherwise occupied. The scenario that played with the greatest frequency was one in which he was taunted and insulted and made to look ridiculous. This made him depressed and worried about the big night. The one that played with the second greatest frequency was the one in which he ends up thrown out of the club after punching one of Abby's friends, and looking ridiculous. Dooley began to realize that he really cared what Abby Homily thought of him.

Dooley's dread of, and preoccupation with, Friday night made him useless at work, where his investigation of the bowling alley bombing and the all-

186

out mob war had fizzled out, ground to a halt and hit a dead end—all at once. He visited with informants and despite his use of guile and threats, came up empty-handed each time. There were those who knew nothing and refused to try to find something out, and there were those that clearly knew something and refused to divulge anything. This in itself was not unusual, but Dooley got the distinct impression that fear was *not* the motivating factor this time, whereas fear was *always* the motivating factor in the past. As impossible as it was for Dooley to believe, this time these lowlifes seemed to be taking a moral stand about something.

Perkins popped his head into Dooley's office. "Hey, Hank!"

"Hi, Perkins." Dooley was sitting at his desk, wearing a vacant expression and scribbling on a note pad while he waited for inspiration.

"What's up, Hank? Hey, you seem a bit distracted."

"Do I?" He stopped scribbling, straightened up a bit and looked at Perkins. "I guess I'm tired. I don't know."

"How's that bowling alley investigation coming along?"

"What bowling alley?"

"The bombing—the bombing of the bowling alley. You *do* remember that you are currently assigned to investigate the bombing of the Spizzatura Lanes, don't you?"

"Oh, yes. Yes, of course. The bowling alley." Dooley went back to scribbling.

Perkins waited until he was certain he wasn't going to get a real response from him. "Well?"

"Well what, Perk?"

"Oh, man! Have you got a problem!"

Dooley looked up, suddenly alarmed and angry. "How do you know about my problem?"

"What problem? Look, Hank, when you get back to planet Earth, drop me a line, huh?"

"Sure, Perkins, I'll do that." Then without missing a beat, he launched into something else. "Perk, do you think it's possible for a person to have a twenty-year long crush on somebody? I mean, does that sort of thing really happen?"

"Oh, sure. I've had a crush on what's-her-name, Eleanor Parker, ever since I first saw that movie about the army ants. You remember that movie where she goes down to South America to marry the guy who was in *The Planet of the Apes*?"

"I'm not talking about ants or apes, Perkins. I'm talking about human beings not actors. I mean, for a real person—one that you really know—do you think it's possible?"

"Like a neighbor or an old classmate, you mean? I don't know. They'd probably look pretty beat-up after twenty years, dontcha think? Whoever you had the crush on wouldn't be the same person anymore. I know I'm not the same guy I was when I was twenty-four. You got a crush on some old flame, or something?"

"No, it's not me. It doesn't make any sense."

"I suppose it's possible. What if they didn't have the chance to act on it during that time? Then, when they get the chance again, they act on it. That would make sense, right? Like if they'd been married and then they're single again. Or, what if they lost touch for a long time? Then it would make sense."

"Yeah, but this is not one of those cases of people losing touch with each other. It would have been easy for this person to contact the other during that time. And marriage was not in the equation for either person. I just don't understand how a person can have a crush on someone and not act on it for twenty years and then, all of a sudden—boom—they act on it."

"Are you suggesting that the bowling alley bombing was the result of a crush somebody had on someone? That seems kinda far-fetched even for you, Hank."

"The bowling alley bombing again! Is that all you can talk about?"

"But, you just said 'boom-they act on it'. And in case you forgot, that *is* the case you're working on. I just thought you tried to tie it in somehow, that's all. No reason to get your panties in a bunch, for Pete's sake."

"Sorry. No, I'm not saying there's a connection. I just wonder—I mean, I don't even recall seeing this person during that whole time."

"Oh, it's you! You have a crush on someone—no, wait a minute. You don't have the crush. Somebody has a crush on *you*. Am I right?" He looked closely at Dooley for the slightest sign and when Dooley averted his eyes, he knew he was right. "Ha! I thought so! Who is it? Is it somebody here at headquarters? It's not some fag crush, is it?" He scrunched up his face in disgust. "You keep saying 'person' rather than 'girl' or 'woman'."

"No! It's nothing like that. It's a woman. This person doesn't work here. I can't really say who it is, Perk."

"Come on, Hank. You know I can be trusted. Who is it?"

"I can't say. I can't tell anybody—not even you."

"Then it must be somebody we both know." Perkins sat back and looked at the ceiling. "Who would we both know who doesn't work here? You said she *doesn't* work here, right?"

"Please, Perkins. I knew I shouldn't have said anything."

Perkins looked back up at the ceiling. "Who could it be? Judge Hollister! She's known us about that long."

"No, it's not Judge Hollister."

"I heard she's been doing De Palo, the City Councilman these days. Man, back when she was in the DA's office, she looked pretty damn good." Perkins suddenly became animated. "Hey, do you remember she had those tight gray pinstripe pants and we'd sit there waiting for her to split the seam when she sat down? Ha, ha! Yeah, but she's gotten a little thick over the years. Still, you could do worse and probably have, right? Oh, wait a minute, you said you haven't even seen this person all this time. We see Judge H. almost every month, so that lets her out."

"It's no use you trying to guess who it is and I can't say anyway, so just drop it, will you? Let's change the subject. Look, you asked if I had anything on this bowling alley case and I have to tell you that not only do I *not* have anything, but, in fact, I haven't even been working on it these past few days. There's no information out there and no clues. I don't even have anything to hush up at this point."

"That can be tough. Well, since we figure it was a Feci job, why don't you just pick up a Feci and bring him down here and we'll make him confess?"

"I've been trying not to make a habit of that. My ratio of convictions per arrests is so low that I'm scared they'll call me before the board."

"I wouldn't worry about that, Hank. You know how many arrests I've made over the last year and a half?"

"I know it's a lot."

"Hundreds. I haven't had a single conviction since last March. Most of them get thrown out for lack of evidence. I've had a few thrown out because the guy I was trying to pass off as the suspect in the case wasn't really that guy."

"I got a conviction in a kidnapping case one time like that. I picked up a guy who worked as a toll-collector at the tunnel and we faked his ID so that we could book him as the child's school bus driver, who was the real kidnapper. The real kidnapper had beat it out of town before we could get to him."

"I haven't been so lucky."

"I've been thinking that maybe it would be a good idea to try to actually solve this one for a change. What do you think of that, huh?"

"Don't be absurd. Why make your life harder than it is already? Come on, let's you and me go down to Little Italy and pick the ugliest one of the bunch and bring him back here and give him the works. What do you say, huh? Come on, Hank. Chances are fifty-fifty that whatever galoot we pick up is actually guilty of this bombing anyway. Come on, you'd have something to show the Captain, then you can move on and put this thankless assignment behind you."

Dooley thought of his options and had to agree that Perkins's solution seemed the most expedient and sensible under the circumstances. The Captain had said he really wasn't expecting any real solution to the whole mess anyway. "What the hell. Okay."

Chapter 29

The two men headed out the door and were back within an hour, accompanied by a typically greasy-looking Feci they had culled from the treasure trove of greasy Fecis down at the headquarters in Little Italy. They brought him into interview room 2 and posed several questions to him.

"Arrggh! Stop, please!"

Dooley stopped applying pressure to the twisted arm. "Look, Ennio, we didn't bring you down here to scream in agony. You can do that on your own time, if you want. We asked you a perfectly good question and we expect you to answer it properly. Can you do that for us?"

"Ugh! I *did*! I told you the truth!"

"Who cares about the truth? Did Detective Dooley say he wanted a truthful answer? He wants a *proper* answer, you slimy little greaseball."

"If you don't want the truth, Dooley, then why do you hurt me like this? You of all people?"

"What the hell is that supposed to mean, 'you of all people'?" Perkins turned to Dooley. "You know, Hank, everybody says the Fecis are stupid. I hear it all the time: 'Oh, the Fecis are so stupid!' 'The Fecis are dumb as dirt!' I didn't want to believe them, but, now I'm starting to agree with the popular opinion." He turned back to their guest. "Ennio, if you represent average Feci intelligence, I think I'd have to go back to school to learn negative numbers again so I could measure your I.Q." He jabbed Ennio in the ribs with a nightstick as he screamed in his ear. "Now, let's try this again. It was a Feci that planned that bowling alley bombing as part of a plot to wipe out the Spizzatura family, wasn't it?"

"That's not true. It was *not*. Aaarrgh! I'm telling you, it was *not* a blow against the Spazzaturas."

"Here, Ennio." Dooley handed him a cafeteria napkin.

"What am I supposed to do with this?"

"Wipe up your blood. You don't want to ruin that shirt, do you? That's a nice shirt."

"Thanks."

"You see, Detective Dooley is a nice man, a considerate man. He cares about you, yet you disrespect him by refusing to answer his questions. You're being unreasonable and stubborn and you're making him sad. Look, everybody knows that the Fecis and Spizzaturas have had an uneasy truce for years. Everybody knows that the Fecis and Spizzaturas have been itching to take over the other's territory. We believe that, since old man Feci died, this mysterious new Big Boss has been setting things in motion to force a final conflict to destroy the opposition and terrorize the hell out of everyone in this City." Perkins paused as he ran out of breath. "Come on, Ennio, don't play stupid with us. Tell us what we want to know. Because, if you don't, so help me, you're going to wish you got the Faccia di Feci instead."

Ennio Feci looked at each of his interrogators for a moment. "Look, guys, the two families have been running the rackets in this City for years without any friction. I'm not wet behind the ears. I've been in this game since I was in short pants. I'm telling you that there is no turf war. Figure it out for yourselves. What would we have to gain? Everything is running so well. And it's running well for both families. You have no idea how much our profit margins are up. I wish I could show you the annual report, but I can't. It's proprietary information."

"Annual report? What the hell! Sounds like Union Carbide or something. Perk, did you know we were dealing with a Fortune 500 company here? Since when does the Mafia have annual reports?"

"Since the new Big Boss took over. I know it's weird, but we kinda like it. We have a lot invested in this racket and I wanna know what's going on in the family. It's enabled the divisions to be more transparent and accountable. It increases trust and, more importantly, it has affected the bottom line. We're all happy as pigs in shit. Sorry, no offense meant."

"None taken."

"Profits are up, expenses are down. You should see the charts. I personally made over seventy thousand dollars last year—take home. I've got a retirement package set up so that, when I get too old to break kneecaps, I can walk away and finish out my life in relative comfort and security. Why would I risk that? Everybody in the family is making more money and certainly making more than they did before sh…" He stopped himself.

"Before what, Ennio? Were you about to tell us the Big Boss's name? Who's 'Sh…'?"

"I don't know what I was gonna say. All I meant was before, you know, the new Big Boss took over. Don't get me wrong. The old man was great, but now we're all doing better personally and there's been a long period of calm for both families—for the whole City, in fact."

"He's got a point there, Perk."

Perkins raised his voice suddenly. "Hey, what's the matter with you? You've had a really lackadaisical attitude all afternoon. Other than you twisting his arm until it almost snapped, I've been doing almost all of the hitting. I've asked most of the questions. All you do is sit there, agreeing with him and handing him napkins so he doesn't bleed all over his shirt. Are you feeling okay?"

"I'm fine."

"Then what is it? We're beatin' the shit out of a Feci. You should be happy. I would've thought you'd be dancing the Tarantella on his face. Instead, it's all I can do just to get you to pick up the rubber hose or slip on the brass knucks. What gives, man?"

Dooley picked at some lint on his trouser leg. "I don't know, Perk. It's just—I don't know."

"Look, fellas, if this afternoon just isn't working for you, maybe we should postpone it. I could come back another day."

"Will you shut up? Let me and my partner work this out without your help, huh?"

"Sorry. I just thought that my presence here is making things worse for you. Maybe you need a little time alone to work it out."

"No, you're not making it worse, Ennio. As a matter of fact, I thought that you've been a great sport about the whole thing. Right, Hank?"

"Perk is right. It's not your fault, Ennio. You're performing admirably."

"Well, I'm glad of that at least. But, I feel bad. I hate seeing you guys not getting along."

"We're getting along fine, thank you. Hank's had a bad day that's all. Isn't that right, Hank?"

"Yeah, that's it. I must've gotten up on the wrong side of the bed. I've got a lot on my mind."

"I'll tell you what, Hank. Let's put Ennio in a cell for a few hours and you can go get a cup of coffee, regroup and then start again with renewed vigor, huh? How about that plan?"

"You guys realize, of course, that a lawyer is going to spring me in about an hour or so."

"If that's the case, Dooley and I will just re-arrest you later on some other trumped-up charge. Will that work for you, Ennio?"

"Sure. So, what do you want me to do? Should I just go now?"

Perkins looked at Dooley and they both shrugged. "Yeah, get lost." Perkins waved Ennio Feci away and watched as he hustled out of there as fast as his Capezio shoes could carry him.

"I'm sorry, Perk. I know I'm not acting myself. I think I'll take your advice. I'm going to head on over to Lingstrome Avenue and get me some coffee."

Dooley drove over to the Riviera, but just as he was parking the car, he spotted Smacky, whom he had not been able to locate for days, in front of what used to be Twitchell's Pharmacy. Smacky was watching workmen changing the sign to the Rexall corporate logo.

"Smacky, I've been looking everywhere for you. Where have you been hiding out?"

"Oh, hi ya, Detective Dooley. How are you doin'?"

"I put the word out that I wanted to do some business with you, Smacky. How come I didn't hear from you?"

"Well, I'm not so sure I wanna do business with you, Dooley."

"Are you kidding me? You always need cash. Why would you turn down the chance to make a nifty fifty bucks?"

"Nah, I don' know nothin', Dooley. Nothin'."

"Oh, come on. Since when do you not know something? I need your help. We've always been able to deal before, Smacky. Besides, you should be glad to help. This is serious stuff we're talking about here. This is all-out chaos and mayhem. Are you going to just stand by and let a mob of greasy Italians tear apart the very fabric of our American dream?"

"Very pretty speech, Dooley, but I don't know who you're trying to kid. Everybody knows what's going on with you and you-know-who."

"What are you talking about? Who's 'you-know-who'?"

"Don't play dumb with me, Dooley. Look, my asshole don't have a PhD like some people's do, but I can still tell when someone is trying to bullshit me."

"I really don't know what you're talking about, Smacky. What the hell do you mean?"

"Nothin'. Just that you'll be changing bosses pretty soon, that's all. Everybody knows it, so you might as well give up the little play-act. You're not convincing nobody." Smacky started to walk away.

"What about the fifty bucks, Smacky?"

"I don' need no fifty bucks. Not fifty *dirty* bucks, anyway."

"You didn't used to be so picky about where your fifty bucks came from."

He continued to walk away and answered over his shoulder. "Yeah, well we play for different teams now, so I have to be picky." Suddenly, he stopped and turned. "Hey, Dooley."

"What is it?"

"Your shoelace is untied. Ha, ha!" He turned and walked away, still laughing.

Dooley looked down this time without thinking. His shoelace *was* untied. While he bent to tie it, he thought about where he could turn next in his sputtering investigation. He didn't have many options left. There was a warehouse manager he hadn't talked to in years who worked on Railroad Avenue and had tenuous mob connections. He decided to drive over there to see if he had heard anything, but he popped into the Riviera for a quick pick-me-up first.

"Hi, Marty. I need some coffee."

"What's the matter? You look dazed."

"I must be losing my mind. I talk to people and they say the damnedest things and they act like I'm supposed to know what it all means. I think I've lost my edge. I don't have that cold-blooded sadistic streak that I used to have that was the envy of everyone in my industry."

"You were never sadistic, Hank. You were callous and heartless, but never sadistic."

"Whatever you call it, I think it's gone and I don't know what to do to get it back."

"Didn't you say you were going to work nights, too? Maybe you're just tired?"

"I'm not really working nights. I'm keeping an eye on Abby—I mean the Captain's sister. It's just a couple of hours in the early evening. I need a refill."

"You haven't touched the first cup yet, Hank."

Dooley looked down into his cup. "You're right!"

"You know, I've seen this sort of dazed, absent-minded behavior before. Guys complaining that they've 'lost their edge', just like you did. You won't believe me if I tell you what it turned out was wrong with them."

"What did it turn out to be, Marty?"

"Love."

"No way, Marty."

"Every time."

"How could that be? Look, I'm supposed to go to the Private Junction nightclub with her and her friends tonight, right? If I'm in love, how come I'm not looking forward to it? In fact, I'm dreading it. Besides, I'm way too old to fall in love. You're the romantic here, not me."

"Is she smart?"

"Yeah."

"Is she pretty?"

Dooley nodded.

"Is she fun to be around?"

"Yeah, I guess."

"Do you live alone?"

"You know I do."

"Can you think about anything else for very long without going back to thinking about her?"

"No, not really."

Marty gave him a look, his eyebrows arched high and he threw his hands out to the side with his palms up. "Hank, you're a man and she's a woman."

"What's that supposed to prove?"

"Nothing, Hank. Not a thing."

"Marty's right. It don't matter what you say." It was the old guy wearing his overcoat, with his hat pulled down over his eyes, digging into a plate of spaghetti and meatballs again. "It's obvious to me you're in love."

"You again? Didn't Marty's meatballs kill you the last time? How can it be so obvious to you? You don't ever look up from under that hat of yours."

"Have I ever told you that I loved a Cuban woman once?"

"Yeah."

"Don't think for one minute that I wanted to fall in love with a Cuban. I hate Cubans. They're savages, every one of them. They stand for everything I loathe in this world. Somehow, she got to me and I ended up tying the knot."

"Why'd you marry her if you hate Cubans so much?"

"It didn't make any sense to not marry her. I thought she had what I wanted and I had what she wanted."

"So, how'd it turn out, old man?"

"I was wrong, of course. She didn't have what I really wanted. That's why I'm here."

"What was it you really wanted?"

"Spaghetti and meatballs. I should've married an Italian."

"You should've married Marty."

While Dooley drove across town to visit his last informant of the day, he thought about the clothes he bought for that night. 'I'm way too old for those clothes. I'll probably look so stupid that they'll use me as the warm-up act: Dooley the Clown! Look at his funny costume and laugh as he tries and fails to pull his life out of a hat.'

He pulled up in front of Magyar Moving and Storage. The guys on the dock told him where to find Paul Banki, his syndicate contact. He went up the stairs to the grimy office. "Paul, remember me?"

"Yeah, I remember you. Frank Dooley, right? How ya doin', Frank?"

"Hank. Still kickin'. You know how it is."

"Hank, sorry. What do you need from me?"

"I'm right smack in the middle of an investigation of this mob war and I can't get my wheels out of the mud. I was wondering if you…"

"What is this, some kind of a gag?"

Dooley stood and stared, dumbfounded.

"You really thought I'd fall for that crap?"

"What is it with you people? Every time I say I'm trying to investigate the all-out mob war I get the same kind of response."

"Well, Frank, come on. What kinda response did you think you were gonna get? Really, man."

"Don't 'really, man' me! If you know something and you're holding out, it's going to land pretty hard on your head, Banki!"

"Have you gone batty on us, man? What is there to know? You of all people, with your new position, should know better than to waft in here like a stinky breeze and claim you're investigating some mythical mob war. If this is some kinda shakedown, I'm not impressed. Things have been running pretty smooth these last couple years and the grievance committee has been very responsive and accommodating. I doubt anything you try is gonna make it past them. No, pal, those good old days are over in this City. If you thought getting in with them was gonna give you a blank check, think again. Now, get lost before I call in and complain to the Big Boss."

"Okay, we'll play it your way for now. Just remember when the shit hits the fan, that I warned you."

"Fair enough. See you in the funny papers, Frank."

Dooley had no choice but to leave. As he walked down the stairs and back out onto Railroad Avenue, a phrase that Paul Banki used jumped out in his mind: 'Very responsive and accommodating'. It seemed so familiar. Where had he heard that before?

He drove back to Headquarters to report back to the Captain and to face the music. When he got to Homily's office, the Captain was talking with Sanchez and appeared to be in a good mood.

"Dooley, come in! Sanchez here was telling me how his investigation was progressing. I haven't gotten a report from you in a few days."

Dooley entered and stepped forward with trepidation. "Hi Sanchez."

"Hey Hank, my man. You look a little off your game, man. What you been smokin', huh?" Sanchez laughed heartily. "Or is it somethin' else, man? Hey, is that it? Is it somethin' else, my man? Heh?"

Dooley noticed that Homily laughed, too. "Yeah, I've had a grueling week, Sanchez. This all-out mob war is driving me nuts."

"Ha, ha! That's a good one, man. You really kill me, Hank, my man. Get him, Captain. Ha, ha! You know somethin', my man? Your sense of humor was always a riot. I *hated* you other than that, but I guess now I can't afford to hate you anymore, eh?" He laughed some more and bid the Captain good bye before sauntering out of the office.

"I'm starting to think it really is time I give up coffee."

"What do you have for me, Hank?"

"I've been all around town and hitting up all my contacts—active and dormant—and I have a big, fat zero. Zilch. Everybody's clammed-up. They're either deathly afraid, which I doubt, based on their demeanor, or they just don't know anything. They're all acting strange and I can't get a peep out of them. And believe me, I tried, Captain."

"Okay. So, how is it going keeping an eye on Abby? Any trouble there?"

Dooley was surprised that the Captain hadn't reacted at all to the bad news about his investigation. "Huh? Oh, no, sir! She lives her life like clockwork and so I have an easy task keeping her under surveillance. Other than that second letter, she's received no additional threats. The lab boys say that letter came from the same source as the first. Who that might be, I haven't a clue. I haven't seen anybody who could remotely represent a threat around her neighborhood. It looks good on that score."

"That's great."

"She did throw me a curveball, but I hope that'll turn out okay, too. I found out she planned a social engagement at the Private Junction tonight. I'll have be there to make sure there's no trouble." He expected the Captain to react strongly upon hearing the name of the nightclub, but again he was surprised.

"Fine. Keep up the good work." Dooley stood and waited for more, but Homily had gone back to his paperwork and looked up only when he realized Dooley hadn't left yet. "Something else, Dooley?"

"No, I guess not. I'll get going now. I have a long night ahead of me."

Before Dooley got to the door, Homily addressed him again. "You know, Hank, I was thinking about it and sometimes our lives are laid out in a way that seems preordained. Stuff happens that looks like it came out of left field, but I'll have you know that, in retrospect, it all makes sense. It was inevitable and you have my full support and blessing."

"Good. It makes me feel better knowing you've got my back, Captain." He walked out wondering what the hell Homily was talking about. The Captain seemed to be suffering the same disease as everyone else.

Chapter 30

Dooley had trouble finding a parking spot close to Abby's house. Even the fire hydrant spot was taken. A black Cadillac Fleetwood limousine, obviously waiting for someone, was parked there with its blinkers on. Dooley went around the block once and had to park up the street near the corner. He was so nervous that he ran the back wheel up onto the curb and had to redo the park.

As he passed the limo on the way to Abby's door, he thought about giving the driver a ticket, just for the inconvenience it caused him. In the end, he decided there wasn't enough time and he didn't want to be late.

Dooley took a deep breath as he walked up to the front door of her house. He wished he had a cup or two of coffee right about now. He rang her bell.

"Who is it?" The voice was distorted and tinny as it came out of the intercom speaker.

"It's Hank Dooley." He was unsure if it was Abby's voice or that of one of her friends that he heard.

"Come on up."

The buzzer alerted him that the door was unlocked and he took a deep breath as he pushed it open. He wished the staircase was longer. Despite his new and improved attire, he still was venturing into uncharted territory and would have liked more time to prepare. Though, he couldn't really figure out what more preparation he could have done at this point. He smoothed his jacket and fiddled with his collar as he ascended.

When he got to the door, he listened for voices, but could only hear some kind of jazzy samba music playing on the stereo. He listened for a few seconds more, but heard nothing. Then he heard footsteps and the door being unlocked and opened.

"Well, look at you! You'll be the handsomest man there, I bet." Abby was smiling broadly and nodding her approval as she looked him over and sized him up. "Come on in, Detective Dooley."

Dooley couldn't help but chuckle at her exuberant praise. She looked quite fetching herself, though definitely not ostentatious. "You look very pretty in that dress, Abby. I'd never guess you were the Captain's little sister."

"That's the idea, silly man. Make yourself comfortable." She closed the door behind her and ducked into the kitchen as he strolled into her living room.

He looked around, finding no sign of Abby's friends. "Where are your friends, Abby? Am I the first one here?"

She emerged from the kitchen, wringing her hands nervously in front of her. "Well, you see, my friends couldn't make it tonight after all, so you're the *only* one here. I hope you don't mind if it's just the two of us?" She scrunched up her face with worry.

Dooley felt an itch, but he was so relieved that he wouldn't have to spend the evening with strangers that he paid it no mind. "Oh, I'm sorry for you, Abby. I hope you're not too disappointed. Look, if you don't want to go with just me, I can…"

She practically leaped at him in response. "No! Don't say that! We'll go anyway. You're all dressed to the nines and I've been looking forward to going. You got your hair cut, didn't you?"

"Yeah, yesterday." He smoothed his hair down. "I needed to get it cut anyway."

"Well, we can't waste a perfectly fine haircut, now, can we? You don't mind, do you? I mean, going with just me? 'Cause if…"

"Oh, no! I'll be completely honest with you. I really wasn't looking forward to going out with your friends anyway. I mean, I'm sure they're perfectly nice people, but I don't know them and I don't know what I would talk to them about. No, in fact, I would be proud to be your escort tonight. So, maybe it's best."

"Instead of being proud to be my escort, how would you feel about being my *date*, Hank Dooley?"

He felt a stirring in his heart at her suggestion. He knew she liked him and that she had had that crush on him, but this was the first solid evidence that she might be as interested in him as he was in her.

"I guess from your expression that you approve of the idea. We should be going or we'll miss the floor show." Abby turned off the stereo, gathered her purse, threw on a shawl and they left the apartment. "If you and I are on a date, I think I should be calling you something other than Detective Dooley, so I'll call you Hank Dooley instead. All right?"

"Sure. Abby, if you'll wait here I can bring the car up to the door."

"That's awfully sweet of you, but that won't be necessary. I hope you don't mind, but I engaged a limo for the evening. He'll be waiting out front when we get downstairs."

"Good grief! You really do go all out, don't you?" He was very glad he had decided to not issue the driver a ticket.

"I just figured that we might not be inclined to drive at the end of the evening. I thought it would be more fun. And I got a really good price because my firm does business with the owner. There he is now."

Indeed, there was the black Cadillac Fleetwood limousine waiting for them at the curb. The driver was leaning on the front passenger side door until he saw them emerge, at which point he opened the rear door for them and saluted. It was obviously a first-class operation and Dooley wondered about the expense and the reason for it. The interior of the car was luxuriously appointed, with leather and wood and a small bar built into the back of the front seat.

"Lookie, Hank Dooley! They have a mini bar here, just for us two. May I pour us each a drink?"

"I'm not so sure I should be drinking while…"

"Nonsense. Remember that we're on a date. You'll have a drink with me or I'll open the door and toss you out of the car and right onto Peace Boulevard."

"Well, since you put it that way."

"Hey, everybody! Hank Dooley cracked a smile. And it turns out that Hank Dooley has a very nice smile." She poured two Seven-and-Sevens with ice and offered him one. You don't mind me being so familiar, do you? After all, we're both adults."

"Here's to Abby and Hank, then."

"To Hank and Abby." They clinked glasses. "May they—may they *succeed*."

"Succeed at what?" She really did perplex him at times.

She paused a long time, staring into his eyes, then broke into a big grin. "At having a fun time tonight, silly man. What did you think I was going to say?"

"I don't know. Where did you learn to bartend?"

"I have many abilities. You have seen only one or two of them, Hank Dooley—so far, anyway."

"I guess I don't know much about you, do I? And we've known each other almost twenty years—in a way, that is. Hell, I didn't even know what you looked like before I started watching you."

"I hope you're not too disappointed." Dooley didn't respond. "It makes sense that you would know little about me. After all, we hadn't seen each other since I was a girl. I had done nothing with my life and was destined for extreme obscurity, which since then I have achieved, although in a surprisingly ironic form. And you have gone on to accomplish great things in your public service."

"Now, just a minute. I really need to straighten you out on a couple of things, Abby. You have a notion that I'm some kind of Supercop. I can assure you that I am nothing of the sort. In fact, I am…"

"You sell yourself short, Hank. I think you sell yourself short as a cop *and* as a man. I admire you greatly. My brother admires you, too."

"You think so? I'm not so sure, Abby. I think you're off base about that. If you could hear how frustrated he gets with me, I think you'd have a very different take on it than you do."

"I know my brother rides you hard sometimes. He relies on you, Hank. You do the things he can no longer do since he became a Captain. I know my brother. He'd rather be out there with you. But, he needed to help me out so he had to get promoted upstairs and out of the field. Who else does he lean on as hard as he does you? He can't rely on di Miceli or Perkins or Armstrong or Sanchez the way he relies on you."

"You seem to know a lot about what's going on in the Department. Still, I wish I could believe you."

"I didn't make it up, Hank. I know what my brother tells me. He tells me you're the go-to guy on his team. He says you have special abilities that make you indispensable and that you've been able to solve cases that were thought hopelessly unsolvable."

"He's probably thinking of this special intuition that I have sometimes." He thought briefly of his anus and shifted a little in his seat.

"Whatever it is, it's pulled his fat out of the fire many times. He hasn't had an easy time of it since becoming Captain, you know. There was a lot of opposition to him getting the job in the first place."

"I remember. It got pretty ugly at times. I didn't know you knew about it. I thought he kept it from his family."

"He kept it from his wife and kids. I was closely associated with it. My consulting firm recommended him for the promotion. The Commissioner was against our recommendations. He knew I worked for that firm and he thought there was a conflict of interest."

"I thought there had been some talk of organized crime getting involved, too."

"Would you like me to freshen up your drink, Hank?"

He thought about it for a moment. He was not a drinker, but he felt relaxed for the first time since he could remember. "Why not? Go ahead."

"Better be careful. I might end up taking advantage of you." She prepared two more drinks for them. "Hank, you're really a lot like my brother in some ways. He has this deep desire to make a difference for people. He gets frustrated sometimes by protocol, as I'm sure you do."

"It does get frustrating. I try not to let it bother me too much and I try to not let it dictate how I go about my job. Your brother is a great Captain because he understands that rules can interfere with good police work and if we crack a few eggs in order to solve a case, well, that's okay."

"Do you feel you make a difference for people—I mean really make a difference?"

"I get frustrated and a little down about it. I don't think I make as much of a difference as I could, maybe. Hell, half the time I'm putting innocent people behind bars while the real culprits go free. You know how it is. But, I guess the City gets exactly the police work that it deserves—no better, no worse. Nobody wants to cooperate with us. They'd rather let a psychopath go free than to fink him out to the police." He finished his drink and replaced the glass in the mini bar. They sat in silence for a while as the driver navigated his way to the Private Junction.

"Hank?"

He turned toward her.

"Have you ever been interested in anyone?"

"You mean, seriously interested? I guess not. Probably because I don't think anyone would want to put up with me. I suppose I never found the right woman, either."

"Do you ever think about settling down, Hank?"

"I don't know that I'll ever find the right woman. I think a cop has to be with someone who understands the profession. Other than cops, believe it or not, the people who understand the business better than anyone else are the criminals. I'm not about to settle down with a murderess or a prostitute. Besides, living alone isn't so bad. At least I don't have anybody worrying about me."

"Yeah, but you don't have anybody worrying about you." They fell silent again.

Waiting for a traffic light to change on Turtle Street, the greenish glow of a streetlight was illuminating Abby's face. Dooley studied her for a moment. She had grown into an attractive woman over the past twenty years. She was pretty to be sure, and her face had an intelligence about it, but there was something else, too. "You're a pretty confident person, aren't you?"

"I never thought so. I'm good at my job, I suppose. What makes you say so?"

"I don't know. It struck me that I know a lot of cocky people. They posture and strut, but they're covering up their insecurity. You seem very sure-footed."

"You make me sound like a goat."

"I didn't mean it that way."

"We'll get a chance to test your sure-footed theory tonight with these heels." She lifted her left foot until it was parallel to her thigh and wiggled it around. She left it up there for an extra beat or two.

Dooley looked at the foot in its shoe. Then his eye took in the gentle curve of her ankle and calf before she lowered the foot back down.

"What was your best case, Hank Dooley?"

"What do you mean?"

"The one case that was your greatest achievement."

"Oh, well, I'm not sure I should talk about that one. It's kind of nasty."

"I'm a cop's sister, remember? What was it?"

"Okay. Do you remember about three years ago at Beach Point, there was a—well, there was a body part that washed up on the sand?"

"Are you talking about that Greek tourist kidnapping?"

"That's the one. Anyway, all we had was a pair of testicles—nothing else. In eleven hours I had the guilty party behind bars and the three hundred thousand dollars recovered and returned to the rightful owners."

"Oh, yeah! I read about that case in the papers. What about the testes? What ever happened to them?"

"We kept them as evidence. They're at Headquarters on a shelf in a jar."

"What about the Greek? What became of him?"

"That's an interesting story. When he found out he wasn't getting his testicles back, he sued the Department. We settled out of court."

"What did he get? I hope the City didn't have to shell out too much money. It sounds like you guys did the best you could for him."

"The City didn't pay him a penny."

"How'd they get away with that?"

"The Department offered him the kidnapper's testicles. He said that would satisfy him. I guess he felt it restored his honor."

"You gave him the kidnapper's balls?!"

"Yep."

"How'd you get them? You didn't take them yourself, did you?"

Dooley shook his head. "No way. That's not my bag. The D.A. took 'em."

"Hank, there's no way the kidnapper would have agreed to it. He wasn't even named in the suit, was he?"

"No, he wasn't. He didn't really have a say in the matter."

"You didn't even take the guy to a doctor?"

"No, we had him in the courthouse jail and we really wanted to wrap it up, so we borrowed a bolt-cutter from the bailiff. It was all done painlessly."

"Did you sedate him?"

"No, he sedated himself. He got so scared when the moment came, that he hyperventilated himself until he passed out cold. Then—snip. We dried them with some napkins from the cafeteria and presented them to the Greek. That was probably this City's court system's finest hour, too."

Chapter 31

The Private Junction occupied its own large plot of land out near the airport. It was a remote enough spot to be attractive to those patrons who needed a nearby getaway. Famous faces were known to have frequented the night-club, accompanied by their paramours. It was all very discreet. Unlike all the uptown nightspots, there were never any photographers allowed in the Private Junction. This was the place to go to escape being seen.

The club, originally owned by a famous crooner, was first called The Wing Tip. Since then, it has changed hands three times, its fortunes rising and falling along the way. The lowest point in its history was during the mid-sixties when it was Club Tarmac and the entertainment featured drag queens impersonating the likes of Tallulah Bankhead, Marlene Dietrich and Judy Garland. The present owners, known to be part of the Feci crime family, bought the vacant property three years ago and put a lot of money into its renaissance. Surprisingly, despite the notorious reputation enjoyed by its current owners, it was not the scene of any known criminal activity and has become the envy of the nightclub industry.

The limo pulled right up to the entrance and the valet quickly advanced to get the door on the driver's side, where Abby was sitting. Except for the pink and blue neon sign and the dazzling lights under the awning, the building's exterior was entirely dark. They got out and quickly walked the few steps to the entrance, where a doorman greeted them. "Good evening, Miss—a pleasure to see you. Good evening, Sir." Dooley got the distinct impression that the doorman knew Abby. Once inside the bustling club, the concierge greeted them with precisely the same words as those used by the doorman, after which he led them to a choice table at the front, next to the dance floor/stage, where a jazz orchestra was playing some popular tune. As they sat down, Dooley wondered how the concierge knew which table to seat them. Abby hadn't spoken a word since arriving at the club.

"Are you a regular here?"

"No. Why?"

"I don't know. I got the feeling that those two seemed to know you, like you're a regular customer."

"What would you say if I told you that I have never been a customer here before tonight?"

He looked at her and cocked his head slightly. He knew she was telling the truth, strictly speaking, but there was something. "I thought you said you'd been here before?"

"Yes, I did say that. I've been here in the capacity of a consultant. My job, remember?"

As soon as they had settled in their seats, the waiter arrived to take their drink order. "Good evening, Miss. Glad to see you. Good evening, Sir." At least this guy didn't say, 'a pleasure,' like the other two had. They ordered their drinks and took in the surroundings. The club had a dance floor in front of the band. There were probably fifty tables on the ground floor and a balcony that ran around the perimeter in a horse shoe shape. They admired the ritzy décor and the quality sound of the jazz band.

They sat and chatted about the famous people, of whom there were many in attendance that they could recognize. Their drinks arrived and they ordered appetizers.

"I hope you don't mind my ordering the appetizers for us."

"No, that's fine. It's your night out, Abby. And anyway, what the hell do I know about appetizers? The meals I usually eat are hardly appetizing— well, never mind about that."

"Do you cook for yourself at home?"

"Not usually. The last meal I ate at home was a baloney sandwich quite a while ago."

"How long ago was that?"

"I was watching Highbridge winning the championship against Chicago. Whenever that was."

"That was four years ago. You haven't eaten at home since then?"

"I guess not. Four years? Time flies, huh?"

"You need somebody to cook a good meal for you, Hank Dooley."

"Are you a good cook, Abby? I mean, do you like to cook?"

"I practice all the time. I've been cooking since I was about twelve. About the time I saw you that first time. It's fun to cook, but it's a lot more fun to

210

cook when it's two people. I've been looking forward to sharing my skills with someone special."

"I think I would be very interested in such an interaction with you, Abby. I've had some really cheap and unsavory meals over the years. It would be an honor to have a decent and fresh meal like the one you're suggesting."

They talked a little about her brother and her mom. Dooley had remembered her mother as a cheerful woman, despite having her only son in uniform and on street patrol. Abby had much to say about the toll it took on the family and how her mother had learned to cope.

After ordering a second round of drinks, Abby grabbed Dooley's hand and dragged him up onto the dance floor. They joined dozens of other couples and danced a few lively songs, including jazzy versions of the Beach Boys' *Help Me Rhonda* and a similarly jazzy rendition of *I Heard it Through the Grapevine*.

When they cleared the dance floor in preparation for the performances, Abby and Dooley returned to their table and chatted some more. Dooley was surprised at how easy it was to talk to her. He felt clever and interesting and he had long forgotten that he had feared that his attire would make him the comic warm-up act for the main attraction. Abby seemed to be really enjoying his company and was as relaxed and natural as he had ever seen her. He hadn't failed to notice that she had taken the liberty of touching him on his hand and arm and even briefly on his knee once. They were warm touches—not provocative, but more than just friendly.

At half-past nine, the cabaret floorshow began. There were some dancers in exotic costumes, with plumage and glitter, performing some acrobatic ballroom moves with synchronized choreography. They gyrated and postured for twenty minutes while the band belted out some jazzy, tropically-tinged calypso tunes. Then, after a brief interlude, the main attraction came out to an enthusiastic greeting from the patrons. She was a short, slight woman, perhaps in her late thirties, with long, wavy red hair and dressed in a midnight blue sequined gown and elbow-length red satin gloves. Despite her small stature, she had a rich, full voice and she imbued her vocalizations with just the right amounts of cynicism and pathos to enable her songs to strike home to full effect. She and the band, which was playing with all the breadth and depth it could muster, very quickly had the audience riding along the emotional roller coaster of her repertoire.

Whether it was because of her talent alone, the emotion-softening effects of the liquor or the electric atmosphere of the club, the songs' poignancy affected Dooley with an unexpected force. He suddenly felt close to Abby as they shared the experience. The fifth song especially hit its mark like cupid's arrow and Abby placed her hand in his as they sat and listened to the heartache of the sad-faced chanteuse pouring forth in waves of fathomless feeling. The lyrics of her song broke down the barriers that had kept their emotions contained.

Woman's heart can navigate and tenderness keeps it afloat
But if a man don't play it true, love sinks like a boat
She endures, though her being yearns for his touches so erotic
Her heart's aflame and loins burn for love that's so narcotic
Tragically she loves all alone, dulling her ache with whiskey
And every night wishes on a star, 'cause reality's too risky
Baby, you can cure this love disease; this is the big chance
Come sail across the roiling seas without a backwards glance

When the teary-eyed singer had sung her last desperate note and the band had closed out with a dramatic flourish, and while the audience exploded with a thunderous ovation, both Abby and Dooley sat stunned and motionless for a long time. The sentiment of that song spoke to them both, and they became choked up by a flood of feeling. They turned and gazed at each other and as Dooley looked into Abby's eyes he felt that he could really see her now and he realized that the desire he had been feeling for her was not entirely of a sexual nature. He suddenly understood that she really appreciated him—as a detective and as a man.

The singer had cleared the stage and the band struck up some more dance music and the crowd started making their way to the floor. Abby stood up without releasing her grip on Dooley's hand and wordlessly led him back to the dance floor, where they swayed to the slower rhythms. They held each other close and Dooley buried his nose in her hair and breathed in her fragrance. He could feel her ribs expand as she inhaled. He was aware of everything about her: the feel of her, her warmth, her softness, the texture of her dress, the indentation of her bra strap, the moistness of her hand in his, her freckled shoulder.

She pulled her head up and looked into his eyes and smiled. "Hank, I hope you don't mind this guard duty *too* much." She smiled and put her head back down against his chest.

They danced through several songs and sat back down at their table, where Dooley ordered coffee. They talked for a while about life and love, their favorite movies and music, where to get the best slice of pizza and which was the best bagel shop in the City. Then, around a quarter past midnight, after Dooley had several more cups of coffee, they decided to pay the tab and go. To Dooley's surprise, seemingly without being summoned, the limo was already waiting right out front when they exited the club. The valet had the passenger door open for them, and as they passed the club's employees, each of them offered warm and respectful farewells.

"They let you stay parked here all evening?" Dooley's question to the driver might as well have been addressed to a deaf-mute. All he got in response was a salute and a smile.

Abby poured two tiny glasses of Drambuie as the limo pulled out into traffic and headed back into town. "You drink a lot of coffee, Hank. Is that how you maintain your big, strong physique?"

"No, my physique—or what's left of it—hangs on despite how badly I abuse it." He sipped the liqueur, savoring the rich bouquet and relishing the sweetness.

Abby scooted over and sat pressed against him, with her body turned toward him and one hand pressed gently against his chest. "Oh, come on. You're being modest. You were always a big strong manly man. You were twenty years ago and you are today."

"You've changed a lot these twenty years, Abby."

"Well, I hope so! I was just a skinny, silly little girl twenty years ago. I'm not that anymore, am I? I'm not too skinny and I hope I'm not too fat. And I'm not silly anymore. Am I, Hank?"

"You're just right, Abby. Funny, but I've never been really comfortable with any woman before. Yet, I'm totally comfortable with you. It feels different, as if we were made for each other. I feel that we understand each other somehow. You know, a cop doesn't get that feeling very often."

"Thank goodness. I'm so glad you approve. I'd hate for you to disapprove of me, especially after so much..." Abby stopped herself.

"After so much what?"

"Huh? Oh, just after so much time, you know I mean after so many years. You know, getting older and all." She smiled at him.

"You're not getting older yet. Hell, you're still young. You're in your prime. You're a very attractive woman and you have a lot going for you in many other ways, too."

"I work very hard to make a contribution."

"Tell me, Abby, what exactly do you do for a living these days? What is this consulting firm anyway?"

"I guess you might say I'm a supervising consultant."

"I thought I remember hearing that you had wanted to be a teacher."

"I did want to be a teacher. I couldn't, though."

"Why not? I bet you'd be great with kids."

"You can't be a teacher if you don't graduate from college."

"Didn't you go to college? I thought you went to college. I thought I remember your brother talking about paying for it."

"All right, if you must know, I *did* go to college. I just didn't graduate."

"Why not? Too many parties?" He laughed, but Abby looked unhappy. As soon as Dooley read her expression, he changed his question. "Did you have to quit to get a job or something?"

"No, my brother was willing to pay for my education. I just couldn't cut it." She sat up straight and hugged herself, scrunching up her shoulders. It was obvious to Dooley that it was painful for her to talk about it. "That's why I ended up at Apex Business Institute instead."

"Oh, come on. You're a smart girl. You should've blown them away in college. Your brother was always singing your praises."

"Thanks for saying so. My brother has always been my biggest cheerleader, but he is prejudiced. I was never very good in school. I had to have a lot of help just to get through high school."

"What kind of help?"

"I have a problem recognizing letters properly. I always have. I can just barely read and I have trouble writing. I couldn't see it myself, but I'd get my tests and term papers back and they'd be covered in red pencil. I'd have reversed letters and misspelled words. I can't help it. The words look right to me when I write them. It's not that I'm stupid, it's just a thing. I can't explain it."

"It must've been tough for you."

"You have no idea what it's like to watch your friends advance and to be left behind, and to have to get special tutors and still be dumped into the dumb class. I vowed to stick it out and achieve and make something of myself, because that's what my brother said he wanted and what our mother would have wanted if she were still alive. More importantly, that's what I knew *you* would expect of me, Hank."

"Me!? Why would you care what *I* thought?"

"That's *all* I care about. That's all I've *ever* cared about." Abby unfolded her arms, turning back toward Dooley and reached across to caress his cheek. "I've loved you ever since that day I first saw you at the old 37th Precinct station when I was twelve years old. I used to look for you every time my mother had any reason to bring me by the 37th. I'd beg her to let me come along just in case I might catch a glimpse of you. I wanted so much to make myself a success so that you'd be proud of me and notice me and oh, it seems so childish now that I hear myself talk about it. But, I couldn't help myself, Hank. I had a love disease, just like in that song. I promised myself that I would earn your love, so I worked and worked at improving myself and I found a way to become respectable and important. It seemed an impossible task at first. You seemed so distant and so unattainable. You were off doing important things and I knew that I would have to do something really important to appear on your radar screen. I tried to achieve something by taking the conventional route. When that led to nothing, I grabbed the opportunity of a lifetime—guaranteed to show up on radar. It was a long, hard climb and I fought hard for every inch and I faced unbearable scorn and ridicule, just so that one day you would notice me. And you *did* notice me, Darling." She looked at Dooley with tears in her eyes. "It took this bowling alley job to finally bring us together, but everything seems worth it right now. Now that you're here with me tonight I know my life wasn't wasted. Not one blessed minute of it."

Dooley was flabbergasted and for a second he almost felt like laughing. "You're funny, Abby. You make it almost sound like this evening was the reason for the bombing of Spazzatura Lanes, rather than the other way around."

Abby looked desperately earnest. "I promised myself and God that I'd do anything to have you in my arms, Hank Dooley. It took me eight years to achieve this moment, not counting the initial planning, which was another two and a half years."

He wasn't sure what to say. "I didn't realize I was so hard to get."

215

Abby looked hurt. "Don't poke fun at me. I was lost and drifting until this plan came to me. It was like I was in a gray fog, until that day when I realized what I had to do and that fog burned away. Since that moment, my life has had meaning."

Dooley was perplexed at the conversation. "Abby, exactly what are you talking about?"

"I did it all for you, Darling, *all* of it—every contract, every payoff, every rubout, every staff retreat."

Dooley finally really heard her. "Abby, you never told me what company you work for?"

"It's a company downtown in Little Italy. Although we've been expanding so much that we're building that fifty-one story office tower on 5th Avenue."

"What does this company do?"

"It does lots of things. It provides security, it enforces regulations, it runs entertainment venues and it owns and operates transportation firms. I'm the top person there, Darling." She beamed with pride.

"Pretty big deal, huh? I guess you didn't need college after all. What's the name of this company? Have I ever heard of it?"

"You certainly have heard of it. You are *very* familiar with it, Hank. They've been in the papers recently for supposedly attempting a hostile takeover of another company."

"Was this attempt *very* hostile?"

"The papers say it was the most hostile type of takeover." She kept smiling.

"And you had something to do with this attempt, Abby?"

"I told you. I am the top person there. But, you can't believe everything you read, Darling. It wasn't really a takeover attempt at all. That was just a lot of yellow journalism, written to sell papers. What's really happening is a good thing."

"Abby, are you trying to kid me?" He could clearly see she wasn't. "You're serious, aren't you? Do you know what you're saying? I'm trying to do some good in the world. I went into police work because it's a noble profession. I wanted to help people."

"You're in the right profession, Hank. You're just working for the wrong people."

"I don't follow."

"Do you know who killed the last mayor?"

"No."

"Well, *I* do. And I know where he is at this moment."

"Where?"

"He's in a can of dog food on a shelf in the nearest A&P right now." She waited for a reaction. Dooley was stunned. "I could go on, Hank. The three men responsible for blowing up that poor clown in front of all those kiddies at the carnival were turned into chum and fed to Nelly and Chester, the sharks at the aquarium. That huge extortion ring operating at the ballpark was put out of business by our team last week."

"Were those the thirty nine men that mysteriously fell from the upper deck during the seventh inning stretch?"

"Exactly. So, you see that we do a lot of good." She could see that Dooley was still skeptical. "You do believe me, don't you? Hank, Darling, hop on board and join the winning team. We need you. The City needs you. *I* need you. You can have everything the way you want it, Hank. I can fix it up for you. You could really help people and make a difference! Would you like that, Darling? I can fix it for you."

"This is all a bit much for me to take in, all at once. Has your brother ever talked to you about my asshole?"

"What? Your asshole? Why would he—oh, yes! He *did* say something about it once or twice, as I recall. He said you rely on it somehow."

"Abby, my asshole talks to me. Well, it doesn't talk, per se, it itches whenever anybody lies to me."

"So?"

"I'm very worried right now because it's *not* itching me."

"But, it's a good thing when your asshole doesn't itch. It means it's clean and healthy, doesn't it?"

"That's right. It also means that you've been telling me the truth."

"Of course I have, Darling. I wouldn't lie to you." She stopped to caress his face. "I love you, Hank Dooley." She kissed him. It was a tender kiss, not a seductive kiss. She didn't try to lick his tonsils like so many women do who are trying to get something from a man.

Dooley returned the kiss, of course—being a gentleman— but he was confused and disoriented. He thought back to the number of drinks he'd had during the evening, then to the number of cups of coffee he'd had afterward. They just didn't add up to him hallucinating as he had done in the recent past. He really seemed to be sitting in the back of a Cadillac limousine, next to the Captain's kid sister, who really seemed to have her head on his shoulder and her arms around his neck.

Did he love her? He certainly had an enchanted evening with her. He also was physically attracted to her. But, who was she? He'd concocted a patchwork assumption of who he *thought* she was, and had been carrying that around like a dossier on Abigail Homily since he started keeping an eye on her. Now, magically, she was presenting herself as an altogether different woman–an extremely powerful and important woman–looking to transform one of the greatest cities in the greatest country the world has ever known into one big Mafia syndicate—with her at the head, promising justice and peace.

Dooley added it all up in his mind. 'No,' he thought, 'this is impossible.' First of all, the idea that the largest crime family in the entire region would have a young woman at its head seemed ludicrous. Secondly, she was not related by blood to the family she purportedly runs. Thirdly, though admittedly the weakest argument against its impossibility, her brother was a police Captain as uncorrupt as they come. After trying to prove Abby's insanity in his mind, his thoughts drifted back to their evening at the Private Junction nightclub. There's no doubt that it is owned by the Fecis, and it was quite clear that the nightclub's employees all treated her with great deference, as if they knew and respected her.

He didn't know what to think. He couldn't wait for the ride to be over so he could get back home to be alone and sort it all out. Abby's voice jolted him out of his meditation.

"What are you thinking, Darling?"

"I'm thinking of you, Abby, and I'm thinking how I don't want our evening to end."

She sighed softly into his chest. "I was thinking of that incredible song she sung about love enduring, waiting. And you came across those seas of time to me, Hank, just like in that song." She sighed and hugged Dooley tighter.

The limo pulled up to her door and the chauffeur opened the door for them. Abby thanked him by name and when she and Dooley walked up to her door, he pulled away into the night.

"I probably shouldn't come in, Abby. A lot has happened to us tonight and we should be careful not to let our feelings run away with us."

"I understand. When will I see you again?"

"Monday, of course." He smiled. He took both of her hands in his. "You are quite a woman, Abby. You've given me a lot to consider. Honestly, I don't know what to make of it all. I don't know what it all means."

She pulled him close and kissed him. It was a less tender kiss and more seductive than the first. "You will. Good night, Darling." She unlocked her door and went inside.

Dooley waited a moment in the quiet, then walked to his car, which was waiting for him like an old reliable friend. It seemed to him that his sedan was the only thing in his life that hadn't changed since the day began.

While he was in the limo with Abby, he had argued the question of her veracity and had almost concluded that she was telling the truth. Now, a mere ten minutes later, he re-argued the question and came up with a much more logical conclusion. He concluded that she was not the head of the Feci clan or a liar, but was in fact completely insane.

He ran the question through his mind over and over again all through the night and into the next morning. He had not been able to sleep most of the night and what sleep he got was fitful. He dreamt that someone painlessly removed his testicles with a Sawzall.

Chapter 32

The next day, Dooley dragged himself out of bed and into the Riviera for breakfast.

"Hi Hank. Did you pull an all-nighter or something? You have no color in your face." He plunked a cup of coffee and sugar dispenser in front of Dooley.

"I had a hell of a night, last night, Marty. Hash and eggs."

"What happened, you have a fight with the Captain's sister?"

"No, I went to the Private Junction with her last night."

"You had a bad time, didn't you? Sorry it didn't work out, Hank."

"No, it was wonderful. It was the most wonderful night of my life."

"Really? Then, what's the matter?"

"Abby Homily is insane, that's what's the matter."

"Well, I don't want you to take it wrong, Hank, but what do you expect? Any girl that—never mind."

"What? Any girl that what? Any girl that falls for me is nuts?"

"I didn't want to say it, but yes."

"You're probably right. More coffee, please. She certainly doesn't *seem* loony."

"Those are the craziest ones."

"You know, Marty, it's possible that you're wrong. It's possible that she's perfectly sane, but then that would mean that the rest of the world is crazy."

"That would explain a lot."

After devouring his hash and eggs, Dooley made it into the office, where he sat and ruminated for two hours about his conundrum. He kept coming back to the belief that Abby was telling the truth. What other explanation could

220

be offered for the Captain's laissez-faire attitude toward the investigation? What could explain the odd comments made by several street-wise informants and their incredulity when he claimed to be working on the mob war?

Dooley looked up her number in the phonebook and thought about calling her.

Perkins drifted in around noon and the two chatted for a while, but Dooley was so distracted that Perkins finally got exasperated with him and called him on it.

"All right, Hank. What gives? I look at you and talk to you, but it's like you're not even there lately. And we haven't heard a peep from your asshole for a week or more. Maybe you should take that thing to a proctologist for a checkup."

"That's something that's been on my mind. My asshole's been tingling a little bit, on and off for days, but not when I'd expect it to. For instance, Ennio was telling us the truth—at least part of the truth—yesterday. He was on the level about the Fecis having nothing to gain by a war."

"Okay, I'll agree with that. But, there's something else going on here. You've sort of disappeared the last couple of days. Is it about this case? Help me out here."

"No, it's not this case, Perk. You know that Homily has me checking up on his sister. He was worried about her."

"Abigail? Hey, I never did find out why she's being watched. Is it because she's in some kind of trouble? Is she on drugs or something?"

"No, she got a threatening note—two notes—that warned Homily to lay off the syndicate or she'd pay the price. So, since I live near her, I was supposed to check up on her just to make sure she's okay. I'm starting to think you're the only one in the department who doesn't know why."

"It doesn't make any sense."

"Sure it does. It turns out that I'm only a few blocks from her."

"That's not what I mean. I mean, why would they send *her* a note?"

"I suppose because she's the only family the Captain has—aside from his wife and kids, that is. If they wanted to pressure him…"

"That's the point. He's got a wife and kids. If you were a Mafia kingpin, would you send a threatening note to the Captain's kid sister? Or would you send one to the Captain's home?" Dooley had no answer. "Not only that, but the Captain has never been particularly hard on the syndicates' operations. He's been especially soft on organized crime since becoming the Captain. So, why would they try to get him to lay off their operations? He's already laying off. None of us are anywhere near solving any investigations into either the Fecis or the Spizzaturas. There's just no heat on them, as far as I can tell. No, it just doesn't add up, Hank."

"That's all true."

"The only one of us who even got near any of the mob's business is gone now, so he's not even a threat anymore."

"Who do you mean?"

"Pfeiffer."

"Pfeiffer?"

"You didn't know that? You got all his cases, didn't you? Didn't you see his files on the Feci family? To him it was like a religious crusade."

"I looked through all of those files. There were no files on the Fecis."

"I thought Homily gave you all of Pfeiffer's cases. Maybe he…"

"No, he held out on me. Remember I told you he wasn't too upset about Pfeiffer? You know, I don't think there's anything wrong with my asshole, after all."

"Whew! That's a relief. I was worried about it, Hank. It's been one of the few things we could really count on—sort of like Old Faithful."

"I've been a fool and I've been distracted. I haven't been listening to my asshole. It's been talking to me this whole time and I've been ignoring it, because I couldn't understand what it was saying. But, I'll tell you this. My asshole really has its finger on the pulse of what's happening out there. I've been occupied by a romantic dalliance and I've allowed it to dull my senses."

"Say, Hank, this wouldn't be related to Abigail Homily, would it? Because, you know, that wouldn't be anything to be ashamed of. As far as I'm concerned, if you're going to dull your senses, she'd be a decent choice to do it with. She's a handsome woman and she's got a good job."

"Do you know what she does?"

"I heard she's some kind of consultant—real white collar stuff. Am I wrong?"

"Not too wrong."

"She might be a good catch, Hank, if you're interested in settling down, that is. A cop wants a wife who has a career. You don't want a wife who sits at home, worrying all day and fucking the mailman. Plus she's a cop's sister. You know that makes all the difference. Yep, she's a good one, I say."

"Why would you think I'd want to settle down? I've done all right for myself."

"All right? Is that what you call it? Hank, your last girlfriend was Rosalie Jimenez's mother, remember?"

"Hey, don't knock it 'til you tried it. She was pretty good, Perk."

"Come on, you do the math, Hank—Abigail Homily vs. Rosalie Jimenez's mother. You can't go on this way forever. You're getting too old for quickies with fat Puerto Rican mammas. I can tell just by looking at you that you're seriously considering it. You must like her, too. Am I right?"

"Yeah, I do like her a lot. There's may be a real connection there. I can't be sure because I've never really had that with anyone before, but I think it's real serious."

"Then you should go for it."

"Yeah, but there's a fly in the ointment, Perk. I can't tell you what it is, but it would require a major attitude adjustment on my part—if it's true, that is."

"It must be a pretty big fly, huh? What, is she a swinger or something? Is she a slut? I wouldn't think that would bother you any."

"No, nothing like that."

"Is it because she's the Captain's sister? Is that it? I don't see him causing any problems with you. He's already got his hands full with his work and his family."

"It is related to her being his sister, but not for the reason you think. I can't really say what it is."

"I still say go for it, Hank. You're not gettin' any younger, my friend. When do you see her again?"

"I'm supposed to see her again on Monday."

"My advice is to tell her exactly what your doubts are and what's holding you back and see what happens. If it's meant to happen, it'll happen. If it's not meant to happen—well, sayonara."

"But Perk, what would you do if you found out your wife was part of an evil organization that you've spent your whole life believing is the cancer that's tearing apart society? If it turned out that she may be responsible for destroying countless lives and terrorizing the citizenry of this City? If she's made her living breaking the bodies and dashing the hopes and dreams of decent law-abiding people, what would you do?"

Perkins mulled it over for a second. "I'd take her to dinner, then go down on her. With a woman like that, you definitely want to stay on her good side."

That sparked an idea for Dooley. "I could take her to lunch."

"Right now?"

"No, Tuesday."

Chapter 33

Dooley spent his entire weekend trying to act as if his life was normal. And for all he knew, it was normal. He'd already formulated a plan to handle his greatest dilemma around the question of Abby and paid a visit to the Riviera luncheonette on Saturday evening for a late dinner and to lay the groundwork for his plan.

"You look better, Hank. Everything okay now?"

"I think so, Marty. I have a kind of a doubt about the whole thing, but I think you can help me work it out."

Marty dropped a cup of coffee and the sugar dispenser on the counter for him. "Look, Hank, I helped you tape those Feci gangsters during their lunch, but they never knew they were being taped. I don't want to do anything that they'll trace back to me. I want to live some more."

"I'm not going to get you into any hot water, I just want to bring Abby here for lunch on Tuesday."

"Why would you want to do that?"

"If I'm going to have a relationship with Abby Homily, I need to know if she is who she's claiming to be. No one else is going to tell me even if they know. So, I think this is a surefire way of finding out if she's crazy or not."

"Maybe you're the crazy one. You ever think of that?"

"Of course I have. The thing is, Marty, I don't really care if she's crazy or not, but I need to know what I'm getting into here."

"Okay, I'll go along."

"The thing is, I'm going to bring her here before they arrive and we're going to sit at their table."

"What the hell! You really have a death wish, don't you? They have that table reserved for every Tuesday and Friday."

"What time?"

"Noon. But you're gonna get you and the Captain's sister killed this way, Hank." He refilled the coffee cup.

"Not if she is who she says she is."

"But, what if she isn't? What if she's just a nice girl with a screw loose? They'll mess you up and she might get caught in the crossfire. You shouldn't do it. I heard that those guys impaled an old lady once, just because she said something disparaging about the hotel she stayed in when she visited Sicily."

"Do you really believe that shit?"

"No, I don't, but I still wouldn't wanna mess with them."

"Bring me a plate of spaghetti and meatballs like you served to that old coot the other day."

"That's the other thing."

"What?"

"Do you really want to subject Abby Homily to the food in this place? Just because she's a cop's sister doesn't mean she has an iron stomach."

"Just don't feed her a grilled rat and I think she'll be all right."

"That happened only once, as far as I know."

Dooley couldn't wait until Monday to see Abby again. He finally admitted to himself that he was in love with Abby when he woke up from a dream in which she appeared as the motorman on a speeding express train. He felt depressed when he woke up and she wasn't really there, taking him and all the others on board to the next station. As far as he could remember, he'd never had that feeling before, regardless of what the dream was about. He dropped by her place on Sunday around eleven o'clock, hoping to see her. Abby just happened to be returning from church and so she invited him up for some coffee.

"I wondered if I could stand not seeing you again until tomorrow. I had the best time of my life Friday night."

"Me, too, Abby. I tried to go back to my regular life yesterday, but I couldn't do anything without thinking of you. I even dreamt of you."

"Ooh! Was it a sexy dream?"

"Well, it was strange. I was on a speeding express train, roaring through the tunnel and the train is racing along at some ungodly speed and it was packed with passengers and they were all celebrating, but I couldn't hear them. You were standing there in the motorman's cab operating the train, smoking a big cigar. Then, the train became a ferryboat and I was standing at the front and the water was choppy and I could see you standing at the slip, waiting for me. You had a catcher's mitt on your left hand and there was a group of Southern Baptists clapping and singing *Michael Row Your Boat Ashore*—you know that song?"

"Sure." Abby waited a bit. "That's all?"

"Yep. Then I woke up."

"You're right, that's not very sexy. It's really nice outside. Why don't we take a walk? We can go over to Calvin Gerner Park."

"Sounds perfect. Let's go."

They left the apartment and walked the tree-lined streets to the park, chatting about growing up in their respective neighborhoods.

"I bet you can't guess where I was born."

"I gather from the challenge that you were not born in this City, am I right?"

Dooley nodded.

"Pittsburgh?"

"Close! Cleveland, but I moved here when I was less than two years old."

"You're one of the Cleveland Dooleys? Let's sit on that bench over there."

"Abby, there's no way you're head of the biggest Mafia family in the entire region."

She just smiled at him.

"Nah, I just don't buy it. The other night, I was a little drunk and my asshole took the night off. But, here in the light of day, it just doesn't add up."

"Why doubt it, Darling?"

"You just don't look like a Mafia kingpin."

"And what's a Mafia kingpin supposed to look like?"

"Well, like Old Man Feci did, for instance."

"Hank, Darling, it's not the 1950s anymore."

"All right, if you were the head of the Feci clan, you wouldn't be allowed to wander around without lots of protection like you do."

"What if I told you that I've had between three and six men close by, watching me every minute we've been together since we first bumped into each other last week?"

Dooley thought about what she said, then looked around the park.

"You can't see them, but there are four men watching right now."

He laughed, nervously at first, then fully amused. "Invisible henchmen? Come on, Abby!"

"I pay top dollar for the best talent in the industry." She leaned in close and gave him a peck on the cheek. "You don't have to believe me, Darling. I think it's kind of cute that you don't. You're like a little boy that way."

They sat for the better part of an hour, holding hands, watching people pass by and greeting an ebullient pup out on his walk. When they got tired of sitting, they strolled around the path themselves. Abby stopped him as they got near the fountain. She faced him, wearing a serious expression, stood quite close and hugged him tightly.

"I love you, Hank Dooley. I always have loved you, and now that I actually know you I still love you."

Dooley returned the hug, though he felt a little odd, sharing true affection in public with a respectable woman. It seemed strangely normal. "I suppose I love you, too, Abby. I certainly can't stop thinking about you. I can't get through a whole day without wanting to be with you."

"Me, too, Darling."

"Hey, Abby, I have an idea. Why don't we meet for lunch during the week? We could switch up—one day a place of your choice and the next day, one of mine. What do you say?"

"That's a fine idea. I wonder why I didn't think of that? Let's start tomorrow. I want to take you to a nice little place near my work. They serve scrumptious Italian seafood. Do you like seafood?"

"Sure, I do. I'm on a see-food diet. That'll be fine. I'll meet you there at noon tomorrow. Then, on Tuesday we'll go to one of *my* favorite places."

Chapter 34

"Hi, Hank. Who's your friend?" Marty gave her the once over.

Dooley presented her. "Marty, this is Abby, the Captain's kid sister."

"Ah, nice to meet you at last, Abby. Some kid sister!" He laughed to put her at ease. "Hank is one of my best customers, you know. In fact, he's often my *only* customer."

"Then, I hope he's a good tipper."

"He is, but he takes me to the cleaners in free coffee refills."

"Hank does like his coffee."

"Like flies like—never mind. The usual place at the counter, Hank? Or something more appropriate for the occasion?"

Dooley looked around the empty room. "I think something a little fancier this time. Don't you agree, Abby?"

"Oh, any old thing is fine with me, darling. We could sit at the counter if that's what you usually do."

"No, Abby, you took me to that cozy little Italian bistro yesterday, so I think we should have the best table in the house. We'll sit over there, Marty, by the air conditioning unit."

"Are you absolutely sure, Hank? I think this one over here would be better, if you know what I mean. It's Tuesday, you know. That's the best table in the house on Tuesday, if you catch my drift."

Dooley looked directly into Marty's eyes. "Yeah, I do. I think it's the right table for the occasion, though. Sit right here, Abby." She sat with her back to the entrance.

"I guess you know what you're doing, Hank. I'll bring some coffee. What will Miss Abby have to drink?"

"I'll have some iced tea, please."

"Coming right up."

"Your friend seemed quite nervous when you suggested sitting here."

"He's just worried because I have such a lovely companion with me today." He reached across the table and clasped her hand in his. "He wants to make a good impression, that's all."

"Is that so?"

The door opened and Dooley's eyes darted up. He relaxed again when he saw it was just the old fellow who's got the Cuban wife. The man took his customary table and sat down without removing his hat.

"Are you going to try the grilled meatloaf, Abby?"

"Should I? I was more in the mood for a tuna salad sandwich."

"Then, that's what you should get if that's what you want."

"Coffee and your tea, Miss. What can I get for you, today?"

"Abby will have a tuna salad sandwich and I'll have the meatloaf."

"Really?"

"Really what?"

"Meatloaf?"

"Why the hell not?"

"No reason. And do you want that tuna salad on a roll, Miss?"

"On wheat toast, please."

"Thank you." Marty glanced out the window. "Uh, Hank, are you sure you don't want to sit over there by the window? You'd be much more…"

"We're fine here. We're not moving. This is the best table, right at this moment."

"Okay, Hank. You know what you're doing, I guess." Marty took care of the old guy next, then went back behind the counter and to the kitchen.

Abby waited until Marty disappeared from sight. "He's such an odd guy, Darling. Funny he can make a go of this business with his nervous manner."

"He looks out for me. He's not usually this nervous. I've never brought anybody here before. I'm sure he's worried about making a good impression on you."

"I don't know. I think if I had your gift, I'd be scratching right about now."

Marty suddenly called Hank's name from the kitchen door, then nodded in the direction of the entrance.

Dooley had spotted them walking in. "Ah, more customers, Abby. See? I'm not always the only customer here."

Four men entered the Riviera. Dooley knew their faces from the files. Fat Tony, Sal, Luigi and Bertie—four of the most powerful Fecis.

Fat Tony spoke first. "Sal, go get Marty. He let some stronzo and his bimbo girlfriend sit at *our* table."

Luigi stopped Sal before he could move. "Don't, Sal. It's him. It's that Detective that the Boss was talking about—and that's *her* he's with."

Abby turned around toward the entrance and faced them.

Dooley straightened up and addressed the bunch. "What's the matter, fellas? Want your table back?"

Fat Tony looked at Dooley, then at Abby. "Nah, don' worry about it. I was upset when I saw youze sittin' here. But I see who you are and who you're with and so it's okay. Hey, Boss, I didn't know you wuz on another shoppin' spree. How much is this detective gonna set us back?"

Bertie grabbed Fat Tony's arm. "Shut up, will ya? Tony, you jerk, this is *the guy*." Luigi gestured with his head and pointed to the ring finger of his left hand. "It's Hank Dooley."

Fat Tony finally caught on. "Oh! I'm sorry, Boss. I didn' know who this cop was. We seen him here before, but didn' put two plus two together. I'm sorry."

"That's all right, Tony. You couldn't know. I'm not buying this one, boys. This one is special." She turned and looked into Dooley's eyes as she spoke those words. "This one is the *future*."

That comment made the guys all look around at each other for some guidance. They didn't understand her meaning. In fact, they often failed to understand her—partly because she was a woman and partly because she was not Italian. In fact, they really didn't know what her background was, Homily being such a peculiar name. She always seemed to be motivated by something higher and farther than they could ever comprehend. They trusted her, though—regardless of the mystery about her and perhaps *because* of it—and this, despite the fact that, half the time, they hardly even trusted each other. They respected her very highly. In fact, they almost revered her. It was clear in the way they acted in her presence.

"You knew my guys were going to be here. You were testing me, weren't you, Detective Dooley?"

He was a little ashamed of himself and her reproach stung him. She hadn't called him anything but Darling for days. This ploy was certainly not an act of love on his part, but he was still a police Detective. Even though she had told him that she was the Big Boss of the Fecis, and he could see it here with his own eyes, Dooley was, truly astounded. He had never seen anything so surreal in his entire life. He would have been less unbelieving if Abby Homily had transformed herself into raging baboon right before his eyes.

"Why did you stage this encounter? You knew what the outcome would be. I told you already what I was."

"I had to be sure, Abby. I knew you weren't lying to me, but you *could* have been crazy. I had to be sure and no one was going to confirm it for me since your identity as the Big Boss was kept so secret. The only way I could be sure was to see it unfold before my eyes like this."

Sal got upset at Dooley's answer. "Hey, what's he talking about, Miss Abby? You ain't crazy! Hey, Flatfoot, Miss Abby is the best Big Boss this family ever had—and the Fecis go back a hundred years. She's taking us to the next level. And if you don't believe me, you should see our annual report. The figures and charts tell the whole story. This family is on the move. Could a crazy broad do that?"

Luigi picked up on Sal's boast. "Yeah, cop, *everything's* up over the last five years between twenty-eight and forty-six percent across the board! Why, if she's crazy, I'm Abraham Fucking Lincoln, for chrissakes."

233

"I'm not crazy, guys, but I am in love. I think it was admirable the way you went about it, Darling." She was holding Dooley's hand in both of hers. "It shows integrity and tact."

"Miss Abby, are you really in love with him?"

"Yes, I am, Sal."

"But, he's a cop! Fecis don't love cops, they *buy* them—as insurance. That's been the Feci way for generations."

Bertie nudged him. "You know that don't matter when it boils down to love, Sal. You went batty over that Meter Maid, Kathy what's-her-face."

"Yeah, but a Meter Maid is not the same thing as a cop. And I didn't marry her. I just fu—Excuse me, I just dated her."

"Gentlemen, you are forgetting that my brother is a cop—a Captain, in fact."

"You can't choose your relatives, Miss Abby. That's easy to forgive."

"You're right, Sal, you can't choose your relatives. And I say that's all the *more* reason to accept Hank Dooley. It's free choice. It's more than that. It's fate and it's our destiny." She lost her audience again. Whenever she started talking like an airy-fairy visionary, their minds drifted off toward more mundane thoughts like money, food and broads. If Old Mr. Feci hadn't given his blessing and been so totally confident in her, they would never have allowed her to run their family business.

"Abby, are you really responsible for the Spazzatura Bowling Alley and Family Fun Center job?"

Fat Tony jumped in to protect his queen. "Don't tell him nothin', Miss Abby!"

"There's no reason to keep secrets from the man I love, Tony. Of course I'm responsible, Darling. I brought it up at the executive board meeting last month. The job was costed out and it was voted on and it passed unanimously. It was a small item on that day's agenda."

"A small item? You know I should be arresting all of you for it. Why did you bomb the place, Abby? I would've thought you'd be against this sort of senseless turf violence."

"I *am* against senseless turf violence, but there is no mob war, and this was certainly not senseless. We owned the Spazzatura Bowling Alley and Family Fun Center." She could read the utter astonishment on his face. "It's true. Ask your asshole, Darling. We got it last year as part of a settlement with the Spazzaturas. There was a complicated transfer of assets, which included the bowling alley, Fairyland Amusement Park, and the International Terminal at the airport along with some other smaller properties— some three dozen Mandelbaum Supermarkets, and so forth. Anyway, in the bargain, we agreed to gather together some of our worst slackers and most egregious abusers. The Spazzaturas did the same. Then, we threw in personnel who were resistant to the new direction in which we were moving and got rid of the whole lot *and* the bowling alley in one stroke. That dump was obsolete, losing money and would have needed expensive renovations just to keep it open. So, you see, Darling, by blowing up the joint, we were preserving peace not destroying it like everybody thought."

"See why we love her, cop?"

"Yeah, cop, she's doin' some real good in the world—not like some people who pretend to, but just go around bustin' heads. She's a true professional and she came to us as a gift from God, who got tired of processing all those dead bodies we wuz sending up there."

Dooley was speechless. He'd devoted his entire adult life to fighting people just like these. They had represented all that was wrong with society—all that was evil, cruel and unjust. Now, here he was, in the midst of these miscreants, and all he could feel was the love emanating from them. "Like I said, I really should arrest all of you."

"But, you won't, Darling, will you?"

"I don't want to."

"Of course you don't. You know that wouldn't be right. Here, move over a little and let's make room for my guys. Come on, boys, sit down and let's all have lunch together." They all got busy and moved two tables over so they could all sit together.

The old guy looked up from his spaghetti and meatballs. "Hey, I don't know that you should be movin' those tables like that."

"Don't worry, pal. We know what we're doin' here. Jus' keep eatin' them meatballs on your plate."

"It just doesn't seem right, seein' those tables together like that." Despite his misgivings, the man did return to the spaghetti and meatballs and gave up his protest.

Marty, seeing the tables being moved together and having discerned that there was to be no bloodshed, came out of the back and took their lunch orders. And once they had their beverages in front of them, the group started feeling much more at ease with each other.

Dooley looked around the table at all the faces and he laughed. It was a deep, relaxed laugh. They mobsters looked back at him with puzzlement. When he composed himself, he felt he owed them an explanation. "I'm sorry, fellas, I'm not laughing at you. I'm laughing at the irony of me eating lunch with you. Hell, I never ate lunch with *anybody* before this week. I never expected I'd end up with you as my colleagues." He laughed again.

"Hey, cop, it's not that funny, really. You and us, we're in the same business. Law and order, you know what I mean?" Luigi took a sip of his ice water. "We was just two sparring families, trying to get control. You see what I'm sayin'?"

"Hank, Darling, let me put it this way. I always loved you, right? When I was a teenager and told all my friends, they made fun of me, saying that what I really loved was the uniform, and that I didn't even know you, the man. I knew they couldn't be right, because I never had any interest in any other policemen. When we bumped into each other on the street a few days ago and you were in regular plain clothes, I still felt the same about you. So you see, the uniform is not important, Hank."

The meaning was not lost on him. "How the hell did you become the head of this mob of gorillas, Abby? You're not even Italian."

"Old Mr. Feci hired some business students out of Apex Business Institute, which we own. I was one of those students—the top of my class, actually. It turns out that I have a talent for this stuff. I can't read or write worth a damn, but I understand good business and I have a head for numbers. Anyway, he was getting old and tired and he wanted to move the family forward, expand the business without violence. He liked my ideas and he implemented some of them, with great success. We started outsourcing much of our work. We reduced staff, some through attrition and some through layoffs and some through elimination. We improved our delivery time on drug trafficking by instituting modern supply-chain models. By the time Old Mr. Feci was immobilized by his first stroke, we had gone from 3rd place of the families on the East Coast to 1st place—when measured by net profits, that is. We'd become the envy of every organized crime family in the industry."

"And it was all because of her, Flatfoot!" Sal beamed, proudly.

"Were you okay with Abby taking over, Sal?"

"No way! Not at first. When the Old Man was ready to pass on, he called us Generals to his bedside and told us who was gonna be the new Big Boss. I couldn't believe my ears, at first. I mean, here's this young broad from outside the family gonna be our new Big Boss? And her being a cop's sister? I figured he'd gone senile on us. But, he showed us the charts and spreadsheets and she made a presentation in our new conference room and we all understood how wise his choice really was. She's the best in her field. She's got a natural talent for this stuff. I'll be honest with you, and I almost hate to admit it, but I like not having to kill people anymore. It's a big load off my mind." The other men nodded agreement with Sal. "I like pulling a regular paycheck. I can budget my new cars and mistresses now. And I got some stashed away in retirement accounts and money market accounts, making eight percent or better."

Marty started bringing out the plates of food.

"I don't know what to say. It all seems so right. But, what about the Faccia di Feci?"

The entire table broke out in hearty laughter.

Abby answered him through giggles. "Hank, Sweety, have you ever actually *seen* anyone with the Faccia di Feci?"

"No, I guess I haven't."

"The Old Man's father, Francesco Feci, invented it. It's a myth—very effective at keeping the superstitious and fearful in line. No one has ever gotten a Faccia di Feci, Darling." She put her teacup down and held his hand.

"Hell, Flatfoot, none of us would even know the first thing about how to give someone the damn thing!" Sal and the others laughed some more, but his face got suddenly serious. "Hey! That's a trade secret, Flatfoot, so don't let slip to anybody or we will figure out how to do a Faccia di Feci on you!"

"Darling, I know you're not for sale, but maybe I could *earn* you."

"Earn me? How would you do that?"

"By achieving a sustained peace in this city. By being someone you can be proud of. I have more than nine thousand people in my employ. I know I can make a difference."

"You can't spell worth a damn." He smiled at her.

"I never knew how I could attract your attention, even with all that I had accomplished, without being too obvious. Turns out, all I had to do was need you and you'd come to my rescue. The letters did the trick, didn't they? But, I bet you knew it was me right away. Your asshole finked on me, didn't it?"

Fat Tony popped up out of his chair, knocking it to the floor behind him. "What the fuck! His asshole stinked on you?"

Luigi grabbed his arm. "Not stinked—*finked*, Tony. Finked. Calm down, will ya'? This is the guy whose asshole talks to him, remember?"

Fat Tony calmed down and took his seat. "Shit, I got upset."

Marty came around and refilled the beverages for the group. They ate amicably, mainly chatting like old friends, sharing stories of days gone by and of old-time criminals, cops and gangsters. They recollected massacres and near-misses, crooked deals and double-crosses and argued the merits of Lincolns vs. Imperials.

At about the time when everyone but Fat Tony was finished eating, Dooley turned back to Abby. "I was wondering something, Abby. I was wondering what we were going to tell your brother. But, then I realized that he must know all of it, already."

"He knows already. He's the one who suggested the letter. He's been on our payroll for four years, now. You recall my telling you that we secured his promotion to Captain."

"See what I mean, Flatfoot?" Sal beamed with pride.

Abby hiccuped and suppressed a belch. "Oh, my! Excuse me, boys. Hank, Darling, with all due respect to your friend Marty, over there, this place is a dump. You should be eating in finer establishments. You, too, guys. You're killing yourself with this so-called food."

"Hey, come on. Be fair, Miss Abby. We gotta have some fun in life. We like eatin' here. It's good enough for us."

"Yeah, it's what you call comfort food."

"Okay, I won't press the issue. You've been very accommodating and responsive to all our changes. I'm not going to dictate what you guys eat, too."

"Thanks, Boss."

"Are you doing anything for dinner tonight, Darling?"

"I don't have any plans. Why?"

"Can I cook you that steak I promised you last week? Remember, you took a rain check on it the last time I invited you."

"Sounds delicious. I'll bring some wine."

"No, you'd better let me supply the wine. Why don't you bring dessert, instead?"

"I'll pick up some seven-layer cookies. I've had a yen for them for a couple of weeks, now."

"You might want to stop on the way and pick up a can of coffee, too. Hey, you'll never guess what I bought yesterday."

"I have no idea."

"I bought a copy of *Love Disease* by that singer we heard at the Private Junction." She snuggled closer to him, humming a small portion of the melody to him. "I'll play it for you. That's our song, remember?"

Dooley turned red as a beet. "Yes, I remember, Abby." He took a sip of coffee, just to do something to conceal his embarrassment.

"Speaking of dinner, Darling, Friday is the monthly Friends of the City dinner at Chez Palacios. Why don't you come with me as my date? All the movers and shakers come to that dinner. We'll be at the table with the Spazzaturas, the State's Attorney General, Sergio Gonzalez, his mistress and the Mayor and his new girlfriend."

"We've been goin' to that dinner for years, Flatfoot. I guarantee you're gonna be scratchin' your ass all night. Ha, ha!"

239

"Sal is right. There's a lot of B.S. slung there."

"Speaking of which—Abby, if I asked you to marry me, you'd have to promise me something."

"What is it, Darling? I hope you don't expect me to give up my career."

A cloud of tension descended on the whole room. There was murmuring among the Fecis and all eyes were now on Dooley. Plans for murder were already being formulated in the seconds before he answered her.

"No, nothing like that." They all breathed a sigh of relief. "Abby, I've never been really serious with a woman before, mainly because sooner or later they always lied to me. I want you to promise to never lie to me."

"I didn't intend to lie to you, but if it's so important to you that I promise, then I promise I'll never lie to you, Darling."

"Good, because I already spend half my day at work scratching my ass. I don't think I could stand doing it at home, too."

Abby leaned over and kissed Dooley enthusiastically. "You're so special!"

"You know, cop, even though we work for her and she could order any of us murdered at any time, she's like a kid sister to us. If you think you're gonna marry her without marrying all of us, you're as dumb as you look."

"Do I have to sleep with all of you apes, too?"

"No, but just for that wisecrack I might make you do our laundry, smart ass."

"Are you asking me to marry you, Hank, Darling?"

Dooley dropped to one knee beside her chair. "Will you marry me, Abby Homily?"

"Absolutely!" Abby leaned over the corner of the table and they shared a long kiss. The boys all cheered.

Fat Tony put down his fork. "What the fuck! This calls for a celebration. Somebody make a toast."

Abby raised her glass of iced tea and proposed the toast. "Here's to love and the future of the City!"

They all clinked their glasses and cups and drank to the bright future of their beloved City.

www.ingramcontent.com/pod-product-compliance
Lightning Source LLC
Chambersburg PA
CBHW030538030726
47495CB00004B/1042